THE PHAROS AT ALEXANDRIA

for Liz Kessler

For more information about Katherine Roberts, visit www.katherineroberts.com

First published in Great Britain by HarperCollins *Children's Books* 2005
HarperCollins *Children's Books* is a division of HarperCollins*Publishers* Ltd
77-85 Fulham Palace Road, Hammersmith
London W6 8JB

The HarperCollins *Children's Books* website address is:
www.harpercollinschildrensbooks.com

1 3 5 7 9 8 6 4 2

Illustrations by Fiona Land

ISBN 0 00 711283 1

Printed and bound in England by
Clays Ltd, St Ives plc

Katherine Roberts

HarperCollins *Children's Books*

OTHER BOOKS BY KATHERINE ROBERTS

The Seven Fabulous Wonders Series

The Great Pyramid Robbery
The Babylon Game
The Amazon Temple Quest
The Mausoleum Murder
The Olympic Conspiracy

The Echorium Sequence

Song Quest
Crystal Mask
Dark Quetzal

Spellfall

www.katherineroberts.com

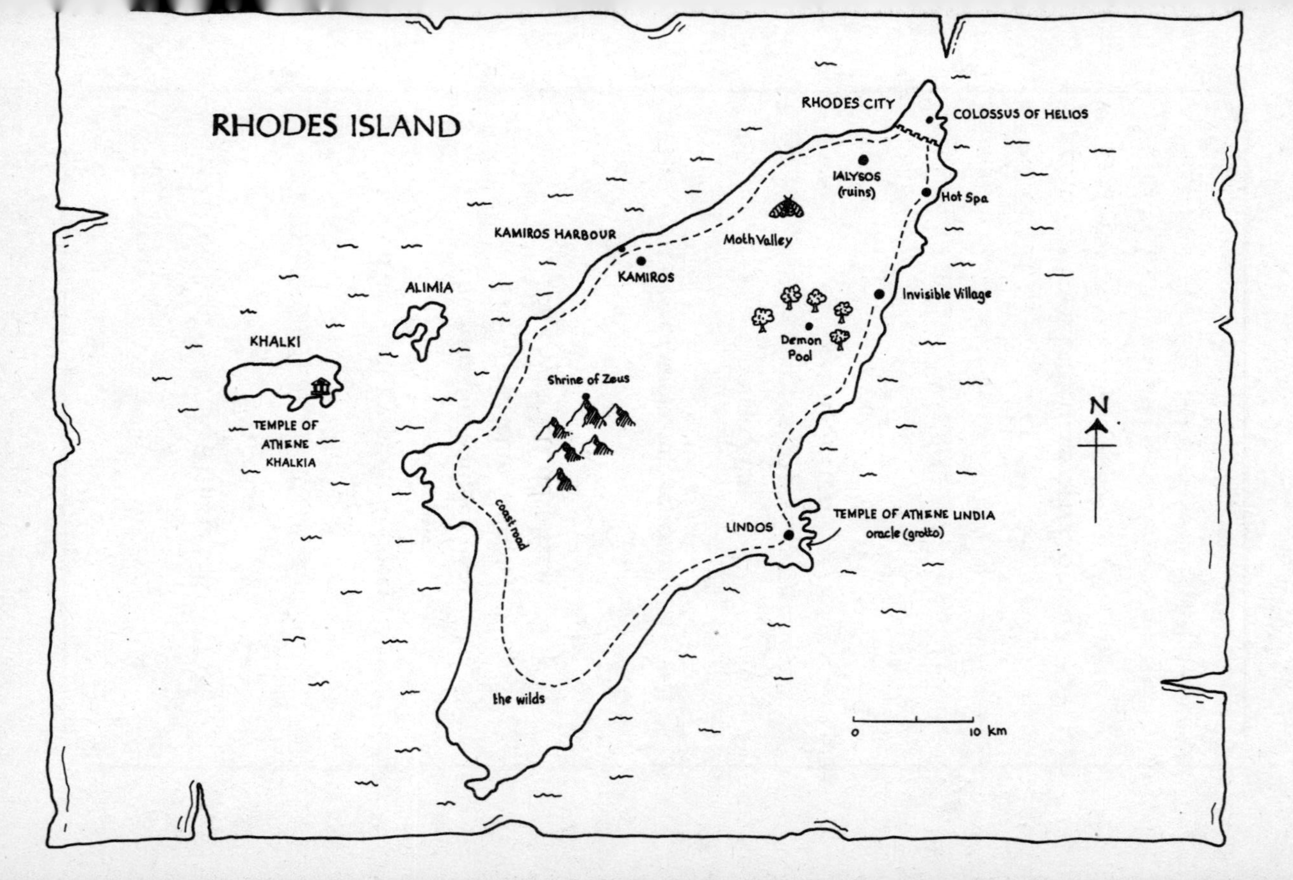
RHODES ISLAND
RHODES CITY
COLOSSUS OF HELIOS
IALYSOS (ruins)
Hot Spa
KAMIROS HARBOUR
Moth Valley
KAMIROS
ALIMIA
Invisible Village
KHALKI
Demon Pool
Shrine of Zeus
TEMPLE OF ATHENE KHALKIA
N
coast road
TEMPLE OF ATHENE LINDIA
oracle (grotto)
LINDOS
the wilds
0
10 km

Prologue

EARTHQUAKE

THE DAY THE earthquake turned Aura's world upside-down began like any other.

Before breakfast, she took her sponge sack and her knife, left her mother sleeping in the hut, and went diving. She worked alone. Occasionally, she would glimpse other divers from the neighbouring islands through the clear turquoise water, but she never spoke to them and they kept well away from her. This suited Aura just fine. She loved swimming through the colourful sponge beds with shoals of fish tickling her bare legs and the water whispering in her ears. Down here, deep beneath the human world, she could forget she was a half-breed and an outcast – at least until her breath ran out and she had to surface again.

She ignored the first warning tremors that stirred sand from the bottom. Small quakes were not uncommon around the islands, and underwater was the safest place to be when Poseidon shook the earth. Also, she had just spotted an unusual blue sponge tantalizingly out of reach in a crevice.

Aura smiled, thinking of her mother's delight when she brought it back. Then the worst happened. As she worked her knife under her prize, the seabed cracked open like a giant clam, sucked her upside-down in a powerful rush of bubbles, and bit closed on her ankle.

The pain was so sharp and unexpected she swallowed water. That had been a big one! Panicking, she twisted her foot until blood swirled, but it was held fast. The sea, that had been calm when she'd dived, was already cloudy with falling debris. Boulders covered in feathery anemones bounced down the underwater cliff around her.

She forced her knife into the crevice and levered with all her strength, trying to free her foot. More blood darkened the water as the rock scraped her ankle raw, but she remained trapped. She gripped the ledge above her head and pulled. Nothing worked. Her lungs were bursting. Being half telchine, the old race from the sea, Aura could hold her breath longer than a human diver. Even so, if she didn't get out of this crevice, she was going to die.

Great Poseidon, she prayed. *Help me!*

She had grabbed the sponge out of instinct. It glowed with a light of its own and felt unusually warm, but she had no time to wonder at this. As her lungs emptied of air, black holes appeared before her eyes and something very strange happened. Through the holes, she glimpsed... *the roofs of a city... a harbour... tiny people fleeing... buildings collapsing... the ground rushing up to meet her...* As suddenly as it had come the vision faded, and her head filled with rainbows. They were beautiful and painful and like nothing Aura had experienced before.

If she hadn't been so desperate, she might have been more afraid. But she was drowning, so she didn't stop to question why the god had answered her when he never had before. *I'm Aura of Alimia, daughter of Leonidus of Rhodes and Lindia the telchine!* she told him. *I'm trapped underwater. My foot's stuck! Please open the rock so I can go back to my mother. She needs me.*

The rainbows faded. Poseidon didn't speak to her again. He was really angry now, opening canyons in the seabed and spitting dead fish from the guts of the earth.

There was no time left for prayers. If the Sea God wouldn't help her, she would have to help herself. Aura thrust the sponge into her sack and gripped her knife in a determined fist. Her layer of telchine fat was keeping her prisoner. She set the blade above her ankle, gritted her teeth, and carefully sliced the flesh from the bone. There was a moment of blackness, when the knife slipped out of her hand and spiralled into the depths. Then her foot scraped free in a cloud of blood, and she was out of the trap.

Weakly, she kicked for the surface. The bubbles had stopped coming out of her mouth and nose a while ago.

She became aware of water in her lungs, heavy and cold. *I should be dead*, she thought. Yet now she'd stopped trying to hold her breath, the pain in her lungs had gone. She swam as if through a dream, kicking with one leg only, her injured foot trailing behind her, while the light grew slowly brighter above.

Her head broke the surface. She gasped air into lungs that were once more on fire, coughed and coughed until she thought she'd be sick. As her heartbeat speeded up to normal, so did the amount of blood flowing from her ankle. The dreamlike feeling vanished.

Waves reared all around her with foaming crests. Beyond them she glimpsed a harbour, its boats smashed against the rocks. The earthquake must have been worse than she'd thought. This was Khalki, the main island off the coast of Rhodes. She had been carried a long way from where she'd dived. Aura looked anxiously for her home, but couldn't see the smaller island of Alimia past the heaving sea. She was too weak to swim there now, anyway.

Stay away from Khalki! Her mother's warnings echoed in her head. The humans who lived there would make fun of her fat thighs, her webbed feet and scarred fingers. They would call her a sea-demon and hurt her because they wouldn't understand. Yet she had no choice.

If she didn't get help, her mother would die.

PART 1

HUMAN WORLD

To you, O Helios,
the people of Rhodes raised this bronze colossos
high up to heaven after they had calmed the waves
of war, and crowned their city with spoils taken from
the enemy.

Chapter 1

KHALKI

BY THE TIME Aura reached Khalki's harbour, the initial terror that had kept her moving was wearing off. Her teeth chattered as she crawled out of the water and dragged her sponge sack up the broken steps. Her body felt heavy and clumsy now that she was back on land. Her wound, bearable in the water, became a blaze of agony that made her feel sick.

Khalki's quayside was in chaos. Everywhere she looked, people groaned in pain from injuries caused by the falling buildings and wept in despair. Fishermen and sponge divers raced to rescue their catch from the damaged boats. A ship that had been driven against the harbour wall in the heavy seas swarmed with sailors trying to free the broken mast and sails before it sank. Everyone seemed to be shouting and running. No one spared Aura a second glance.

All her instincts screamed *hide*! But she was sensible enough to realize she needed help. When two white-robed priestesses hurried past carrying a stretcher, she caught the nearest one's cloak and said, "Please, help me..."

"Stay there, dearie!" the older one said, seeing the blood on her ankle. "Someone'll be along to help you in a moment. We've worse cases in the village. Half the houses fell down the cliff. We're taking all the injured up to the temple so Goddess Athene can heal them."

"But my mother..." Aura managed through chattering teeth.

The priestess's face creased in sympathy. "Got separated from your family, did you? Don't worry, she'll know to look for you up there."

As she spoke, the quayside trembled with an aftershock, and waves surged against its cracked walls. A frightened hush fell over the harbour. Aura broke into a cold sweat. By the time she looked round again, the priestesses had gone.

With the help of one of the mooring posts, Aura struggled to her feet. She closed her eyes as the quay spun. The sack of wet sponges was heavy, and she shifted it to her other shoulder. Teeth gritted in determination, she limped towards a line of boats that seemed to have survived the quake.

Two of the Khalki boys stood in the boat at the far end of the flotilla, legs spread for balance, arguing. The older one, who was muscular and stocky with curly dark hair, seemed to want to row across to Rhodes for help. The younger boy looked as if he had been crying.

Aura recognized them. They were brothers who sometimes dived for sponges near Alimia. Their names were Milo and Cimon.

"Please help me!" she called from the cracked quay. "I need to get back to Alimia. Can I borrow your boat?"

They looked round in surprise, taking in her dripping silver hair, her bleeding ankle, and the empty sheath strapped to her thigh.

The younger boy, Cimon, made a sign at her with his fingers crossed. "Look out – it's the sea-demon! Go away, telchine! This is all your fault. Our roof fell in. Father got hit on the head, and Mother can't make him wake up."

A pang of anxiety went through Aura, as she thought of what might have happened to her own roof. "I can't make the earth shake, silly!" she said. Then she realized the boy must be just as scared as she was. She said more gently, "It was Poseidon – you know that. Please let me borrow your boat. I'll bring it straight back, and… I can pay you."

"Leave us alone!" Cimon said, splashing water at her with his oar. "Swim back where you came from, and take your evil sea-demon eye with you. Or I'll set my brother on you!"

"Don't be silly, Cim," Milo said. "You can see she's hurt too bad to swim all that way."

His gaze rested on Aura's sack. "Got sponges in there, have you?"

Aura nodded warily.

"Anything good?"

She fought another wave of dizziness. "Maybe."

The older boy smiled and beckoned to her. "Let me see."

Aura looked doubtfully at the rocking boats. She thought of the way her body always let her down when she was out of the water, even without a wounded ankle.

"No, Milo!" Cimon said, realizing what his brother was up to. "Don't let her step in our boat! She'll sink it for sure!"

"Don't be silly, Cim. She's not going to do that if she needs it to get home." Milo folded his arms and stared challengingly at Aura. "Well, telchine girl? Do you want to borrow our boat, or don't you?"

Aura thought of the beautiful blue sponge in her sack. She thought of the way it would feed her mother for several days. Then she thought of the collapsed houses on Khalki, and what might have happened on Alimia in her absence.

She bit her lip and stepped carefully into the first boat. Milo's dark gaze followed her. It wasn't easy to lift her injured foot high enough, but she managed it. Next, she had to put her weight on it, ignore the pain… and she was in the second boat, though it rocked crazily and she had to flail her arms for balance. Cimon crouched and held on to the sides with a worried look. But Milo stood with the easy balance of the island-born, watching her every step with a gleam in his eye.

The sun glinting off the water was too bright. Aura concentrated only on the boats. As she lifted her foot over the last one, Cimon scuttled away from her, and the whole line jolted against one another. The shouts of the people on the quay faded. Aura's injured foot, slippery with blood, slid between the two linked boats. She screamed as they closed on her ankle.

Milo shouted something that might have been a warning. But it was as if Poseidon had shaken the earth again. The boat heaved up in front of Aura and sea and sky whirled into one.

She fell sideways. Cimon leapt clear. Milo jumped towards her, no doubt to push her in so he could have his laugh. She grabbed his arm and pulled him off balance. The three of them ended up in the water together, spluttering and cursing. The boys splashed wildly to keep their heads above the surface, while Aura slipped under like a fish. She wanted to laugh at their reversed positions, only she didn't have the strength.

Before she had time to be glad she was back in the sea where her weight was no handicap, someone grabbed her sack. She struggled, but she was tangled up in the cord. She gulped water and choked. Her ears roared, and rainbows flickered in her head.

For a terrifying moment, she thought Poseidon was about to speak to her again. Then something snapped, and darkness carried her away.

Aura was having a lovely dream. She was back with her parents on Alimia, before her father had gone away. A happy time, when she'd been too young to realize webbed hands and toes were not normal. Her mother had them, too. Her father did not, which made him the odd one out. In her dream, she knelt in warm sand and watched him feed her mother fresh sponges from his catch – browns, reds and yellows. The telchine's eyeless sockets turned to Aura, and she smiled. "Try you sponge, Aura," she said. "Good for telchines. Make us strong grow." But Aura could not chew the tough flesh of the sea creatures that were neither plant nor animal. She moaned and licked her dry lips. A bony arm supported her head. Liquid bubbled into her mouth, and she swallowed gratefully.

"I'm too human, aren't I?" she whispered. "I'm sorry, Mother..."

"Steady, dearie," said a voice she recognized, only she couldn't think from where. "You take it easy. You've had a bad time of it, but you're safe now. The sponge boy brought you in. Carried you up the cliff steps himself. You've a good friend there, I'd say."

Friend? Aura didn't have any friends.

She opened her eyes to see marble columns framing a doorway of sky and sea. Sunlight, streaming in from the east, fell across mats occupied by people with bandaged limbs, cuts and bruises. She struggled to sit up. "What happened? Where am I?"

"In the temple of the goddess Athene, dearie. I'm Priestess Themis. We saw you down at the harbour, remember? I told you not to try moving around. You must have slipped and fallen in."

Fallen in, yes. It was coming back now. Milo and Cimon, the line of boats, her sponge sack... She looked round. She was still wearing the old tunic she wore for diving, stretched embarrassingly tight over plump flesh. Her knife sheath and the sack had gone.

"Where are my things?" she demanded, frightened.

The old priestess pushed her gently back on the mat. "Relax, dearie. Your knife must have fallen out, but your sheath is safe in the courtyard with your sponge sack. They were soaking wet when the boy brought you in. We put them in the sun to dry."

Aura heaved upright again. "No, you mustn't let the sponges dry out! I want them back. Now! I have to go home. My mother's alone on Alimia. She depends on me with Father away."

Priestess Themis gave her a strange, sideways look. "The sponge boy said you lived out there alone."

"No, I... my mother's a telchine. She hides from humans."

"A telchine? Are you sure, dearie? Sea-demons haven't been seen around Rhodes since the gods walked the earth, though she could have had some telchine blood, I suppose – that might explain your webbed toes." The priestess muttered something and put down the water jar she was carrying. She pushed a plate of bread and shellfish towards Aura. "All right, but you rest and eat something. I've just got to consult the goddess, and then I'll fetch your things."

Aura sat back down, glad of the excuse. Her ankle had been neatly bandaged while she slept, but it hurt if she put her weight on it. She picked at the shellfish, while the other patients stared. Whenever she looked at anyone, they made the same sign Cimon had made down at the harbour and shielded their faces from her "evil eye". She did her best to ignore them.

After what seemed an age, Priestess Themis came back with her sheath and sponge sack. As soon as Aura saw it, she knew it had been opened. It dangled too lightly from its cord, and the knot was different. She snatched it from the priestess. Inside were three small brown sponges, not quite dead. The rare blue one had gone.

Her fingers tightened on the sack to match the tightening of her heart. "*Milo*," she hissed.

"That's him! That's the sponge boy who brought you up here." The priestess smiled brightly. "I couldn't think of his name before. Strong boy. Did you meet him diving?"

Strong to carry a lump like me up all those steps, she means, Aura thought. Before the priestess could ask any more questions, she dropped the sheath in the sack with the remaining sponges, retied the cord, and struggled to her feet. She slung the sack over her shoulder and limped towards the door. The browns would be better than nothing.

"Where are you going, dearie?" said the priestess, hurrying after her.

"Home to Alimia," Aura said. "Where people don't steal things."

Suddenly, there were four of them between her and the door – women in white robes soiled with bloodstains.

"You have to rest," Priestess Themis said, catching her elbow in a firm grip. The others nodded and closed around her in a wary, but determined fashion.

Aura pulled her arm free, her heart beating faster. "Let me go! My mother will be worried about me." As the priestesses eyed one another, she remembered her father's lessons in human manners. "Thank you very much for looking after me and bandaging my foot, but I'll be all right now. You can give my bed to someone else."

Priestess Themis shook her head and caught her elbow again. "I'm afraid you have to stay, dearie. I'd hoped not to alarm you unnecessarily, but the goddess says we're to look after you until someone can come over from Rhodes to collect you."

"You can't keep me here!" Aura protested, her stomach jumping. "I don't even know anyone on Rhodes..." Then she remembered her father had originally come from Rhodes. She supposed it was possible he had relatives over there he hadn't told her about. Were they worried about her, because of the earthquake? It seemed very strange. "I'm not allowed to go to Rhodes," she said.

"I'm sorry, but we must do what the goddess orders. You should rest that ankle, anyway. It's a nasty cut. What happened? Did you fall when the earth shook?"

As they spoke, they were hustling her back to her mat. Another priestess, a skinny novice with long black hair who looked about Aura's age, ran up with a flask. Priestess Themis took out the stopper and tried to make Aura drink. The novice stared, her blue eyes round. Suspicious, Aura pushed the drink away. "I'm not thirsty."

"It's just something to help you sleep," the old priestess said soothingly. "Then when you wake up, you'll feel much better—"

"No!" Aura dashed the cup to the ground, making them jump back, and barged through the women. She made it out of the door and down the steps into a sun-baked courtyard, before her ankle caused her to stumble. She was caught by a temple guard. He held her firmly, one hand covering her eyes, while she struggled and shouted at him to let go.

The priestesses caught up and pushed her back against the rim of the fountain. Water splashed Aura's hair. But there was not enough to escape into. She was trapped on land... clumsy... hurting.

Priestess Themis poured another cup of the potion and forced it between her lips, while the guard pinched her nose to make her swallow. When she did, the guard took his hand from her eyes. The novice watched in silence.

Aura's limbs went floppy. The guard heaved her on to his shoulder. He carried her up the steps and past the lines of wounded, back to her mat. He set her down on it with a grunt of relief.

"The goddess knows best," Priestess Themis said, smoothing the hair out of Aura's eyes. "It's no life for a young girl, out on that little rock. There's no need to be afraid. They'll be able to look after you properly in Rhodes City, and Athene will watch over you. She's got a temple there too, you know. She'll help look after everyone, now the Sun God has fallen. Go to sleep now, dearie, don't fight it."

There was something Aura ought to remember. Briefly, she was transported back underwater, her ankle trapped in the crevice, praying to Poseidon… but it was getting hard to concentrate.

As the potion dulled her thoughts, she heard the priestess whisper to the novice.

"Don't look at me like that, Electra! Athene says it's for her own good. The poor girl's delirious. Thinks her mother's a telchine! That boy Milo says he's never seen any mother, and by all accounts the father vanished years ago. She must have been living out there all alone, poor dear. Sooner she's safe in the city, the better. They say sponge diving turns everyone crazy in the end. Did I ever tell you about the old man down in the village who claims he can hear sponges scream as they dry out...?"

Their voices faded. Aura drifted in and out of strange, jumbled dreams. The potion kept her too weak to get up and run out of the door. Whilst the priestesses prayed in hushed voices, the injured were carried one by one into the sanctuary, a small room at the heart of the temple, where they lay before the statue of Athene. When it was Aura's turn to see the goddess, she was not carried back to her mat like the others, but left in the small, windowless room. The door to the sanctuary closed, and she heard a bar fall.

It was like a weight falling across her heart.

During the night her head cleared a little, and she heard someone moving softly around the room. For a moment she thought she was back home in the hut on Alimia and smiled. Then the incense made her sneeze, and she remembered. This was the Temple of Athene Khalkia, where they had poured a potion down her throat so she couldn't take the sponges she'd found back to her mother.

She let out a cry of protest.

"Shh!" came a nervous whisper. "Or the guards'll hear us, and then they'll make me leave. I'm not supposed to be in here."

With an effort, Aura turned over. She lifted arms that felt as heavy as temple columns, and rubbed her eyes. She focused on a thin face shaded by black hair, and recognized the novice from the first day. The girl crouched at her feet, fingering the webs between Aura's toes. Her bandaged ankle felt stiff, but whatever the priestesses of Athene had treated it with must have been good, for the swelling had gone.

"What's the matter?" Aura said in a cracked voice, relieved about her ankle at least. "Never seen a sea-demon's feet before?"

The girl gave her an uncertain look. "Priestess Themis says you can't really be a... never mind. Do the webs hurt?"

"Why should they?" Aura almost giggled. She fought her dizziness and sat up. "You're Electra, aren't you?"

The girl nodded.

Aura lurched forwards and grasped her wrist. "My name's Aura. Please help me, Electra! I have to get home. My mother's blind, and she depends on me to bring her food. She'll be very hungry by now."

"A blind telchine?" Electra whispered, staring at the scars on Aura's fingers.

"Yes!"

The sanctuary was gloomy, but the glow from the incense made the statue of Athene glitter. The goddess held a spear in one hand and wore a golden helmet over her marble plaits. Around her neck hung a glowing blue pendant encased in copper wire. Her mind drifting again, Aura thought it was her blue sponge.

She shook her head in an effort to wake up.

"Please, Electra! If you help me get out of the temple, I can swim back to Alimia."

Electra shook her head and pulled free, still eyeing Aura's fingers. "No, you can't. That potion we gave you had mandrake root in it, and your ankle's still a mess even though Goddess Athene's been healing it for you. She doesn't seem to be healing people as well as before, but I expect that's because she's got so much to do with all the injuries from the earthquake. Besides, there are guards out in the courtyard. Priestess Themis told them to keep watch until the ship comes for you from Rhodes. It'll be here in the morning."

A chill went down Aura's spine.

"Did the goddess really tell you to keep me prisoner?" she said.

Electra blushed. "Well… Priestess Themis was the one who spoke to the goddess about you. But I'm training to be an oracle-priestess, so soon I'll be able to talk to her, as well. When I burn the right herbs and touch the goddess's pendant, I can sometimes hear a few words already. I'll get better at it, though! Priestess Themis says I have the gift, and from now on it's just a matter of practice."

Her tone was proud. Aura abandoned the idea of swimming. She didn't think she could stand, even. She remembered how she'd prayed to Poseidon underwater. She'd almost convinced herself that the vision he'd sent her had been brought on by her "drowning". But these priestesses seemed to believe the gods spoke to them.

"What did Priestess Themis mean when she said the Sun God fell?" she asked.

This made Electra giggle. "Oh, she meant the big statue of Helios the Sun God over in Rhodes City! It fell down yesterday during the earthquake. Everyone always said it would fall over eventually, it was so big." When Aura looked puzzled, she added, "You know. The world-famous Colossus? You must have seen it from Alimia. They say you can see it all the way from Anatolia on a clear day."

Aura remembered the big bronze statue she'd seen glittering in the setting sun on the northern point of Rhodes, and the way the ground had seemed to rush up to meet her in her vision. Could her vision have come from Helios, rather than Poseidon? She hadn't even realized the statue had been of the Sun God. "I don't know very much about Rhodes," she admitted.

"If you don't know about the Colossus, you don't know *anything*." Electra shook her head. "Didn't your parents ever tell you about it?"

"I don't think Mother's ever been to Rhodes."

Electra eyed her sideways. "Is she really a telchine?"

"Yes, I keep telling you. Why won't anyone believe me?"

"I believe you." Electra stared at her toes again, then said, "What happened to your fingers?"

"Nothing." Aura hid her hands under her armpits, distracted by the change of subject.

"You used to have finger webs as well, didn't you? You're a telchine, too!"

"I'm only half telchine," Aura mumbled. "My father's human."

"Then why didn't he tell you about the Colossus?"

Aura was getting tired of the novice's questions. "If you must know, he went to the Great Library in

Alexandria seven years ago, and I haven't seen him since."

Electra regarded her sympathetically. "That probably explains why Athene said to keep you here. Except Priestess Themis said her instructions weren't as clear as they usually are, and sometimes I'm not sure the goddess tells us the best things to do—"

She slammed her hand to her mouth and stared up at the statue, as if she were afraid the goddess would strike her down where she stood. "Oh, I shouldn't have said that! Don't tell Priestess Themis, please! I'm sorry about the potion, but I didn't have any choice. I didn't make it as strong as I should have. I hoped you might wake up early like this, so we could talk before you went away. I knew you were telling the truth. I could take a message to your mother, if you like. Tell her where you've gone, and that you're safe. Take her some food, maybe." She broke off uncertainly. "What do telchines eat? Though I suppose, if she's really hungry, she'll eat anything. I know I always do! Priestess Themis makes me fast for two days every week, because she says we hear the gods a lot better when we're hungry."

No wonder the girl was so thin. Aura considered her. "You're not scared to go to Alimia?"

"No… well, maybe a bit. But if I want to be an oracle-priestess, I'll have to learn not to be scared of things like sea-demons."

Aura managed a smile. "Thank you, Electra, though my mother would be more scared of you than you are of her. But you don't have to worry, because I'm not going to let anyone take me to Rhodes now I'm awake."

Electra gave her a doubtful look. "You mightn't have much choice. The guards have orders to hand you over to whoever comes on that ship."

Another chill went down Aura's spine. But the ship would have to pass Alimia to reach Rhodes. She could easily jump overboard. Her mother would be hungry, though, and she might have to hide for a while before going home.

"If you really want to help, you can take her those sponges I caught," she said. "That's what she eats. They're still just about fresh enough. But she needs to get them before they dry out."

Electra made a face. "She eats *sponges*?"

"Of course. She's telchine, not human."

"But they're horrible and slimy and—" Electra scurried across the room as the door opened.

A temple guard looked in and scowled at the novice. "I thought I heard voices! What are you doing in here? Come on out at once! And what's the Alimia girl doing awake? I thought you'd given her something to make her sleep until she was safely on her way to Rhodes?"

Electra squeezed under the arm of the guard, picking up Aura's sponge sack on the way. She smiled up at the man through her fringe. "I was just checking on her. She's fine now."

The guard frowned at Aura, who lay back on her mat and feigned a moan. He grunted as he shut the door.

"Won't matter. She's not going to get very far with that ankle, anyway. At least if she's awake, we won't have the job of carrying her down to the harbour. Near broke my shoulder, getting her in here!"

There was a chuckle from another guard outside, which made the blood surge to Aura's cheeks. But she didn't react. Let them think she was weak and helpless. Then maybe they wouldn't watch her so closely when they took her out.

Their laughter faded, leaving Aura alone in the sanctuary to sort through everything that had happened. Her head was still too fuzzy from the after-effects of the potion to make much sense of it.

Poseidon shook the earth, she thought. And Helios the Sun God fell.

Maybe it's the end of the world.

Chapter 2

VOYAGE

By morning, Aura had decided to tell whoever came on the ship the truth about her mother. If, like Priestess Themis, they didn't believe her, then she would make them take her to Alimia and show them – although she wanted to avoid that, if possible, since strangers would frighten the telchine.

Her mind made up, she stood shakily in the temple courtyard beside the fountain with a guard holding her arm, while a man wearing a robe trimmed with purple picked his way up the cracked steps from the harbour. As he came closer, she saw his hair and beard were streaked with silver and his eyes were grey. She had never seen him before in her life.

Slightly breathless from the climb, the man looked down his nose at her as if she were a sponge he didn't want. With a brief command, he ordered the two soldiers who had followed him to take her down to the harbour and secure her on board the ship. Aura had no chance to tell him anything. She didn't think he even noticed her bandaged ankle, let alone her telchine toes. But as the soldiers took her away, she saw him spread the fingers of his right hand and narrow his eyes after her. He stayed behind to talk to Priestess Themis, his voice echoing in the courtyard as he gave orders to get the quayside cleared, the temple repaired, the steps mended, Khalki's guardian statue righted...

Aura concentrated on keeping her footing down the steps. The after-effects of the potion made her legs tremble, and she was relieved the soldiers were there to stop her falling. She leant on them gratefully and didn't try to escape. The soldiers, for their part, seemed relieved she was being sensible. One of them smiled at her, his eyes crinkling at the corners. "The boss'll be down soon," he said. "We'll be on Rhodes before you know it, then you can have something to eat and a nice rest."

"Who is he?" she asked.

The soldier raised his eyebrows. "Don't you know? Never been to Rhodes City, eh? Well, you're a lucky girl, because that man up there talking to your priestess is none other than Councillor Iamus himself."

When she looked blank, the other soldier added, "Councillor Iamus owns the School of Oratory. He's very rich and important. Nothing much happens on Rhodes or in the islands that he don't know about."

This sounded rather worrying, but Aura asked in a steady voice, "Then why does he want me?"

The soldiers glanced at each other over her head. "Ah, well, I heard it's a request from the Temple of Helios," said the first man with a cough. "He don't tell us the details. We just work for him." But their hands tightened a little on her elbows. Aura bent her head and limped more heavily until they relaxed again.

"Councillor Iamus is a fair man, so you needn't worry," added the one who had smiled at her. "It's the old priest you got to watch out for— " His comrade shot him a warning look, and he cleared his throat and went on, "We sailed over here in the middle of a crisis to collect you, so whatever it is must be important. Things are a lot worse over on Rhodes than they are here. You were lucky, all things considered." He eyed Khalki's cliffs, scarred by the previous day's avalanches, and grimaced.

Lucky? When her best sponge had been stolen, and she'd been handed over to some strange Councillor like a slave?

They had reached the bottom of the steps. The soldiers had to thrust their way through the crowd that had gathered on the quay. They held Aura tightly, as if they were afraid someone might try to rescue her. Obviously, no one had told them how unlikely this was. Aura's cheeks grew hot as some of the Khalkians made superstitious signs in the air. A few mumbled that she'd brought them bad luck and ought to be slaughtered like the sea-demons in the ancient tales, though they shut up quickly enough when the soldiers passed.

The ship had a crimson sail with Helios' sun blazing gold at its centre. The deck was already crowded with people and animals. Many of the islanders had lost their only means of transport and were desperate to get to Rhodes to check on relatives, buy essential supplies, hire labour, find material to repair their houses, and exchange gossip about the biggest earthquake to hit the islands in centuries. Some of the wounded from the temple, being transferred to Rhodes for treatment, moaned on stretchers among them.

The soldiers cleared a space for Aura near the mast. One of them told her to sit, while the other put his hand on her good ankle in a firm manner. Before she realized what he intended, he had locked an iron manacle about it.

"What are you *doing*?" Aura cried, scrabbling away. A chain secured the manacle to the base of the mast, its rattle making her stomach jump. "Take this thing off me!"

Her voice carried. There was a hush on deck as heads turned to look.

"Now, don't make a fuss," said the kind soldier with a smile. "It's just so you don't fall in."

A few of the other passengers laughed nervously. Then a voice hissed, "It's the telchine! She'll put her evil eye on us, and we'll sink!"

Aura's heart jumped again. Cimon and his brother crouched near the bows guarding a bulging sack. Sponges, she bet.

"You sneaky little thieves!" she yelled, forgetting the chain in her anger. "You stole my sponge!"

The soldiers frowned. "We're not thieves."

"Not you... those boys!" Aura tried to get up, but the manacle jerked her off balance. She sat back heavily, bruising her spine. Tears sprang to her eyes. "Why?" she sniffed. "Why are you doing this to me?"

The soldiers glanced at each other. "Do you think the chain's really necessary?" mumbled the one who had smiled at her. "Where's she going to go?"

"She's a sponge diver, ain't she? You want to be the one who has to dive in after her, when she slips over the side? You heard the Councillor. Secure her on board, he said. Chief Priest Xenophon'll only kick up a stink if we lose her. Best to be safe... watch yourself, the boss is coming."

Councillor Iamus jumped aboard, and the soldiers snapped to attention. The Councillor looked at Aura's chained foot and nodded, his face blank of emotion. He didn't come close enough for her to tell him about her mother, and she didn't want to shout it out to the whole ship. He cast a glance over the crowded deck, climbed on the steering platform at the stern, and raised his voice.

"Hear me, Khalkians! We sail for Rhodes City. The earthquake caused much destruction, so I want to make it clear that you come across at your own risk. I can't promise there will be a roof over your head or food to fill your belly when you get there, or that you'll be able to trade for all the things you require. It may be that you'll be called to work on public projects before you go home. Our priorities are these. First, repairing the harbours and public buildings. Second, restoring the temples and statues. Third, sending aid to our sister cities of Lindos and Kamiros, and re-establishing our trade links. Finally, and most importantly, raising the Colossus so that once again the world will know that Rhodes triumphs over land and sea!"

There was a ragged cheer. Councillor Iamus certainly knew how to make people listen. He looked about the same age as her father had been when he went away. Aura experienced an unlooked-for pang of loss. Alexandria was far across the sea. A great city, he'd told her, larger even than Rhodes, where people from all over the world went to study, trade and see the sights. All sorts of things could have happened to him there during the seven years he'd been gone.

As the sails filled and the ship headed out of Khalki, her anxiety for her mother returned. The little island of Alimia lay to their left, tantalizingly close. She tugged in frustration at the chain that fastened her to the mast and stared at the beach until her eyes hurt, trying to see the hut Leonidus had built for them before he left, though she knew it wasn't visible from the shore. Then she did see something – a boat, pulled up on the sand. She relaxed a little. At least Electra had managed to take her remaining sponges over. The telchine wouldn't starve.

"I'll come back as soon as I can, Mother," she whispered, the turquoise sea blurring with tears. "I promise."

The crossing to Kamiros harbour on the west coast of Rhodes was only a morning's energetic row from Khalki, but their voyage round the northern point to Rhodes City's harbours on the more sheltered east side of the island took longer. Long enough for the passengers to settle down and exchange stories about the earthquake, long enough for the animals to stop bleating and squawking, and long enough for Milo and his brother to venture across to the mast where Aura sat hugging her knees.

She turned her face away so they wouldn't see she had been crying. "Leave me alone."

Cimon scowled. "You could at least say thank you! You were really hard work to fish out of that harbour, you know! Then my brother had to carry your fat lump all the way up the steps to the temple!"

"You took your payment for it," Aura said bitterly, still not looking at them. "That sponge was for my mother."

There was a short silence. Cimon whispered something, and Milo said, "What sponge?"

"Oh, don't make as if you don't know!" Aura turned furiously on the boy. "The big blue one you took out of my sack before you handed me over to the priestesses!"

Milo's dark eyes narrowed. "I took nothing out of your sack. Cim carried it up..." He turned to his brother. "Cimon? Do you know anything about Aura's missing sponge?"

The younger boy shook his head. Aura glared at him, and eventually he mumbled, "I think a blue sponge fell out in the harbour. I couldn't dive after it, because we were too busy rescuing you."

"See?" Milo said. "We didn't steal it."

Aura transferred her glare to Milo. "Let me see in your sack, then."

He shrugged. "If you like. Cim?"

Cimon dragged his sponge sack across the deck and opened it to show her the boys' catch. It was a slimy mass of browns and reds, with a few small yellows mixed in. Her blue sponge wasn't there, of course. She grabbed the younger boy's wrist, almost sure they'd hidden it somewhere, but he twisted free easily. The potion had stolen her strength.

Milo was watching her, the same challenge in his eye as when he'd watched her walk across the line of boats. "Satisfied, telchine?" he said.

Aura blinked to stop the tears returning. "Why did you bother fishing me out of the harbour? You get a message from Goddess Athene, too?"

The boy gave her a peculiar look. "Sponge divers' code. You fainted. You might've drowned."

Aura bit back her next words. Sponge divers might be fiercely competitive when it came to their catch, but they always helped other divers in trouble. She'd never been in trouble before, so this was new to her. The thought that Milo had helped her, despite her telchine blood, gave her a warm feeling inside.

"You didn't have to carry me all the way up to the temple," she said more gently. "You could have left me down at the harbour for the priestesses to collect with their stretcher."

"I'm not scared of you, telchine-girl."

She frowned at him.

Milo shrugged. "You fell in because of me. Now we're even. So you needn't put your evil eye on us, need you?"

Aura sighed as the warm feeling vanished.

"I'm not scared of you, either!" Cimon interrupted. "Not now you're Councillor Iamus' prisoner."

"I'm not his prisoner!" Aura's heart jumped again.

Milo shushed his brother and glanced at the soldiers, who were talking to the Councillor in the stern. "Why did they arrest you?" he asked.

"I don't know." The tears threatened again. What was wrong with her today? She didn't normally cry so much.

"You must have done *something*. Everyone's saying this ship only came over to Khalki because of you."

"Apparently, Goddess Athene told Priestess Themis to send me to Rhodes."

Milo's scornful expression said what he thought of that. "Maybe it's because of your father?"

Aura gave him a sharp look. "Do you know something about my father? Tell me!"

The boy's dark eyes avoided hers. "There's rumours… I heard the sailors talking before the soldiers brought you down. They say that when the Sun God fell, Chief Priest Xenophon told everyone it was the sea-demon lover's work, and the traitor must be found. Two priests were killed, and there was some trouble during the night around the broken statue. In the morning, this ship set sail." He gave her a sideways look. "You say your mother's a telchine. So how many people in love with sea-demons do you know?"

Aura's stomach fluttered. Councillor Iamus stood on the steering platform, his hair blowing around his face and his grey eyes fixed on the approaching coastline. He had seen them talking, but he didn't seem to care.

"It must be a mistake," she whispered. "Father's not a traitor. He's never done anything bad."

"Are you sure, though?" Milo lowered his voice, too. "He's been gone a while, hasn't he? My folks say when he first came to Khalki, he acted very strange. Tried to break into the Temple of Athene, and then swam over to Alimia when the guards chased him away. He didn't come back, and everyone assumed he'd drowned. But years later, he started coming over to Khalki to trade for stuff. He used to collect blue sponges. He'd pay a fortune for the right colour, but he never sold any on to the Rhodian traders as far as they know. Then you turned up with your webbed feet..." He glanced at her scarred fingers again. "Seems to me, if someone wanted to hide, a deserted island like Alimia would be a good place to go."

"My father's not a traitor!" Aura said fiercely, the tears back in her eyes. But something he'd said made her pause. Blue sponges... like the one she'd found during the earthquake, when she'd had her vision? "Milo, did you tell Priestess Themis my father tried to break into the temple?"

"Of course not. Why should I?" Milo touched one of the scars that ran up the insides of her fingers. The gesture was gentle, and a shiver rippled up her arm. The boy smiled, as if he knew the reaction he'd caused. Cimon rolled his eyes and dragged their sack back into the bows, where he curled up and used it as a pillow.

Aura pulled her hand away and hid it under her armpit. "Why are you going to Rhodes?"

"To get a physician to come and take a look at Father, since Athene isn't healing people properly any more." The boy gazed back at Khalki, and his eyes darkened. "The priestesses think he's broken a bone in his neck and say he shouldn't be moved, which is why we couldn't take him across with us. We were going to row across to Kamiros and walk from there, but this ship's going straight to the city. It'll be much faster. We've got to hurry, because the priestesses say if Father wakes up and tries to move before the physician gets to him, he might never walk again."

"I'm sorry," Aura said. At least her father was safe in Alexandria. She hoped. "I didn't cause that earthquake, you know."

"I know that!" Milo's teeth bared, and he gave her a proper smile. "Or did you think that's why Councillor Iamus had you arrested? Look, I got to go. The Councillor's watching us. When we land, I'll see what I can do to help you."

Aura bit her lip and touched the boy's arm. "I'm grateful for you fishing me out of the harbour," she said. "Thank you."

She watched him thread his way back across the deck to rejoin his brother, and closed her eyes. *Could* her father have done something terrible she didn't know about? Was that why he was so reluctant to talk about his past, and had forbidden her to go to Rhodes? And what about the blue sponges? Why had he never mentioned them? He must have collected them to feed her mother, only she couldn't remember her eating many blue ones...

"Harbour ahead!" one of the sailors shouted, sending the crew running to their positions.

Fear lodged itself like a stone in Aura's belly. She made herself look at the approaching city. On the acropolis hill beyond the town, white temples dazzled against the sky. Spread below them were more houses than she had ever seen in her life, laid out in neat squares across the entire northern tip of the island. A second acropolis rose from the innermost of Rhodes' five harbours, crowned by a huge temple gleaming with crimson and gold paint. Ships and boats of all sizes made a floating city in the sheltered waters, and people and animals crowded the streets and quays so thickly that she couldn't see how any more would possibly fit. A confusion of shouts and cries carried across the water.

A sweat came over her as she imagined the Rhodians staring at her and pointing at her differences. Then she realized the people she could see were busy clambering through the wreckage and getting on with their lives, taking no notice of the incoming ship. Many of the huge statues guarding the harbour entrances were missing arms or heads. Some lay smashed along the quays, and the bronze limbs that had fallen into the sea gleamed under the water. Further inland, most of the big public buildings were ruins. Rubble filled the streets, where gangs of slaves supervised by soldiers lifted great chunks of stone and marble on to carts to be carried away. Dust lay over everything, coating the flowers in the gardens and dulling the red roofs.

As the ship bumped the side, Aura looked for the fallen Sun God, but couldn't see him. Slightly disappointed, she turned to ask Milo if he knew where the famous Colossus had stood, only to see the brothers leap for the shore with their sponge sack and run down the quay. They did not look back, even once.

She hugged herself miserably. So much for the sponge divers' code!

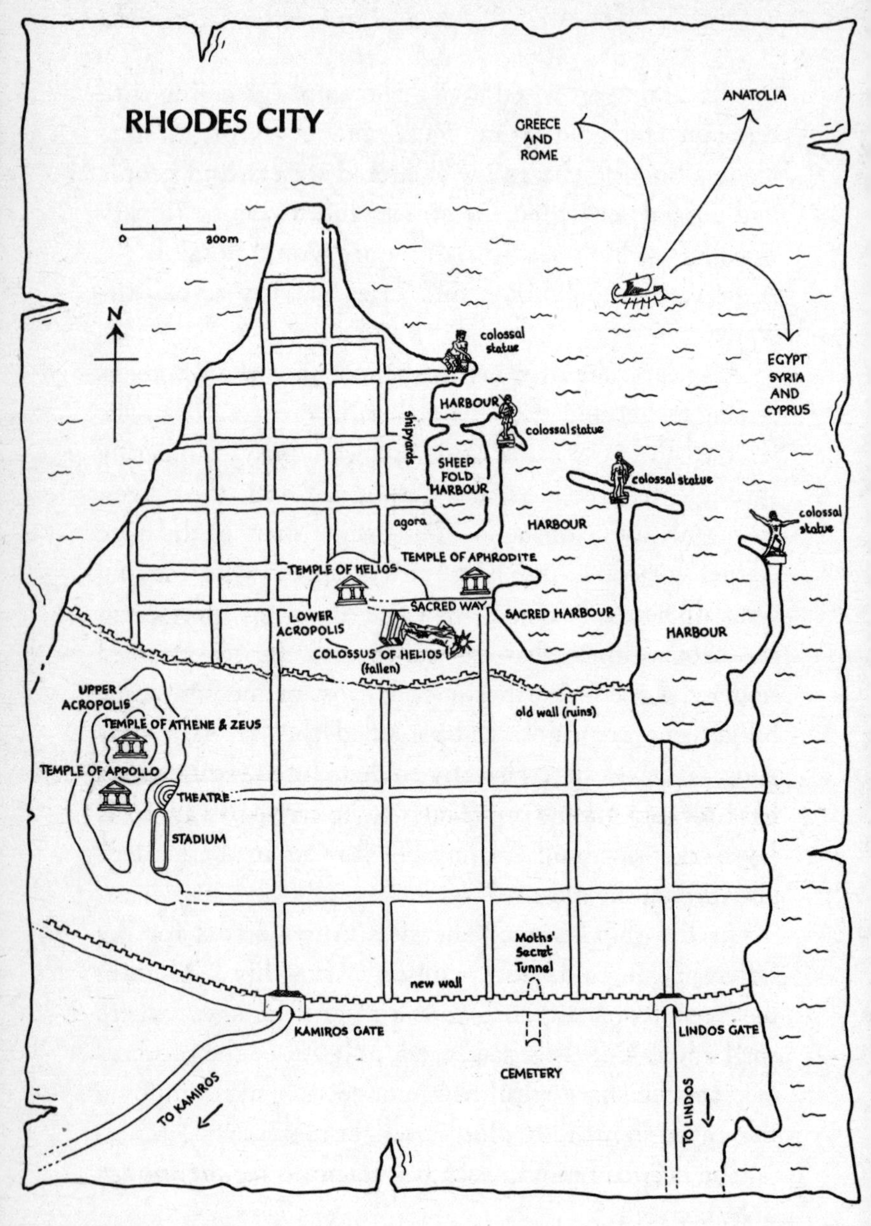
RHODES CITY
0
300m
N
GREECE AND ROME
ANATOLIA
EGYPT SYRIA AND CYPRUS
colossal statue
HARBOUR
colossal statue
shipyards
SHEEP FOLD HARBOUR
colossal statue
colossal statue
agora
HARBOUR
TEMPLE OF HELIOS
TEMPLE OF APHRODITE
SACRED WAY
SACRED HARBOUR
HARBOUR
LOWER ACROPOLIS
COLOSSUS OF HELIOS (fallen)
UPPER ACROPOLIS
TEMPLE OF ATHENE & ZEUS
old wall (ruins)
TEMPLE OF APPOLLO
THEATRE
STADIUM
Moths' Secret Tunnel
new wall
KAMIROS GATE
LINDOS GATE
CEMETERY
TO KAMIROS
TO LINDOS

Chapter 3

SUN GOD

THE HUSH THAT had fallen over the Khalkians upon seeing the extent of the destruction dissolved into excited chatter as they collected their animals and bundles. The deck emptied quickly. A few people cast sideways glances at Aura as they stepped over her, but most of them seemed to have forgotten her. Councillor Iamus strode off towards the market place. Finally, only the soldiers remained.

Aura's fear returned as they approached the mast. "Where are you taking me?" she whispered. "I haven't done anything wrong!" As they unlocked the chain from her ankle, her thighs wobbled. For once, she wasn't embarrassed. She was too afraid.

The soldiers shook their heads. "Poor girl's trembling like an animal at a sacrifice! I thought those priestesses on Khalki were supposed to have given her something to keep her calm?"

"Must have worn off," grunted the other. "You'll be all right," he told Aura. "See that big temple up on the hill? That's where we're going. It used to be the old acropolis before the city spread south. People come from all over the world to see our Colossus. It's a shame you didn't visit us before the earthquake, but even lying on the ground it's quite a sight. Just think, you'll be able to tell all your friends about it when you get back to Khalki!"

"I live on Alimia," Aura reminded them, too frightened to care whether she saw the famous statue of the Sun God or not. "And I haven't got any friends."

The soldiers glanced at each other again. "Oh, come now!" said the kindly one. "Of course you have. Every girl your age has friends."

She thought of Milo and Cimon. "Not me."

They were negotiating the gangplank. Aura bit her lip as her bandaged ankle knocked against the side. But at least her thoughts were clearer. She took careful note of where the soldiers were taking her, memorizing the route in case she got a chance to escape. They had left the chain on the ship.

The road up to the Temple of Helios was bordered by trees and tubs overflowing with red blossoms. Before the earthquake, Aura supposed it must have been impressive. But now some of the tubs were broken, the trees uprooted, the marble paving cracked and uneven. She limped heavily and made sure she stumbled often.

As they climbed, the crowds thickened. Her escort smiled knowingly. Most of the people lined the southern edge of the avenue, gazing towards the old city wall that divided the newer houses with their parks and gardens from the crowded streets of the original town. In the valley lay enormous chunks of stone and bronze, which had demolished several houses. They stretched from what looked like a jagged bronze tree stump at the top of the hill, all the way down to the wall itself. It took Aura a moment to realize what she was seeing. Although she'd seen the other big statues at the harbour, she couldn't help but stare.

The soldiers allowed her to stop for a proper look. "There's our famous Colossus of Helios, brought down like all the rest!" one said. "Just goes to show we all meet the same fate in the end, god or mortal."

"I always said Chares built it too big," the other man said. "It was only a matter of time before it fell over. No wonder he killed himself. Better off dead by his own hand, than face Chief Priest Xenophon's wrath!"

Aura blinked at the fallen Sun God. The huge statue had broken at the knees, and broken again as it crashed to the earth. The jagged piece at the top of the hill near the temple was Helios' huge bronze feet and lower legs, still attached to their plinth. The Sun God's head, surrounded by the spikes of his golden crown, lay against the base of the city wall. Children kept climbing on it to slide down the polished spikes, much to the annoyance of some men in crimson tunics, who were trying to chase them off. Seeing the spears in their hands, Aura guessed these were temple guards. But

Helios' body was in five gleaming pieces, each segment filled with rubble and tangled iron bars. Adults as well as children were peering curiously inside, swinging on the bars, and climbing over the huge stones. There weren't nearly enough guards to stop them.

"People are stupid sometimes," one of Aura's escort muttered. "Look at 'em down there! They'll be the first to complain if that rubble falls on their heads. Looks like old Xenophon's given up trying to keep 'em away."

"Got more important things to do, I expect. Like explainin' why the gods aren't answering people's prayers any more. People don't give as much gold when the gods don't answer, do they?"

They chuckled and returned to their argument about why Chares had built such a large statue in the first place. Aura sidled away. Both men's attention was on the fallen Colossus. They seemed to take it for granted that she would want to stand and stare like everyone else.

She took a deep breath, barged into the crowd and stumbled back down the hill. The soldiers gave a shout and darted after her. Aura shoved people out of the way, using her bulk to get through. For a moment, seeing the harbour shining below her through a gap in the crowd, she thought she was going to make it. Then she tripped over the raised edge of one of the cracked paving stones and sprawled face down. Her ankle wrenched painfully.

After that, her escort stopped trying to cheer her up. They dragged her to her feet, gripped her elbows, and marched her past the crowds into the Temple of Helios. A few of the tourists stared after them, but they were too interested in the fallen Colossus to take much notice of an overweight girl with a bandage around her ankle, being hustled into the temple by two men from the city garrison.

Aura's eyes barely had time to adjust to the gloom, before an ancient priest draped in stiff, jewel-encrusted robes of red and gold scraped out of the shadows and squinted into her face. His skin was shrivelled and yellow as if he didn't get out in the sun much, and his beard was white. For a moment he seemed wary. Then he chuckled. His knobbly fingers clutched a stick, which he had seemed to need to cross the floor, but now used to poke Aura's stomach.

"Fat lump of a thing, eh? Just like her mother, if that priestess was telling the truth."

"No," Aura said quickly, taking an instant dislike to the creepy old man. "She wasn't. I'm not—"

"Silence, you! I'm Chief Priest Xenophon. You address me as 'your holiness', and only when I give you permission to speak." The stick poked her again. The priest's eyebrows, smaller versions of his beard, came down. He squinted at her feet. "So you're from Alimia, eh? And it's true you have webbed toes – though not, it seems, your mother's powers." He chuckled again. "Who'd have thought Leonidus would manage to breed with the sea-demon? All these years he's been hiding you and the telchine away on that island, and I never even guessed! But Helios sees everything. No one can hide from the Sun God, and he's delivered you to me at just the right time." He jammed the end of his stick under her chin. "Where's your father, girl?"

Aura set her jaw, determined not to tell him anything.

Xenophon's brows lowered again. His thin lips worked as if he were chewing something he didn't like, and he scowled at the soldiers. "Where's Iamus? Why didn't he come up with you?"

Aura's escort glanced at each other. "I think he said something about seeing the fishermen, Your Holiness, in case any of them have found anything—"

Xenophon slammed his stick against a pillar, making Aura jump. "I already told him that's a complete waste of time! Any fool can see the Sun God fell into the valley! How's the Gift supposed to turn up at the bottom of the sea, for Helios' sake? It's obvious the traitor stole it. He probably got his sea-demon lover to cause that earthquake so the Colossus would fall in the first place."

The soldiers exchanged another awkward glance. "Ah, there are the other statues to consider, Your Holiness..."

"Pah! As if that matters, when we've lost Helios' Gift! Things are already falling apart. The gods do not speak sense, and they aren't healing people like they used to. If someone tampers with the Gift, we might lose its power altogether. There'll be plenty of time to look for the rest of the pieces later. Go to the harbour and tell Iamus I need him up here straight away... no, wait, you'd better bring the girl through to the sanctuary first. My temple guards are busy keeping those idiot tourists off the Colossus, and I don't want her taking it into her head to run off while you're gone."

Aura was still trying to make sense of this, when the soldiers took her elbows and guided her after the Chief Priest of Helios. They passed through a heavy bronze door into a windowless room rather like the one where she'd been held on Khalki, but decorated more impressively. Every surface seemed encrusted with gold, ivory or precious stones. In the centre of the floor, a man-sized statue of the Sun God stood in a chariot drawn by four winged marble horses. Around his neck hung a blue pendant, very like the statue of Athene in Khalki and very like her lost blue sponge... Incense filled the room, and through its smoke the pendant glowed in welcome, making Aura dizzy.

When her head cleared, Xenophon was looking thoughtfully at her bandaged ankle. "Unwrap that," he instructed her escort. "I want to see the damage."

The soldiers guided Aura to the edge of the plinth and sat her down. She bit her lip as one of them knelt and rolled the bandage away from her ankle, pulling off the scab. The old priest moved the soldier aside with his stick and squinted at the cut. "Hmmm! Not as bad as I was led to believe. Athene Khalkia's healing powers are obviously working better than that priestess claims. The girl's been having you on, with all that limping. A knife wound, I'd say." He peered up at Aura, his little eyes suddenly bright. "How did it happen?"

She set her jaw. "None of your business."

Xenophon's eyes narrowed. He pushed a yellow fingernail into the tender, healing skin. Aura pressed her lips together, determined not to let him know how much that hurt. He peered into her face again and told her to stand up. She thought it was a test and – since there was no point pretending any more – deliberately put her weight on her injured foot to show him she was not weak.

He chuckled at her defiance. "I thought so." He seized her wrist and lifted her hand to the nearest lamp. "Webbed toes, but not the fingers. Scars, though. What happened? Someone cut the webs off for you? That must have hurt a lot." His eyes gleamed, as if the thought of her pain pleased him.

Aura glowered at him. "I did it myself, if you must know."

The chief priest met her gaze for the first time. She'd surprised him, she knew. Maybe now he'd realize he couldn't bully her.

"So…" He breathed, dropping her wrist. "You've a strong will. But experience has taught me everyone has their breaking point, even sea-demons."

He motioned the soldiers back. Before she realized what he intended, the stick cracked across her half-healed ankle.

Aura fell to her knees, aware of someone whimpering. The marble floor heaved like the deck of Councillor

Iamus' ship, and she was sick with the shock and pain. Xenophon shuffled back in distaste.

One of the soldiers helped her up, saying nothing, though his expression made it clear he didn't approve. He guided her back to the plinth so she could take the weight off her foot. In the smoke, Helios' pendant and the horses' golden hooves spun around her. Her ankle was bleeding again. It hurt more than when she'd made the first cut. Injuries always hurt a lot more on land than they did underwater.

She raised her gaze to see the priest smiling. It made his face crinkle like a raisin.

"That should stop you running off before I've finished with you," he said with a twist of his lips. "And you can stop looking at me like that. I don't believe you have the telchine evil eye. If you had your mother's power, you'd have used it by now. Why do you think I sent Iamus to collect you?"

"You've no right to treat me like this!" Aura managed through gritted teeth. "I'll complain to… to…" Who did people complain to on Rhodes? She'd never had to worry about such things, living on Alimia.

He raised an eyebrow at her, amused by her defiance. "You'll complain to the Council, maybe? Do you really believe they'll take your side against mine? I think you'll find I have every right to detain you and treat you exactly how I wish. You're the daughter of a known traitor who has been caught several times desecrating the statues of the gods, and now he has dared attack the

Colossus of Helios, which I raised to protect and care for the people of Rhodes."

He watched this dawn on her face. "Oh yes, it was me who had the vision to build that Colossus you saw on your way up! Chares might have built it, but Chares was just a common sculptor. Without me, his name would be nothing. I want you to remember that, Aura of Alimia. I am the real power on Rhodes, not Iamus or his precious Council. If you defy me, I can make things very uncomfortable for you. On the other hand, if you co-operate, maybe I'll let you live happily ever after on your little island with your poor blind mother. I thought she'd died off years ago. I should have known better."

Aura froze. "You leave my mother alone," she whispered.

Xenophon smiled. "And let Leonidus spirit her away somewhere to work more sea-demon magic? I think it best to keep the two of you safe until we find him, don't you?"

Aura leapt up, forgetting her ankle. A cry of pain escaped her as she staggered round the plinth towards the door. The soldiers blocked her way, apologetic but firm.

"Please," she whispered, all the strength flowing out of her. "I'll do whatever you want… anything! Just don't hurt my mother. Please."

Xenophon's smile was cold. "So you do have a breaking point, after all. I'll admit I was beginning to worry. All right, I think I can handle her from here."

He waved the soldiers out and closed the door on their backward glances, transforming the sanctuary into a jewelled tomb. Aura sank against the plinth.

Unhurriedly, his stick tapping the marble, the old priest returned to sit beside her. "Now then," he said in a conversational tone, hitching up his robes. "Let's start again, shall we? Where's your father hiding? And what does he plan to do with Helios' Gift?"

The questioning went on and on. Aura told the chief priest as much as she could, terrified he would hurt her mother if she lied. She told him her father had gone travelling seven years ago to find out more about telchines so he could help his blind wife return to her people, though she was careful not to mention Alexandria or the Great Library. She told him she knew nothing about Leonidus' past, other than the fact he'd been born on Rhodes, which was the truth. She told him she had never heard of Helios' Gift, which was also the truth. She kept the story Milo had told her about the blue sponges to herself, though she was starting to suspect they might have more to do with this than she'd thought. She explained how she dived for sponges so her mother wouldn't starve, since her blindness meant she could no longer hunt for herself. "She can't eat anything else," she finished. "You mustn't try to make her, or she'll be ill."

Xenophon pulled a face, struggled to his feet and tapped his way around the sanctuary. "So you claim you don't know what your father's up to, and you haven't seen him for seven years? Yet as soon as the Colossus fell, someone was waiting down in the valley to steal Helios' Gift. Rather a coincidence, don't you think?"

When she didn't answer, he gave her a thoughtful look. "Presumably you eat human food, Aura? Are you hungry?"

Aura closed her eyes. "No," she lied.

He scowled at her in frustration. "You will be. I could have food sent in for you, or I could give orders you're not to be fed. It's entirely your choice. Maybe you're willing to starve yourself, but your mother will be here very soon. Are you willing to watch her go hungry too, I wonder?"

"You don't need to bring my mother here! I already told you I'll do whatever you want."

"Except tell me the truth, it seems!" Xenophon snapped. He slammed his stick against the plinth beside her leg, making her jump. "Not to worry, though. If Leonidus is any sort of man, he'll come racing back here soon enough once he learns I have his wife and daughter. Then I can do what I should have done years ago, and dispatch him to Hades after his idiot of a father."

It took a moment to sink in. Aura staggered to her feet and flung herself clumsily at the old priest. "No! You can't mean to *kill* him!"

Xenophon gave her a prod in the chest with his stick, forcing her to sit back down. "You just told me you know very little about your father, Aura. Either that's a lie, in which case you know why I have to kill him, or it's the truth, in which case you can believe me when I say your father has dark secrets in his past that you know nothing about. Now, I've wasted quite enough time with you. I need to talk to Iamus. You can stay here and keep the Sun God company, and maybe by the time I return you'll be in a more biddable mood. While I'm gone, you'd better bandage up that ankle again. You're bleeding all over my floor."

He tapped his way to the door and slammed it behind him. Too late, Aura found the strength to rush after him. She flung herself against the door in time to hear the bar fall into place on the other side. She put her ear to it, but the bronze was thick, and so were the walls. She couldn't hear anything outside the sanctuary. It occurred to her, with a little chill, that this meant no one outside could hear her, either. Screaming for help would not be much use.

She closed her eyes. Tears came, and this time she didn't try to hold them back.

One by one, the incense burners and lamps went out. It grew cold in the sanctuary. Aura picked up the soiled bandage, sat on the floor with her back against the plinth, and made the best job she could of her ankle. Then she took one of the dying lamps and limped around the sanctuary, examining the walls for other ways out. There were none that she could find, and the riches piled around Helios' shrine mocked her – she couldn't eat gold or jewels. She was very thirsty and, in spite of what she'd told the chief priest, hungry too. She banged on the door and shouted till her voice was hoarse. No one came.

Remembering how the god's pendant had seemed to glow when she'd come in, she used the last flicker of the lamp to examine it. Close up, it did look a bit like a dried-out sponge, only brighter in colour. She thought of the blue sponge she'd found during the earthquake, when she'd had her vision. Tentatively, she pushed her fingers through the wires. "Helios?" she whispered. "I'm a prisoner in the temple. Please help me!" But aside from a small tingle from her injured ankle, there was nothing. She shook her head, feeling foolish.

Eventually, weariness overcame her. She climbed into the golden chariot, found an embroidered cloak left as an offering, and curled up at the Sun God's feet. Trying not to think of what Chief Priest Xenophon might be doing to her mother, she shivered herself to sleep.

She wasn't sure what woke her. The last of the lamps had gone out, but there was an eerie blue glow in the sanctuary. It seemed to be coming from above her head. She looked up and saw the Sun God's pendant, shining like a star.

Aura took deep breaths. Careful not to knock her ankle, she stood on tiptoe and touched the glowing pendant again. Rainbows flickered in her head, and she heard words as clearly as if someone were standing right behind her: "*Please speak to me, Goddess! I don't know what to do.*"

Startled, Aura snatched her hand away and searched the shadows. "Who's there?" she demanded.

Her ears hummed, like water pressing against her eardrums.

She laughed at herself for letting her imagination run away with her, then remembered the way Electra had said she heard the voice of the goddess when she touched Athene's pendant. Starting to suspect the truth, she touched the Sun God's pendant again.

"Who are you?" she asked warily.

"*Goddess Athene?*" came the whisper, more eager this time. "*It's me, your novice Electra! I'm sorry I can't speak louder, but I have to be quiet or Priestess Themis will make me leave. I'm not supposed to be in here.*" The words were distorted, but Aura recognized the speaker.

"Electra?" she breathed. "Is that really you? Where are you?"

"*I'm here, Goddess. Right in front of you.*"

"Where's here?"

"*I'm in your sanctuary, Goddess.*"

"No, I mean which temple? Which island?"

"*Yours, of course!*" A nervous giggle. "*The Temple of Athene Khalkia… on Khalki.*"

Aura's breath came faster. She'd been right! She tightened her scarred fingers around the Sun God's pendant. "Electra, this is important. Are you touching Athene's pendant? Is it glowing blue?"

Electra giggled again. "*You're teasing me, Goddess Athene! Of course I'm touching your pendant. I wouldn't be able to hear you, otherwise.*"

Aura closed her eyes in relief. "This is Aura of Alimia," she said, keeping her voice level. "I'm a prisoner in the Temple of Helios in Rhodes City. I think the gods are letting us speak to each other through their pendants. Did you go to Alimia? Did you see my mother?"

There was a short silence.

"*Your mother, Goddess?*" Electra whispered, sounding confused. "*I thought you were born fully-grown from the head of Zeus?*"

"I told you, I'm not Athene!" Aura forced herself to be calm. Electra must be just as frightened as she was. "My mother the telchine, remember? Her name's Lindia, and she's blind. You went to Alimia to take her my sponges. Please tell me the chief priest didn't hurt her!"

Another silence, longer than before. Aura's stomach twisted in anxiety. Then Electra's voice came again. "*Aura…? But it can't be you. I can't see you.*"

"You can't see the goddess either, can you?" Aura said, getting impatient.

"*Oh, I understand!*" The girl's whisper brightened. "*This is a test, isn't it? You're Goddess Athene, but you're testing me by pretending to be the sea-demon's daughter, to see if I'm worthy to be an oracle-priestess. I did take the sponges to Alimia, like she said. But when I got there,*

I couldn't find the telchine. I left the sponges in the little hut. It had been smashed up, and there was a message written on the wall. I know now why you told Priestess Themis to send her to Rhodes. But whatever Aura's father did to anger Helios, Aura doesn't deserve to die! Please tell me what I can do to help her."

Aura's breath stopped. She shuddered and asked, "What did the message say, Electra?"

"*It said...*" Electra paused, as if trying to remember the exact words. "*It said, 'Leonidus son of Chares, if you want your wife and daughter back alive, give yourself up and return Helios' Gift'.*"

Aura slipped down into the chariot and hugged her knees tightly. It was too late. They had her mother.

She tried to think. The message had obviously been left by the chief priest's men for her father. Chares was the sculptor who had built the Colossus of Helios and killed himself after it was finished. If Leonidus was Chares' son, that might explain why Chief Priest Xenophon thought he had taken Helios' Gift... But did he expect her father to just turn up after seven years and find the message in the hut? It was so crazy, she felt like laughing. Except it wasn't funny – not at all.

She touched the pendant again. "Electra," she said, trying to make her voice sound commanding, like a goddess' might. "I want you to write another message and address it to Leonidus of Rhodes, care of the Great Library of Alexandria. Bring... take it to Rhodes City and give it to someone on a ship bound for Alexandria.

Pay them a talent out of my temple funds. Tell them it's very important the scroll reaches the person it's addressed to, and that he'll pay them another talent when he gets it. Don't tell Priestess Themis. Do you understand?"

"*Yes*, *Goddess*," Electra said, sounding nervous and excited at the same time. "*What should I write?*"

Aura took another breath. She felt bad about deceiving the novice, but it might take her all night to convince Electra the voice she was hearing wasn't that of Athene, and in that time either Priest Xenophon or Priestess Themis would catch them.

She closed her eyes. A letter to her father. She had never written one before, having never learnt her alphabet or had access to a scribe. She needed days, weeks, months, to work out what to say. But she didn't have them.

"*I'm ready*, *Goddess*," Electra prompted.

"Write this," Aura said.

Father,

Do not come back to Rhodes!

Chief Priest Xenophon plans to kill you!

I am all right and will care for Mother.

Something evil is happening here.

Love Aura

Chapter 4

TELCHINE

WOULD ELECTRA TAKE such a message? Perhaps she should have sent a more anonymous warning, the sort of thing a goddess might say? Too late now. The novice had gone.

Aura thought about trying to use the Sun God's pendant to contact another temple and ask for help, working on the theory that some of the other gods and goddesses might have been fitted with them, too. But what if the chief priest was waiting for her to do just that? He could easily be in one of the other temples of the city, listening, and she would have no idea who she was talking to. She abandoned the idea and worked the pendant free of its chain so she could examine it more closely. The blue object inside the wire cage was definitely more sponge than stone, though she had never seen one that glowed so brightly out of the water.

As she was trying to bend the wires apart, the bar on the door scraped open and light flooded the sanctuary. She leapt to her feet, the pendant falling out of her lap, and shaded her eyes. Framed in the doorway, two men clutched the elbows of a squat woman with enormous thighs, webbed feet and a cloud of silver hair. The sanctuary, airless and stale from the incense, filled with the wild scent of the sea.

"*Mother!*" Aura cried, stumbling towards the light. The guards shoved their prisoner towards her and backed out quickly, slamming the door behind them.

Aura tried to catch her mother, who fell awkwardly where she had been pushed. The telchine's webbed hands had been bound behind her back, and her eyeless sockets stared about her in confusion and terror.

Fury at the way her mother had been treated lent Aura extra speed. She launched herself at the door and managed to jam her good foot into the gap before the guards could drop the bar. "Wait!" she shouted. "We need water and food and more oil for the lamps! Where's Councillor Iamus? I demand to see him! The chief priest can't keep us here like this! There must be laws—"

She gasped as the guards put their shoulders to the other side of the door, squashing her toes. But she did not give way.

"Be sensible, telchine-girl," one of them muttered. "Take your foot away before we break it."

"Not until you give us some food!" Aura said. "Live sponges for my mother, fruit or fish for me. Your chief priest won't be very pleased if you let his hostages die of starvation."

There was some worried muttering from the guards.

"Nobody said they weren't to be fed..."

"...probably forgot in all the confusion..."

"We'll get you some," a gruff voice said in the end. "But only if you behave and take your foot away. The chief priest's busy, but he'll be back soon. Are you going to be sensible?"

Aura glanced at her mother. She knelt on the floor, her face tilted to the sound of their voices and her empty eye sockets staring sightlessly at the wall. Aura wondered if their combined weight would be enough to force the door.

As if he had read her thought, the other guard drew his sword and showed her the blade through the gap – a chilling glitter.

"You won't get far, even if you do manage to get out of the sanctuary," he said. "The chief priest's stationed men all around the hill. You're injured, and your mother's blind. So, what's it to be? Sensible, and you get fed. Trouble, and we don't bother."

"How do we know you'll come back?" Aura said.

"Do you have any choice?"

Aura bowed her head. When the guards eased the pressure off the door, she withdrew her foot. She flinched as the bar thudded down.

As soon as they were alone, she rushed to her mother's side. The telchine's hands were freezing, and the thong cut into the flesh of her wrists. Aura tugged at the knot. She couldn't see what she was doing. She took a deep breath to stop her tears and groped in the chariot for the Sun God's pendant.

"Did they hurt you?" she asked.

The telchine spoke slowly, as if every word had to be dragged from a far place. "They me surprise," she said. "I try hide in water, but they say you hurt if I trouble make. Lindia love Aura. Not let them you hurt. They me tie. They me carry to human boat."

Aura slid her arms around her mother. Her sea-scented flesh was trembling. At times like these Aura felt like the mother, comforting a small child. "I'm sorry, Mother! I was stupid. I trusted the priestesses of Khalki, and they gave me a potion so I couldn't come back to you. The Chief Priest of Helios wants to kill Father! But I sent him a message warning him not to come to Rhodes, so you needn't worry. I'll get you untied. Then we'll think of a way to get out of here. I've discovered something that might help us..."

As she worked at the knot, she told her mother about the conversation she'd had with Electra last night. "The statues of the gods wear pendants with a sort of blue sponge inside that enable someone in the Temple of Helios in Rhodes City to speak to someone in the Temple of Athene on Khalki," she explained, breaking off her efforts to suck at a fingernail. "Only I don't think the priestesses on Khalki realize that. Electra thought I was the goddess speaking to her, and apparently Priestess Themis gets regular instructions from Athene, or at least she did before the earthquake. But I think they're from the chief priest *pretending* to be Goddess Athene."

The knot was loosening. She worked at it in silence for a moment, using her teeth as well as her fingernails.

Her mother struggled to her feet as the bindings fell away. "Aura, you me listen!" she said urgently. "Sun God's temple very bad place! We out get. Now!"

"We will, Mother. As soon as we can. And when we do, I'm going to take this pendant with me. I think it's got power—"

The telchine shook her head wildly. "Aura not bring bad thing! Very dangerous!" She backed away, knocking over a brazier and stumbling blindly through a heap of jewels. Her webbed hands beat at the walls in rising panic.

Aura hurried after her and caught her round her ample waist, pulling her into the Sun God's chariot so she wouldn't hurt herself. She eyed the pendant, which glowed faintly on the floor where she'd dropped it.

"Mother, do you know what Father did before he came to Alimia? One of the Khalki boys said he used to collect blue sponges... I think they might have something to do with the gods' pendants, and I think I found one under the sea." She told her mother about the unusual sponge she'd found during the earthquake, when she'd prayed to Poseidon and had her vision of the falling Colossus.

She thought her mother wasn't listening, being too panicky about what she called the "bad thing". But when she explained how she'd got trapped in the crevice, the telchine's webbed hands felt for her bandaged ankle.

"Aura, you hurt are!"

"It's almost healed, don't worry. I was deep underwater when I cut it, so I didn't lose much blood. The priestesses healed it while I was in the temple on Khalki." She told her mother how she'd nearly drowned on her way to the surface. She even laughed a little, because it seemed such a small thing compared to their present predicament.

Her mother's fingers lifted wonderingly to her lips. "Aura, you water-breathe?"

Aura closed her eyes, remembering that peculiar coldness in her lungs before she'd surfaced. So much else had happened, she'd almost forgotten. "I don't know what I did." *Water-breathe*. It sounded right.

"You water-breathe like real telchine!" Her mother trembled again, this time with excitement. "You up grow, Aura!" A pause. Then, softer: "You have eye-power too, maybe? Use eye-power so us escape? I not eyes any more. I us not help."

Aura went very still. Her mother never spoke about how she'd lost her eyes, just as her father never spoke about his childhood on Rhodes. Once, when she'd been too young to know better, she'd asked if it were true telchines had the "evil eye" the Khalki boys teased one another about as they dived for sponges. Her mother had thrown Aura face down on the sand and slapped her legs with her webbed hands until she screamed. Then she'd gone off to the far side of the island and collected shells for necklaces, singing in the telchine language, as she did when she was upset. Aura had avoided the subject ever since, though sometimes she wished she did have some real power. Like when the chief priest had hit her ankle with his stick.

"Eye-power?" she whispered. "You mean our evil eye, don't you?"

The telchine squeezed her hands. "Aura, you up grow and you talk to human friend on Khalki, so maybe you ready. But you careful be, or Poseidon you trick."

Aura stiffened. "That vision I had underwater," she whispered. "Was that really from Poseidon? I thought, when I heard about the Colossus falling, it might have come from Helios..."

Her mother slapped her on the cheek with the startling accuracy of one who has been blind a long time. "Visions you forget! Dangerous!"

Aura stood in stunned silence, one hand pressed to her stinging cheek, while her mother paced the floor and muttered about Poseidon tricking them. It seemed telchines got their powers suddenly, as Aura had done underwater when the earthquake came, but her mother had not expected her to grow up so soon. The telchine was so upset, she pressed her webbed hands to her eye sockets, curled up on the floor and moaned.

"Why didn't you tell me?" Aura demanded. "Why didn't you prepare me better?"

"Eye-power dangerous," her mother mumbled. "Lindia love Aura. But now we no choice have. Aura use eye-power to escape. Then leave bad thing here so not us trick any more."

Aura experienced a wave of anger at the way her mother had left her to "up grow" alone, but this was no time for an argument. She took a deep breath. "I'm not afraid," she said, though her palms were clammy with terror. "Teach me."

Lindia picked up the pendant, thrust it into her hand, and started singing in the telchine language. Aura forced herself to be calm. This time, she was expecting the rainbows in her head and barely shuddered.

"Good, Aura," the telchine whispered, retreating to the back of the sanctuary. "Now close eyes and wait we."

Aura stood with her back to the chariot, her eyes shut and her head full of rainbows. Her hands sweated with tension as they clasped the Sun God's pendant. She could feel the power building inside her with every breath.

The door opened a crack, and she heard a plate slide across the marble floor towards them. Time seemed to stand still. She fought the urge to open her eyes. There was a crash as the plate hit the door, followed by the thud of a large, fleshy body.

"I warned you!" growled a voice, and night air cooled Aura's cheeks as the door was pushed wider. "Hey! What's the girl doing with Helios' pendant? Give that here, you—"

"Aura, now!" shouted the telchine.

Aura's eyes snapped open. She had time to see a temple guard in the sanctuary, his sword pointed at her mother's throat. Then *something* exploded from her. Blue light engulfed the guard. He screamed, and kept on screaming. The door swung open unchecked. Torchlight dazzled Aura, and for a horrible moment she couldn't remember who or where she was.

A webbed hand seized hers. "Run we now!"

Aura pulled herself together and thrust the pendant into a fold of her tunic. She and her mother stumbled out of the sanctuary. She blinked around the temple. The main doors stood open. It was dark outside. The courtyard, that had been full of sightseers when she'd been brought up here, was deserted. The guard on whom she'd used the eye-power lay writhing on the floor behind them. A second guard pressed back against one of the columns, staring at Aura in terror.

When she looked at him, he flung an arm across his face and waved his sword blindly in their direction. "Keep your evil eye off me, telchine!" he cried.

Aura didn't stop to see what she'd done. She hurried her mother out of the temple, casting wary glances at the shadows. The main avenue gleamed like a river in the starlight, leading down the hill to the harbours. Lines of torches to the north and west lit the streets of Rhodes, where gangs of slaves worked with their mule carts to clear rubble while the city slept.

Aura pulled her mother down the temple steps. The commotion in the temple had alerted the guards, who had blocked the Sacred Way and were spreading out across the north side of the hill, barring Aura and her mother's route to the harbour. Aura gripped her mother's hand tighter and, praying for luck, dragged her down the steep, rock-strewn slope into the valley where the Colossus had fallen. Her ankle jarred on the uneven ground. The telchine stumbled blindly beside her. They made it halfway down, before a spear thudded into the grass beside Aura's foot, making her heart leap. She flung herself into the bushes, still clinging to her mother's hand. The telchine tripped over her, and they rolled down the slope in a wild jumble of arms and legs, boulders blurring with the stars.

They bumped to a stop against the huge bronze head of the fallen Colossus. His crown spiked the night sky as they lay panting, too bruised and breathless to move.

"Telchines!" called a commanding voice from the road above. "You're trapped! Give yourselves up, and we promise you won't be harmed."

Aura's breath was so short, she couldn't have replied even if she'd wanted to. It was a trick, anyway. She didn't think the guards could see them down here in the shadow of the old wall. Some of the men left their positions at the top of the hill and began to pick their way cautiously down the slope after them. Wincing, Aura scrambled to her feet and guided her mother into the tangle of iron and stone that filled the Colossus' neck.

It was very dark inside. Cautiously, they felt their way deeper into the head of the god, crawling wherever they could get through. They groped their way into what felt like one of spikes of the Sun God's crown, and moved some stones until they blocked the entrance.

"They're bound to search in here," Aura whispered. "We must be very quiet until they've gone." She checked for the pendant, afraid it had broken in their fall, but it seemed to be in one piece. Telling herself she couldn't risk the blue glow, she pushed it deeper into her tunic.

A sudden fit of trembling came over her. "Did I kill that guard?"

Her mother touched her cheek in the dark, making her jump. "Aura, no cry you. You up grown now. You well did. But humans afraid of Aura now. If us find, you me leave. Easier you escape without blind Lindia. Find Leonidus, forget visions, and away stay from bad things."

"Don't be silly!" Aura said. "I'm not leaving you with that horrid chief priest! We'll escape together, or not at all." She closed her eyes. *Together*, she vowed, touching the pendant inside her tunic. Though she was beginning to think she'd made a mistake. If the guards guessed they'd hidden in here, they would be neatly trapped.

They clutched each other's hands, hardly daring to breathe, as the voices of the guards came closer. The spike they'd chosen tilted upwards, and Aura kept slipping. To make things worse, little scrapes and rustles came from above their heads, where rubble blocked the narrow end. A mouse, probably. But if it didn't shut up, the guards would hear.

"I'm not rooting around in the Sun God's crown, even if they did go inside," said a voice directly below them, making Aura's heart thud. "You saw what that girl did to poor Cleon back in the temple. If the telchines are hiding in there, they can stay in there till old Xenophon comes to drag 'em out himself."

"But they took the pendant from the temple! We got to get it back. You know how furious Xenophon was when the big one disappeared from the Colossus. We'll probably get the blame for that, as well as for letting the telchines escape."

"You go in after them, then, if you're so keen. I'll wait out here and take your frazzled body back up to the temple for burial rites—" The guards' nervous guffaws cut off as the noises at the end of the spike started up again. "Hear that?"

Aura held her breath. There was a silence outside as the guards listened. Almost as if the mouse knew it was being listened to, the noises stopped.

"Telchines! We know you're in there!" called one of the guards, bluffing again. "Come on out and give us the god's pendant you stole, and we promise we won't tell

the chief priest of your little escapade. How's that for an offer? You can be safe in the sanctuary of Helios' temple before he gets back, and no one's the wiser."

Aura almost laughed. It seemed Helios' guards were just as scared of their chief priest as she was.

After a pause to see if their quarry would reply, a spear banged against the outside of the crown, sending vibrations through the whole head. "All right, telchines! Have it your own way! I'm leaving some men out here, in case you get any bright ideas of creeping out after we've gone. Reckon you've not got long before the chief priest gets back. Think about it."

The guards moved away, but not far. Aura heard them grumbling and snapping twigs to make a fire. For a mad, brief instant, she wondered if they should accept the offer. It would be better than being dragged out of their hiding place by a furious Xenophon. There might be a better opportunity to escape later.

She felt for the pendant she'd stolen, uneasy. Could the thing the chief priest had called Helios' Gift be a larger version of this one? Carefully, remembering how her mother had called it a bad thing, she uncovered the pendant to see if it had been changed by her use of the eye-power.

As soon as its blue glow revealed their hiding place, the telchine sensed it and scrabbled away. "Aura not bad thing bring!" she moaned. "Poseidon trick us again!"

Even as she spoke, a hand snaked from the narrow end of the spike and grasped Aura's wrist.

Aura scrabbled round in panic, trying to summon the eye-power, got stuck in the small space and fell across her mother's thighs. The rainbows left her with barely a ripple, and she knew she'd wasted the power. In the fading light, she saw a boy with a black eye and split lip, wearing a tattered cloak too big for him. A dagger poked from his belt, its silver hilt glittering.

"Put that away!" hissed their 'mouse'. "Or they'll see it glowin' and come in after us, for sure."

Chapter 5

NIGHT MOTHS

IN THE FAINT light from the pendant shining between her fingers, Aura and the boy stared at each other. She wondered where he'd got his fancy dagger, because it hardly matched the rest of him. Underneath the cloak, his clothes were filthy and full of holes. "Who are you?" she whispered, afraid the guards would hear. "What are you doing in here?"

"Hidin', same as you," the boy whispered back. He crawled out of the rubble at the end of the spike and tried to bow, but couldn't manage it in the small space. He grinned instead. "Androcles, boss of the Night Moths, at your service. Good name for a gang, huh? We took it from them red-winged moths that breed in the valley out beyond Ialysos, because no one knows where they hide during the day – just like us!" He peered curiously at her mother, who had scrambled as far away from him as possible. "I guess you're the telchines the guards out there were shoutin' about. What did you do to annoy old Xenophon, then?"

Aura opened her mouth to explain, then closed it again. So far, telling the truth had only got her into trouble. "None of your business," she said, keeping between him and her mother. With the boy crouched in the spike as well, there was hardly room to breathe.

"Suit yourself." The boy didn't seem worried about her evil eye. He wriggled back up into the narrow end and shifted some of the rubble down towards them. "You're the ones in trouble. I was only seein' if I could help. Now you're here, though, you might as well make yourselves useful. Stash that out of the way. Got to make some space for you. Could have done without them guards hangin' about outside, but we'll handle 'em."

Aura shook her head, the hopelessness of their situation returning. "There are only three of us. What are we going to do? Fight our way out?"

"If necessary," said the boy. "He peered past her, sizing up her mother. "Fat, ain't she? What happened to her eyes? Don't she speak?"

"Not to rude strangers," Aura said, putting a protective arm about her mother. The telchine was listening to the boy's rough accent with her head on one side. "And she's not fat. She's a telchine, and that's why she's so big and strong. She's my mother."

"Can she run?"

"Yes."

"Good, then we got a chance. The other Moths'll be along soon. They're getting the cart and tools. We're goin' to cut off this gold spike and take it over the wall. We've bin plannin' how to do it ever since the Sun God fell down. We lifted the smaller stuff on the first night, of course, but this is more of a challenge."

He ran a hand along the inside of the spike, where he'd stripped off the bronze lining to reveal the outer layer of gold. No wonder they had been able to hear the guards so clearly. The thin metal was all that lay between them and recapture.

The boy seemed unconcerned as he patted it. "Solid gold! That earthquake was a real gift from the gods! This here Colossus must have more gold in its crown than there is in the whole of Rhodes City! It's the cuttin' it up and carryin' it off that's the problem. Hidin' it too, of course, till we can melt it down an' sell it on."

Aura realized where the dagger had come from. "You're a thief, aren't you?" she whispered.

"So are you." Androcles cast a sly look at her hand. "I seen them blue pendants before. They belong to the gods. That's why the temple guards were chasin' you, ain't it? You stole it from the statue in Helios' sanctuary."

Aura closed her fingers protectively over the pendant. She felt her mother stiffen. But whatever the telchine might have said about "bad things" was lost when Androcles held up a hand and hissed, "Shh! I think the others are here."

There was a furtive scrape outside, and three sharp taps echoed through the spike.

A guard cursed and shouted, "Oy, you! Get away from there! I thought I told you kids to keep off the Sun God's crown – it's not a playground!"

Androcles leant over Aura's legs and banged the hilt of his dagger against the inside of the spike three times in reply. He bared his teeth at her and said, "Now we'll have some fun!"

The guards' shouts had been joined by the yells and taunts of children. Aura heard people running outside. Stones clanged off the Sun God's head, making her flinch. Others obviously struck human targets, because there were grunts of pain. The fight moved around the other side of the head, and the tapping code began again.

Androcles motioned them to squeeze up after him. "Not planned this for three of us in here," he said. "But your weight'll help."

Before Aura could decide if this was an insult or not, there was a screeching noise above them and a row of sharp metal points, like tiny teeth, broke through the gold. Androcles lay on his back with his feet braced against the inside of the spike and kicked hard as the saw ripped back and forth, cutting the soft gold. Now the Moths had broken through, the fighting below was louder.

Aura rolled over and peered out through the crack.

"Watch your eyes!" Androcles said, pushing her back. "Do you want to end up blind like your mother? Get your weight up this end. Hopefully, it'll snap off, and we won't have to cut right round—"

Even as he spoke, the spike groaned and tilted downwards. There were yells outside as people jumped off, and the twang of ropes. Stars showed through a jagged hole above their heads. Aura slid with her mother and Androcles down into the golden spike. Then the end of the spike snapped off, and the world spun as they fell out of the Sun God's crown.

Aura thudded on her back into grass. Her mother landed with a grunt beside her. Androcles had managed to catch a rope, his legs kicking wildly above them as he pulled himself back up. The Night Moths, who were all dressed in a variety of rags like their boss, cheered and swarmed up the city wall, agile as spiders, taking with them their ropes and the saws they'd used to cut the gold. Slings came out from under their cloaks, and they aimed stones at the temple guards from the top of the wall.

Aura could see more clearly now what they'd done. The gold spike where they'd hidden from the guards had been neatly cut off from the Sun God's crown. It swung, suspended from a net of cords, to the top of the damaged section of the city wall, where the cords strained over pulleys, hauled by someone or something on the other side. Willing hands helped steady the gold on its journey up and over the wall. There must be hundreds of them, she thought, trying to focus on all the running, climbing, stone-slinging children. The temple guards were hopelessly outnumbered.

For a moment, she thought they were going to get away with it. Then she spotted a wizened figure with a white beard limping down the slope towards them. The chief priest was soon overtaken by Councillor Iamus, holding up his long robes so he wouldn't trip over them.

One of the guards, blood running down his face, looked their way and cursed.

"Forget the thieving kids!" the chief priest yelled. "Seize the telchines! Don't look at that girl's eyes! Someone get a blindfold..."

Aura's heart banged. She dragged her mother to her feet and ran towards the disappearing ropes. "Wait for us!" she cried, as the last of the Moths swarmed up the wall.

She didn't see how her mother was going to climb, even with a rope. But something touched her ear, and a voice shouted, "Grab hold, telchine-girl! Tie it round your waist! We'll pull you up." The last person she expected to see lay on his stomach, peering over the wall.

"Milo!" she breathed. He'd come back for her, after all.

The Khalki boy was not as handsome as when they'd parted on the ship. Like Androcles, he had a black eye and cuts and bruises.

"Hurry!" he urged. "They're coming!"

His brother Cimon knelt next to him, looking scared but determined. Some of the Moth boys lowered a second rope for her mother. Aura grabbed the first rope and knotted it round her mother's waist. She gave her a squeeze of encouragement, before tying the second rope around her own. She boosted her mother up as far as she could, then braced her legs against the wall and did her best to climb, while the boys strained to pull them up.

One of the guards grabbed her ankle. "Give it up, telchine-girl!" he said, tugging her from her precarious hold until her whole weight swung on the rope. Her mother was higher, being drawn slowly upwards, but the guards were already climbing after her, jabbing their spears into the cracks to use as steps.

Aura kicked desperately. There was a shout of encouragement from the top of the wall as the guard fell back. But the ropes had stopped going up, leaving them dangling helplessly in space.

"Keep pulling, Milo!" Aura shouted, although she knew it was hopeless. They were too heavy.

The councillor reached the bottom of the hill. He looked at the missing spike, the injured guards, and finally up at Aura and her mother. "Send some men round through the gate, you fool," he ordered the red-faced captain. "See if you can catch the kids on the other side. We'll wait here."

He met Aura's gaze as the captain dispatched some guards at a run towards the nearest gate. Desperate, she fumbled for the pendant.

"Councillor Iamus, be careful, sir! The girl's got the evil eye."

Guards advanced warily from both sides, arms raised to shield their faces from Aura's gaze. She closed her eyes and reached for the rainbows. It wasn't easy. The wind had been knocked out of her during the fall from the crown, and she felt dizzy with hunger. Nor did she want to repeat the horrifying thing she'd done to the man in the temple. But as the spear-climbing guards reached her mother and began to untie the rope from her waist, the eye-power surged free.

The councillor ducked, and her rope swung round so she was looking at the wall when it happened. There was a heave, like when Poseidon had shaken the earth, and stones exploded around them in a blaze of blue light as she blasted a hole through to the other side. Guards fell off the wall and scattered, arms over their heads, yelling in terror. The chief priest waved his stick and shouted at them not to be such cowards. A rock hit the old priest on the head, and Aura saw him fall senseless. Councillor Iamus dragged him to safety. Chunks of wall bounced off the Sun God's head. Aura's rope went slack, and she found herself sprawled on top of the breach, staring at a garden full of rubble and a house with a smashed roof.

Rumbling out of the garden at surprising speed was a cart drawn by two oxen. In the back of the cart bounced the gold spike the Night Moths had cut off the Sun God's crown, ridden by cheering figures waving their saws and torches. More Night Moths ran after the cart and disappeared into the shadows. Androcles stood on the driver's seat, wielding a whip and laughing, his cloak flying like tattered wings in the night.

Seeing them on the wall, he raised a fist. "Hurry up then, Khalki brats!" he called. "Or we'll leave you behind!"

There was no time for questions. The Moths split up to confuse their pursuers. A tall, blond boy called Timosthenes led their little group through the suburbs along paths Aura would not have guessed existed, until they came to the southern boundary of Rhodes City. This wall looked much newer and thicker than the one Aura had demolished with her eye-power. Two soldiers patrolled a gate set in a tunnel beneath it. More soldiers could be seen silhouetted on the battlements against a paling sky.

They crouched in the bushes, while their rescuers held a whispered consultation. Aura's ankle ached, and her feet were bleeding from cuts made by thorns and stones. Her mother had fared better, since telchines had tougher skin than humans, but the unaccustomed exercise had left her wheezing. Aura looked back the way they had come. Seeing no sign of pursuit, she caught her breath and tapped the blond Moth on the shoulder. "Thank you for helping us, but we have to get back to the harbour and find a boat. I have to get my mother home to Alimia."

Timosthenes frowned at her.

"Don't be an idiot, telchine-girl!" Milo hissed. "They'll look for you back on your island, for sure.

Besides, all the harbours will be crawling with soldiers by now."

"So is that wall, in case you hadn't noticed!" Aura snapped back, her temper short because she knew Milo was right. The one place they *couldn't* go was back home. She bit her lip. "Sorry. But they're not just going to let us walk through that gate, are they?"

Milo considered the wall and pulled a face at the blond Moth. "It's true what Aura says. Your Androcles, or whatever he calls himself, hasn't a hope of getting his ox-cart out of the city with that gold you stole."

Timosthenes smiled. "Let the boss worry about that. My task is to get you back to Ialysos safely. Doesn't look like the alarm's been raised yet. Androcles is right – everything's fallen apart since the quake. The soldiers aren't getting messages across the city so quickly. Don't worry about the guards. There's a tunnel under the wall, which comes out in the cemetery. We've just got to wait for that patrol to pass before we can use it. The boss must think you might be useful, or he wouldn't have sent us back to help haul you over that wall."

"You can't force us to come with you." Aura was more worried about the guards. Besides Timosthenes, she counted just three Moths with them still. Even if Milo and Cimon didn't help her, there weren't enough of them to take her and her mother anywhere against their will.

The blond boy shrugged. "I suppose we could always hand you over to those soldiers on the gate and tell them you're Chief Priest Xenophon's escaped prisoners. It'll save us some food if we leave you behind – you both look as if you eat a lot."

The other Moths chuckled as the telchine's blind face turned towards them. She licked her lips. "Aura, hungry I," she whispered.

This encouraged more laughter. "We're all hungry, lady!" one of the others said. "That's what comes of havin' to steal your supper. There ain't never enough to go round."

"Stop it!" Aura clenched her fists, fear growing in her belly at the thought of being back in the chief priest's power.

"Besides," Timosthenes added. "There's another islander back at Ialysos, asking after you."

In the act of reaching for her mother's hand so they could make a run for it, Aura frowned. "Who?" she asked, thinking illogically: *Father! He's come back to make everything all right again.*

The Moth boy smiled. "Some crazy girl who says she's an oracle-priestess. She was carrying a scroll she claims Goddess Athene told her to send to Alexandria, of all places... She was going to pay the sailor who agreed to take it a whole talent!" He shook his head. "Naïve, or what? Boss relieved her of the problem."

"Electra," Aura whispered. What remained of her strength ran out of her like water from a broken jar. "What have you done to her?"

Milo frowned. "The novice from the temple on Khalki? What's she doing on Rhodes?"

Timosthenes shrugged. "Beats me. She was travelling alone, a young priestess all dressed in white, with law and order falling apart around her pretty little ears! Crazy, like I said. It's a good job we found her first, if you ask me." He gave Aura a sideways look. "So, telchine-girl, are you coming with us or not? Because we've got to move now, before that patrol comes back."

Aura bowed her head in defeat. There was no way the Moths could have known about Electra and her message, unless they really had robbed her on the road like they claimed. How Milo and his brother had got tangled up with the Night Moth gang, she didn't know. But she could guess why they wanted to stay. Obviously, the Khalki boys had decided sponge diving didn't pay as well as thieving.

"Best go with them, Aura," Milo said, touching her arm. "They're supposed to have a hideout up in some ruined city in the mountains. You'll be safe from the chief priest there. Me and Cim are going, too."

Aura blinked at him. "Is that supposed to make me feel better? I pity your poor injured father, having two sons as selfish as you!"

Milo's eyes darkened, but he didn't say anything. Aura took a firm hold of her mother's webbed fingers and dragged her into the tunnel after the Moths.

They left the valley and climbed through thick pine forests into the clouds. Aura and her mother were soon gasping for breath again, and even the Khalki boys puffed. But Timosthenes would not let them stop for a rest. The number of Moths escorting them varied, as some of their party melted away into the bushes and others joined them from the shadows. There were girls as well, as dirty and thin as the boys, their hair cut short and knives thrust through their belts.

"Don't worry," Timosthenes said, eyeing Aura's limp. "We'll soon see to your foot, when we get back to base. We've got a healer now, better than that little toy you used on the wall."

The other Moths with them chuckled. But Aura was so exhausted by then, and so worried the soldiers might catch them before they got to the Night Moths' hideout, she missed the significance of the joke.

Chapter 6

IALYSOS

IT WAS EASY to see why Androcles had chosen Ialysos for the Night Moths' base. The mountain town had been abandoned many years ago, when the population moved down to Rhodes. From the plateau, the Moths could keep an eye on the busy shipping lanes and also on the coast roads that linked Rhodes City to the older cities of Kamiros to the east and Lindos to the west. Grass sprouted between the paving stones, and vines wreathed the ruins with flowers.

A girl called Chariclea led Aura and her mother to one of the roofless houses and ordered the Moths who lived there to share the remains of their meal. This didn't amount to much – a few berries, a bruised apple, and a small piece of very smelly goats' cheese. There was nothing a telchine could eat. In desperation, Aura offered her mother the sponge-like pendant she'd taken from the temple. But Lindia shrank away from it and huddled in a corner. At least there was plenty of water, drawn from a fountain with marble waterspouts in the shape of lions' heads, though they couldn't have cared by that time if the water had come from a hole in the ground.

Androcles returned at midday, minus the gold and the ox-cart. He was greeted by whistles and jokes about how long he'd taken, which he answered with grins, slapping people on the back. He checked on Aura and her mother, told them that they both looked thinner already, and disappeared into one of the old temples with Timosthenes, Chariclea, and a handful of other Moths whom Aura assumed to be his lieutenants. They'd gone before she realized she had forgotten to ask where Electra was.

The Moths camping in the house didn't seem to know anything about Electra, but they were kind enough to their visitors. When Aura's mother fell into an exhausted sleep in her corner, one of the older girls put a blanket over her and shooed the others away. She advised Aura to get some sleep as well while things were quiet, because soldiers were sure to come and search the place soon. She didn't seem worried about this. The others joked about how much loot the soldiers would find this time, and how far down the mountain they would get before the Moths stole their treasure back again. It all seemed to be a game to them.

Aura limped to the edge of the plateau and gazed at the tiny islands of Khalki and Alimia, dark now against the setting sun. Tears sprang to her eyes as she stared at her home, so far away and unattainable. To make things worse, the two people she least wanted to talk to – Milo and his brother – had followed her.

There was a long, awkward silence. Unable to bear it, Aura whirled and demanded, "So what are you doing with the Moths? I thought your father was meant to be hurt?"

Milo was staring at the islands as well, the wind lifting his dark curls. His black eye had gone green around the edges. "We couldn't find a physician who'd come to Khalki with us. They were all too busy. They said we should have brought him across with the other wounded."

Aura frowned. "Didn't you explain he couldn't be moved?"

"They said he had to wait his turn, and if it was a real emergency they'd get a message from the Sun God!" Cimon blurted out, and burst into tears.

Aura looked at the younger boy with mixed feelings. A message from the Sun God? Like the messages the priestesses on Khalki used to get from "Athene"? A chill went down her back as she thought of the pendant she'd stolen.

Milo rested a hand on his brother's shoulder. "That's why we came to Ialysos," he said, looking at Aura for the first time. "The Moths are supposed to have a some sort of a healer up here. Didn't Timosthenes say he'd take a look at your ankle?" He paused. "If you see him before we do, could you tell him we need to talk to him?"

Aura kept her voice steady with an effort. "Give me one good reason why I should help you."

"Sponge divers' code? We helped you."

Worry made her tone sharp. "Helped me? If it hadn't been for you making me walk that line of boats back on Khalki, I wouldn't be here! Your father might be injured, but the chief priest wants to *kill* mine. Xenophon was keeping us hostage in his temple to lure him back to Rhodes. I managed to give Electra a message telling him not to come, but then your stupid Moths went and robbed her of it! I can't even find her. She's supposed to be up here somewhere, and I'm responsible for that, too..."

A tear escaped. She brushed it away, angry that the Khalki boy had seen her cry twice now.

"It's such a mess, Milo! Why did Poseidon have to send that stupid earthquake in the first place? Everything was fine before then. Mother's hungry and scared. She doesn't belong here. I have to dive, get her some more sponges somehow, and I have to find another way of warning Father not to come back to Rhodes... but now we can't even go *home.*"

Milo steadied her with a hand on her elbow. He guided her to a cracked marble slab and sat her down. Aura put her head in her hands, knowing she was making a fool of herself, but too upset to care.

Cimon crept closer. "Maybe you could use your evil eye again? That's what you did on the wall, wasn't it? You zapped that old priest! It was brilliant."

"Don't be silly, Cim. She didn't zap anyone," Milo said. "The priest got hit on the head by a falling stone."

"I was there! I saw blue light come out of her eyes."

"Get lost, Cim," the older boy said gently. "Go see if anyone knows where the Moths' healer is, huh? Aura and me have some things to talk about."

The last thing Aura wanted to do right now was talk to Milo, but she was glad when the younger boy went. He'd seen her use the eye-power. Probably half of Rhodes City had seen.

"I know it's a mess, Aura," Milo said. "Believe me, I didn't realize why Priestess Themis wanted to know so much about you and your family, or I wouldn't have told her. She promised Athene would heal you. She didn't say anything about keeping you prisoner or sending you to the chief priest. I'm glad you escaped."

"It makes no difference, though," Aura said. "The chief priest's men left a message on Alimia. If we're not home when Father gets back, he'll come to Rhodes looking for us. Then Xenophon will have him killed, anyway."

Milo was silent a moment. "I can understand why you're upset—"

"You don't understand anything about me!" Aura shrugged him off, her head spinning. She'd been dizzy ever since she arrived on the plateau. She probably did need to sleep, like the Moth girl had advised, but there were too many things to think about first. And if the soldiers came to raid the camp, she needed to be awake to protect her mother.

"You're wrong." Milo took hold of her hand and spread the fingers, tracing her scars.

At first, she tried to pull away. Then she gave up and let him hold it.

"I saw you," Milo continued softly. "On Alimia, when you were little."

Aura stiffened. "What are you talking about?"

"I saw you make these scars. I was diving near Alimia, and I heard you crying on the beach."

She snatched her hand away, her cheeks on fire.

"I watched you. You were so determined. You didn't cry afterwards, like most girls would have done, with all the blood and everything. And you didn't scream while you were doing it, because you dived deep and cut them off at the bottom of the sea. I couldn't follow you that far down, but I waited till you came up again. Before you dived, you had sea-demon's hands. Afterwards, you had human hands. You looked a bit like you do now, all pale and like you could hardly stand. But you kept walking along that beach until you'd bandaged your fingers with seaweed, and then you sat down and fainted with a smile on your face. So you see, I do understand. You don't want to be a telchine, do you Aura? You want to be human like us."

"That's not true!" Aura said, jumping up. She'd only been seven when she cut her hands, having seen how all the divers from Khalki had separate fingers and toes without webs. Not wanting to be a freak, she'd done her best to make her hands look like theirs, not realizing how much blood there would be or how much it would hurt. He'd been watching her? "I cut off my finger webs because they got in the way," she said. Her head spun again, and she staggered dangerously close to the edge of the plateau.

Milo pulled her back. "Strange for a sponge diver. You could swim better with them, I think."

She scowled at the Khalki boy. "I can swim better than any of you, with or without webs! What were you watching me for, anyway?"

Milo smiled. "You're interesting, in a weird sort of way."

Aura laughed. She couldn't help it. "*Me*, interesting? Look at me! Fat as my mother nearly, and clumsy, with webbed toes and the evil eye..."

"And silver hair like a cloud with stars in it. You're not clumsy underwater. You're like a fish, all rippling and quick. And you're brave. Cim's right. I didn't want to frighten him earlier, but you did do some magic back at the Colossus. You were shining like you had blue light under your skin, and then it came out of your eyes and hit the wall, and the wall fell down. You're not like other girls."

Things were getting too confusing. She changed the subject. "How did you get your black eye?"

Milo touched his eye with a wry smile. "I had a fight with Androcles, down at the harbour. Me and Cim were trying to find a physician who'd go to Khalki, so we were flashing our money about a bit. The Moths must have seen us trade our sponges and thought we were simple islanders. They stole all the money we got from the traders. I lost my temper."

"Who won?" Aura couldn't think why she hadn't put the two black eyes together.

Milo shrugged. "Androcles. But afterwards, he laughed and said I was good in a fight, and we could join the Moths if we liked because there would be a share of something big pretty soon. I was about to tell him to get lost. But then one of the others mentioned the healer they had up here, who would take care of our black eyes, and I thought if we joined the Moths we might at least have a chance of getting our money back, and maybe they'd help us rescue you as well. Didn't know you'd be in the head of the Colossus with Androcles, though! That was brilliant – how did you know the Moths were going to steal the gold from the crown?"

"We didn't," Aura said, thinking of the pendant she'd stolen and how they'd fled into the crown in the first place – had it *made* them fall down that hill? She shook her head. Milo's dark curls shadowed his face. The knowledge that he had seen her cut off her finger webs, when she'd thought no one knew except her family, made her feel strangely vulnerable. "What about my blue sponge?" she said. "Did it really fall out in Khalki harbour, like your brother said?"

Milo frowned. "I'm not a thief, Aura."

"So that's why you joined up with a gang of thieves and helped them steal temple gold, is it?"

Milo's frown deepened. "I don't care about the gold. I told you, I only wanted to find a healer for Father. What's so important about your lost sponge, anyway? You can easily dive and find another one. Or do you collect blue ones, like you father did? Is that why you're so upset?"

She wondered how much to tell him. Then she remembered he knew part of it, anyway. So she told him about the pendants around the necks of the statues in the sanctuaries of Helios Rhodos and Athene Khalkia. She told him how they could be used to communicate across the sea, and how she suspected the blue sponge she'd found during the earthquake had the same kind of magic. "If they do have special powers," she went on carefully, "that might explain why my father collected them, though I don't know what he wanted them for. Perhaps he went to Alexandria to see if he could sell them."

Milo stared at her. "That makes sense! My folks say Egypt's full of sorcerers. So you think that sponge you found was one of his collection?"

"Could have been. I don't remember him bringing many blue ones back to Alimia for my mother to eat. If he'd hidden them in an underwater cave somewhere near the islands, that earthquake might easily have released them back into the sea."

"And you think your father stole these magic sponges from the gods' pendants in the temples?"

"I don't know..." She hated to think her father might be the traitor the chief priest claimed he was. "From what you told me, he must have collected plenty of ordinary blue sponges that don't have any sort of power, as well. But if he did steal the ones in the gods' pendants, and he knows the truth about the messages, it might explain why the chief priest wants to kill him."

Milo narrowed his eyes at the dying sun. "Magic sponges that can communicate across the sea...?" He grinned. "My folks always said all those new oracles springing up all over the place were fakes. This could be really big, Aura! I'll help you find out about the blue sponges, if you help me and Cim persuade the Moths' physician to come back to Khalki. You can threaten him with your eye-power if he refuses. It'll be our secret pact. Sponge divers' code?"

The Khalki boy raised his hand in the formal way, looking into her eyes with that infuriating confidence.

Aura didn't know whether Milo was just being friendly because he was scared of her using her eye-power on him and his brother. But she needed a friend. So she sighed and touched her scarred fingers to his strong brown ones.

"Sponge divers' code."

Chapter 7

RAID

THAT NIGHT, AURA had the strangest dream. She was lying in the darkness, bound with copper wires that pierced her flesh. She could not feel her arms or her legs. Raw emotions surged through her. Terror... anger... pain. Then something touched her, and a blue glow lit her prison. She glimpsed rocks, glistening with damp. A cave—

She jerked awake, sweating, the vision of the blue-lit cave still sharp behind her eyelids. She was clutching the pendant so tightly, it had left red marks on her palm. She pushed it back under her tunic with a shudder. Sunbeams, glittering with dust and insects, shone through the broken roof. The ruined city was quiet. A smell of smoke lingered in the air.

For a horrible moment, seeing the Moth girls huddled motionless under their blankets, Aura panicked. What if she'd used the eye-power in her sleep, and killed them in their beds? Then one of the girls sighed and turned over, and she realized they were only sleeping. With a smile for her stupidity, she turned to check on her mother. She found only a flattened blanket.

She hurried outside. The entire camp seemed dead to the world. Angry that there were no guards, Aura thought how lazy the Moths were. Then she spotted two ragged figures patrolling the far side of the plateau, and relaxed slightly. One of them waved her across. As she got closer, she recognized Chariclea.

The girl seemed alert and cheerful. "Your mother's gone to the fountain," she told Aura. "She woke up thirsty. Don't worry, those two Khalki boys are with her. Milo said to let you sleep."

"Where's Androcles?" Aura asked.

Chariclea glanced at her companion – an older boy with dark curls and a cheeky grin. "Boss is busy," the boy said in a tone that warned they wouldn't tell her any more.

"What about Electra, then? You must know who I'm talking about – the novice priestess from Khalki, the one you robbed on the road. She's my friend, and I want to see her. Now."

Chariclea smiled. "Oh, *her.* That girl's not right in the head, if you ask me. Probably still down at Athene's ruined temple. I'll take you there, if you like – doesn't need two of us to keep watch up here, and the company's getting boring." The boy made a rude sign at her, which

Chariclea answered by whipping out her knife and poking it under his chin until he backed off, chuckling.

Aura hesitated, worried about her mother. But Milo had promised he'd look out for her, and she needed to talk to Electra about the gods' pendants.

The Moth girl led her into the forest along an overgrown path. It was cool under the trees, making Aura shiver. She took deep breaths of the pine-scented air as they walked, trying to clear her head. Her ankle ached whenever she trod on a loose stone. Remembering her pact with Milo, she took the opportunity to ask Chariclea about the Moths' healer. "Timosthenes said he'd take a look at my foot," she explained.

The girl glanced down at her bandage. "Looked all right to me, the way you ran across the plateau just now."

Aura made a face. It did feel a lot better than it ought to do after all the punishment she'd given it lately. "Do you have a healer up here, or don't you?"

The girl said in a guarded tone, "We have a healer, yes. It's just... well, you'll understand when you see. Can't take you there right now, though. Boss is too busy. And I thought you wanted to see your friend? Here we are!"

The ruined temple of Athene Ialysos stood in a clearing beside a stream. Its columns were wreathed with ivy, and its roof had gone. Whispering could be heard inside, interrupted by muffled sobs.

Chariclea shook her head. "I can't believe she's still at it! Hasn't stopped prayin' to the goddess since we

dragged her up here. I hope you can talk some sense into her, because if the soldiers raid us while she's goin' on like that, they're bound to hear."

Aura looked nervously down the mountain. "If they know you hide your treasure up here, why haven't they have come looking for the Sun God's gold yet?"

Chariclea looked thoughtful. Then she grinned. "Maybe they've given up. They hardly ever manage to catch anyone, and we usually steal most of the stuff they confiscate straight back again. Or maybe it's like the boss said. Everything's fallen apart since the quake, and they're just too busy to bother about us."

Aura couldn't imagine the chief priest giving up his gold so easily. Then she remembered how he'd been hit on the head during their escape. Maybe he was in no position to give orders.

They picked their way beneath a pediment supported drunkenly on cracked pillars. Pine needles made a soft carpet inside the temple, deadening their footsteps. The inner sanctuary lay open to the sky. A door hung off its hinges. They found the novice kneeling in front of a headless statue of Athene, her cheeks streaked with tears. The goddess' arms had been broken off at the elbows, and her feet were wreathed in vines. This statue looked much older than the one in the temple on Khalki, and it didn't wear a pendant.

"The goddess won't speak to you unless you have one of these," Aura said, pulling out the one she'd taken from the Temple of Helios.

Electra whirled and stared at it, wild-eyed. "Where did you get that? It's a sacred pendant. It belongs to Athene!" She tried to grab the pendant, but Aura held it out of reach.

"Oh, don't be so silly." Chariclea caught Electra's wrist. "I've brought your friend to see you. Least you could do is say hello."

Electra's gaze rose to her face. "Aura…?" Confusion replaced the wild look, and she set her jaw. "I *knew* the goddess was testing me, back on Khalki! You're not a prisoner in the Temple of Helios like you said, so it can't have been you talking to me, can it?" She laughed a little and tried to prise Chariclea's fingers off her arm. "I might have known you'd escape that councillor using your telchine powers. Did you give him the evil eye?"

Chariclea grinned at Aura and tapped her head. "Warned you, didn't I? The girl's crazy."

Electra ignored her, appealing to Aura. "These horrid Moths, or whatever they call themselves, robbed me on the road from Kamiros while I was on important temple business!" She tossed her black hair and scowled at Chariclea. "Let go of me. I'm an oracle-priestess of Athene. The goddess *does* speak to me, and if you're not careful, she'll smite you with her sword of fire!"

"I'm the only one with a sword around here." The Moth girl laughed again, and gave Electra a gentle poke under the chin with her knife, which made the novice go white. "All right, all right, don't faint on me. I'm letting go. You act nice, though. Otherwise, I might have to lock you in here with your precious goddess for your own safety." She nodded at the sanctuary, which smelled foul. Electra had obviously used a corner of it for her toilet. A flattened pile of needles at the goddess' feet showed where she had been sleeping.

Aura put an arm round the girl. Despite the novice's brave words, there were tears in her eyes. Her bony body was strung tight as a bowstring. "Come on," she said gently. "Let's go to the fountain and get you cleaned up. My mother's there with Milo and Cimon, and I don't want to leave her with them too long. What happened to the message you wrote to my father— to Leonidus, I mean? Have you still got it?"

Electra felt for something in the pocket of her stained robe, then stiffened. She stared at Aura, her eyes wide. "How do you know about that?"

So Aura had to explain, all over again, what she thought was happening when the priestesses in the Temple of Athena Khalkia received messages from their goddess. She told Electra her theory that the voice they heard coming from the statue of Athene was actually Chief Priest Xenophon, speaking from his sanctuary in the Temple of Helios. Then she explained how she'd used the communication pendants the night she was a prisoner in Helios' sanctuary to dictate the message Electra had written to Leonidus.

When she recounted exactly what was in the letter to her father, and went on to repeat their conversation of that night word for word, the novice paled. She pulled out a crumpled scroll, scanned it quickly, and looked up in confusion.

"No one knows what I wrote," she whispered. "They didn't even look at the scroll. I don't think any of these horrid Moths can read!" She darted a look at Chariclea, who was sitting on a fallen column scratching the marble with the point of her knife.

The Moth girl whistled softly, as if she had no interest in what they were saying, but Aura suspected she was listening to every word so she could report their conversation straight back to her boss. It couldn't be helped.

"Listen, Electra," she said, taking a deep breath. "The chief priest has lost something he calls Helios' Gift, which seems to have gone missing from the Colossus when it fell in the earthquake. He thinks my father's taken it, which makes a sort of sense. Milo told me my father used to collect blue sponges very like the ones inside the gods' pendants, and during the earthquake I found a similar sort of blue sponge under the sea. I was holding it when I had the vision of the Colossus falling. I thought it was Poseidon at the time, answering my prayers." She ignored Chariclea's scathing look, glanced round the ruined temple, and lowered her voice. "Now I'm not so sure. I think Helios' Gift is a larger version of the gods' pendants, but more important. The chief priest said if someone tampered with it, the gods would not speak any more and their healing powers would be lost.

He said things were already not working as they should be. That seems to suggest this missing Gift has some sort of magic that affects the other pendants."

Chariclea stopped doodling and stared at them intently.

Electra shook her head with a nervous giggle. "Are you saying Athene hasn't any power? That is all comes from a big blue sponge? That's crazy! Anyway, how could your father have taken this Gift thing from the fallen Colossus if he's supposed to be in Alexandria?" She gazed at Aura in triumph.

"I never said he did take it. That's just what the chief priest thinks. But it's disappeared, so I don't think the chief priest can use it to pretend to be a god any more. He said the other pieces were useless without it. But I think telchines have some kind of special connection with it, which is why I could use the smaller pendant in the sanctuary to talk to you that night." She thought it best not to mention the eye-power just yet. "My mother was frightened when we were locked in the sanctuary. She calls the pendant a 'bad thing' and keeps saying Poseidon will trick us. I need to talk to her again. I think she knows a lot more than she's telling, but it's all tangled up with how she lost her eyes, and she never likes to speak of that."

Electra's forehead creased. "Priestess Themis did complain that the goddess was neglecting us after the earthquake," she said slowly. "And Athene refused to speak to me in the temple here. I thought she was angry with me because I'd failed her, but if what you say is true..." She looked at the pendant. "Aura, how many of those things are there on Rhodes?"

"I don't know. But there's a statue in every temple, isn't there? The soldiers who took me to the temple said Councillor Iamus was questioning the fishermen about the other statues guarding the harbours, so they might have had pendants, too..." Even as Electra's eyes widened, she realized Milo must be right about the deception being big. The message system must be all over Rhodes, as well as the smaller islands.

"I've got to get back to Khalki and warn Priestess Themis the goddess' voice might be false!" Electra said, clearly agitated.

"You're not goin' anywhere till the boss says you can," Chariclea got to her feet, knife in hand. "Gods and goddesses don't really speak to us, anyway, don't be so silly."

Electra set her jaw. "Yes, they do! True oracles come from the gods."

"Only when you're half crazy with temple smoke! My father used to think he saw things too, only they weren't visions from the gods – they came from bad wine, and then he'd beat me because they never came true. That's why I ran away to join the Moths. Forget your silly oracles. I'm more interested in what Aura said about messages sent through the statues – now, *that* makes sense. It would explain why we always used to have so much trouble before the quake, with the soldiers knowing where we were all the time, and why they seem so disorganized now. Wait till I tell the boss! Maybe we can go down and smash the statues the earthquake didn't get." She smiled, as if imagining the fun the Moths would have doing this.

"You can't just go round smashing sacred statues!" Electra said. But she didn't sound so sure any more. She eyed the pendant in Aura's hand. "I know! You can use that thing to send a message to Priestess Themis and warn her."

Aura opened her mouth to say it mightn't be such a good idea to contact Priestess Themis. Before she could speak, a blinding blue light knocked her to her knees. She clutched handfuls of pine needles, rainbows flashing behind her eyes.

"Aura!" Electra's voice seemed to come from a long way off. "What's wrong?"

"I... think it's... danger." She could barely get the words out. The temple columns and the treetops spun. She could feel the power building, exactly as it had when she'd been dangling from the city wall. "Get away from me, Electra! Chariclea!" she gasped. "For Poseidon's sake, *run*!"

"If this is some kind of trick, telchine—" Chariclea began, but broke off as a scream split the air. "A raid!" she shouted, grabbing Electra's arm. "If you want to stay free, come on!"

"We can't leave Aura!" the novice said, her voice a frightened squeak. "She needs help."

From the plateau came more screams, and men's voices shouting commands. Some of the screams cut off horribly short. The shouts came closer. Through a crack in the wall of the sanctuary, Aura saw soldiers running between the trees, chasing Moths who had fled the plateau. When they caught them, they bound their captives' hands behind their backs and herded them together so they could link their necks with rope. The Moths yelled curses, bit and kicked, but to no avail. They were outnumbered and out-armed.

"There's hundreds of 'em out there!" Chariclea cried in dismay. "We'll have to wait till they've gone, and try to work our way down to Moth Valley. Maybe we can give 'em the slip there. Shh!"

Aura gritted her teeth against the rainbows. "I've got to... help my mother..."

"Forget it, telchine," Chariclea said. "They'll catch us as well if we go back up there – look out, they're coming this way!"

Horses galloped up to the old temple. Their riders dismounted and ran up the steps drawing their swords. Chariclea dragged Electra behind the goddess' statue. Aura could not move. Her head was full of the rainbows, burning like fire. There was a shout of triumph as the soldiers spotted her. She fought desperately to control the eye-power. She didn't want to do to these men what she'd done to the guard in the Temple of Helios. But they didn't seem to realize the danger.

Then Chariclea leapt between them, knife in hand.

"Give it up, Moth girl!" one said. He wore a full-face helmet, and his gaze was steady and professional. "Your game's over. You made a big mistake when you stole the Sun God's crown. Ialysos is surrounded. Your friends have surrendered. We're taking the lot of you back down to the city. When Councillor Iamus has finished questioning you, you'll be returned to your masters and your families so they can discipline you as they see fit."

"Get lost!" Chariclea shouted. "I'm not goin' back to *my* family! The boss'll soon rescue us."

"Your leader's dead," said the soldier with a note of regret. "He refused to surrender. He fought bravely, but he was an untrained boy against an army."

"That's a lie!"

But Chariclea turned pale, and her knife wavered. The men used the advantage to rush them. Electra screamed as one of the soldiers seized her elbow. Another grabbed Chariclea, while the last man bent over Aura.

Chariclea stabbed her captor in the arm with her knife, causing him to curse and drop his sword. She wrenched herself free and darted out of the temple, yelling at the top of her voice. "Moths! Moths! It's all lies! Androcles can't be dead! *Fight* 'em! Don't give up now!"

She didn't get far. One of the soldiers outside reversed his sword and brought the hilt down on the girl's head as she ran past. She crumpled without a sound, the knife flying from her hand. He quickly bound her hands, lifted her over his shoulder, and carried her across to the other captives.

The man crouched over Aura frowned. "What's wrong with this one? She looks sick to me... Great Helios' crown! She's lit up like a sacrificial fire!"

"Watch it!" warned the other one, waving the others back. "That must be the girl we were told to look out for, the telchine! Get something to cover her eyes with, quick."

Fear of recapture made Aura's heart race. She couldn't hold the rainbows back any longer. The eye-power left her in a rush of blue light. The earth shook. The two men left in the sanctuary slammed back against the walls, their flesh crisped and smoking. The pine needles around the goddess' feet burst into flame. Sparks flew up through the roof, and the overhanging branches – dry with summer heat – crackled alight. The soldiers herded their captives away from the temple in alarm.

Electra stood frozen with both hands over her mouth, staring at the dead men and the flames. She had dropped the scroll, and it was alight as well.

Her letter to her father, burning... Aura wanted to curl up and cry. But the fire was spreading too quickly, leaping from tree to tree. "Run!" she said, catching Electra's hand and dragging her outside.

"Chariclea..."

"They'll take her with them. She'll be all right."

More soldiers raced into the clearing to help fight the fire with their cloaks, spears, scabbards and whatever else they could lay their hands on. Aura and Electra hesitated

long enough to see the captive Moths were safe. Then they were running, faster than they had ever run before, with deer bounding across their path and birds screeching overhead, the flames crackling behind them in the wind.

Whatever plans the soldiers might have had for Ialysos were abandoned when the forest caught fire. The men turned their discipline to fighting the flames, rather than chasing their elusive Night Moth quarry. They used their helmets to draw water from the fountain, passing them up the mountain along a human chain to quench the flames. Another group used swords to chop down bushes and undergrowth in the path of the fire, while others beat out stray fires with blankets from the camp.

Aura and Electra crouched behind a wall near the fountain, trying not to cough. Their eyes watered with smoke as they stared in dismay at the soldiers surrounding it. There was no sign of Aura's mother or the Khalki boys. Electra was very pale and quiet. Aura's stomach twisted in anxiety. Had her mother been recaptured? Was Androcles really dead?

A few soldiers were still searching the ruined houses, wrenching aside broken doors and prodding spears into dark corners. Those Moths who had gone to ground darted out in ones and twos and made a bid for freedom. Some were caught before they could get to the trees, but others got away in the confusion. Bodies were scattered around the ruins – crumpled, motionless children looking like little piles of rags thrown out in the street. Aura was glad she couldn't see their faces. The steps of one building glittered with jewels and gold. A man in civilian dress stood on the top step, arms folded, watching the activity with narrow eyes. Aura's ankle itched in memory of the chain he'd ordered locked around it.

"It's Councillor Iamus!" she whispered, clutching Electra's arm. "My mother's obviously not here. Let's go."

Keeping their heads low, they backed away from the wall and hurried after the escapees down the southern slope of the mountain. It was harder than they thought to find a path through the undergrowth. With the smoke in their lungs, and all the running uphill earlier, every breath was painful.

Electra cast Aura sideways looks as they fled. As soon as they were safe and it became obvious they weren't being followed, she dug in her heels and pulled her hand free. "I'm not going a step further until you tell me what you did to those men back in Athene's temple!" she said, trembling all over.

Aura considered the novice. She owed her the truth. "It was my evil eye," she said.

Electra frowned. "But you killed them, Aura. *Burnt* them."

"I know. I didn't want to kill them. But they were threatening us, and I couldn't stop it." She sat on a boulder and rested her head in her hands. "I couldn't hold the power back. I think it comes through the god's pendant, like the visions."

"From Helios?" Electra whispered.

"I don't know. Why would Helios help me kill the soldiers? Mother seems to think the power comes from Poseidon. I fought it as long as I could, but it was burning my eyes—" She scrambled to her feet as the shouting behind them drew closer. "Come on. We can't stay here, or the soldiers will find us."

Aura's head swam as they walked, and she kept getting glimpses of the cave she'd seen in her dream. She shook them away. At last, they saw one of the escapees ahead of them, moving through the trees. With some relief, Aura recognized the Moth boy who had guided them out of the city.

"Timosthenes!" she called. But the blond boy just scowled over his shoulder and increased his pace.

They were forced to save their breath for negotiating tree roots as their reluctant guide twisted and turned through the undergrowth. Aura's head started to float again. She clung to Electra's hand as lights sparkled before her eyes, worried she was going to faint. The pendant in her pocket was warm, and she kept her hand away from it.

She thought the boy would never let them catch up. But when the slope levelled out in a valley where a heady scent banished the smell of the smoke, he whirled and hissed, "Will you stop following me? You're not Moths, so you can't come."

"Come where?" Aura said.

"Never you mind. We should never have brought you here. They've never come after us with so many men before."

"Please help us," Electra whispered. "We can't go back to Ialysos now. Councillor Iamus is there, and he's the one who took Aura to the chief priest in the first place."

Timosthenes made a face and pointed through the trees. "You take that path, and you'll end up in Moth Valley. You can pick up the road to Kamiros that way, get a boat back to your islands. You'll be safer there than you will with us. I can't be looking out for you, not any more. I've enough troubles of my own, now."

Electra glanced the way he was pointing. "Maybe we *should* go back to Khalki, Aura," she whispered. "Priestess Themis will help us, I'm sure."

Aura shook her head. The scent rising from the valley made it hard to think. But she knew she couldn't trust any priest or priestess until she found out more about the blue sponges and Helios' Gift. "Did you see what happened to my mother – the telchine?" she asked.

Timosthenes grimaced. "I expect the soldiers caught her. Didn't look like she could run very fast to me."

"What about the Khalki boy? The one who gave your boss a black eye? Did you see what happened to him?"

This brought a grin. "No, but I hope he got away. There aren't many people who could give the boss a shiner like that! Maybe he's at the rendezvous." He peered back through the trees. "What happened to Chariclea? Wasn't she with you two?"

Aura exchanged a glance with Electra. "The soldiers caught her, I'm sorry. They trapped us in Athene's ruined temple."

"And you escaped?" Timosthenes' expression sharpened with suspicion.

Aura took a deep breath and met the blond boy's gaze. She said the only thing she could think of that might persuade him to let them come. "If the councillor catches us, we'll tell him you came this way, and we'll tell him about your healer."

"What do you know about our healer?" Timosthenes said, suddenly defensive.

"You said he would take a look at my ankle," Aura reminded him. "He's hiding from the authorities like the rest of you, isn't he? That's why you're so secretive about him. What did he do?"

The boy shook his head. "Him? He? You don't know half of it!" But he sighed. "Oh, all right, since I can't seem to get rid of you, I suppose you'd better come with me. Boss'll soon send you packing if he thinks you shouldn't stay."

"Androcles is alive?" Electra said in surprise. "The soldiers up at the temple told us he'd been killed in the raid."

The blond boy gave her a withering look. "Takes more than a sword cut to kill the boss! We've got the Sun God's magic healer, haven't we?"

The *Sun God's* magic healer?

Several things fell into place in Aura's head, and the visions she'd been getting of the cave started to make sense. She thought she could guess what the Moths' great secret might be. But she kept her suspicions to herself. Electra was spooked enough after seeing her use the eye-power back at the ruined temple, and Timosthenes seemed jumpy, too. She didn't want to alert either of them to the strange behaviour of the pendant in her pocket, which grew warmer and brighter with every step.

Chapter 8

HELIOS' GIFT

AS THEY WENT deeper into the valley, splashing through streams and pushing through the scented bushes, Aura began to guess which direction the boy would lead them. They came to a cliff, and the pendant brightened to show her a crack in the rock partly hidden behind a curtain of vines. Her skin prickled as she ducked inside.

"Hey!" Timosthenes called. "Wait! You can't just barge in there without the password, you'll get—"

His warning came too late. A stick slammed across Aura's shins, and she stumbled to her knees. Someone grabbed her hair, and a blade pricked her cheek. Immediately, with a blaze of power so great it took her breath away, the rainbows filled her head. She squeezed her eyes shut. "Get off me," she gasped. "Quick, before I hurt you!"

"Wrong way round, fat girl," chuckled the Moth boy on her back. "I'm the one with the knife."

"Someone make him get off her!" Electra screamed, rushing in after Aura. "Or she'll kill you all!"

The others scowled. But Timosthenes called, "It's all right, they're with me. They already know about our healer. They were with Chariclea at the temple when the soldiers came."

The boy climbed off Aura, and to her relief the rainbows faded. Shakily, she climbed to her feet.

The cave was bigger than she'd thought, lit by a blue glow coming from the centre of the rocky floor, just as it had been in her dream. Perhaps twenty Moths huddled around the eerie light. Some had blood running down their faces; others cradled injured limbs. Androcles lay in the middle, unconscious, his chest bared.

Electra pressed a hand to her mouth, and Aura felt sick. A sword had sliced right through to the boy's ribs, exposing his entrails. No wonder the soldiers had thought him dead. The halo around him changed colour like the sun playing over the sea. The other Moths appeared to be praying.

Electra stood on tiptoe, trying to see. "Aura, is that what I think it is?"

Aura swallowed. The pendant was now so hot, she could feel it burning through her tunic. She started towards the blue light. But before she could see what was making it, there was a scuffle in the shadows at the back of the cave, and her mother lurched towards her.

"Aura, no! Danger here is! Bad thing stay away from!"

"Mother!" Aura hugged the telchine with relief. "I thought the soldiers had caught you!"

Milo and Cimon rushed up, too, grinning.

"We thought the soldiers had caught *you*!" Cimon said.

"You'll never guess what this healer of theirs is!" Milo said. "It's the most enormous sponge! And it works miracles! Androcles was more or less dead when they carried him down here, and some of the others had broken bones, and look… my eye's better! Seems you were right about there being magic sponges, Aura. If we can borrow this one and take it back to Khalki, Father will be fine."

She realized Milo's eye was no longer black. Electra crept across for a closer look, but the telchine clung to Aura's arm and kept her from following. She moaned, "bad thing, bad thing", over and over.

Aura looked for someone who might answer her questions. Her gaze settled on Timosthenes. "You stole it, didn't you?" she said. "You stole your healer from the Colossus, after it fell. That's what the soldiers are looking for, don't you see? It's the missing pendant the chief priest calls Helios' Gift, the important one with all the power that he needs to send his messages. No wonder the councillor brought an army after you!"

There were some worried mutters from the other Moths.

"We took it because it looked valuable," Timosthenes admitted. "We only found out it was magic when one of the temple guards speared my leg. I was helping carry it at the time, so I was touching the wires. All these blue sparks came out, and suddenly my leg was better and I could run again. We kept a good hold of it after that, you can be sure. That's why the boss hid it away down here. But it's a healer, not a messenger. At least, it used to be a healer." He frowned at the unconscious Androcles and asked, "What's the matter? Isn't it working?"

"It was working just fine till the telchine-girl turned up," called the boy guarding the entrance. There were more worried mutters, and an argument broke out over what they'd do if the soldiers came while Androcles was still unconscious.

Timosthenes told everyone to shut up and questioned Aura and Electra closely about their part during the raid. He frowned at Aura's description of how the forest had caught fire, mumbled something about Androcles being upset about Chariclea, and jerked his head at the back of the cave. Some of the older Moths trailed after him, casting glances at their injured boss on the way.

A space formed around Aura and the agitated telchine. The wounded Moths gave them unfriendly looks. Aura couldn't blame them, and she didn't want to make things worse. But the glowing Gift drew her as fiercely as her mother was trying to keep her away.

She prised the telchine's webbed hand off her arm. "I'm sure it can't be that dangerous, Mother, or it wouldn't have healed the Moths."

The telchine shook her head wildly. "Trick Lindia! Trick Moths! Trick Aura, also!"

Aura exchanged a glance with Milo, who took a firm grip of the telchine's arm. "She's been kicking up a fuss ever since we got here," he whispered. "She seems better at the back of the cave, away from the Gift, or whatever it's called. You go. I'll look after her."

Aura gave him a grateful smile. With a mixture of excitement and fear, she approached the glow in the centre of the cave. The others parted to let her through, and she caught her breath.

At first she thought she was looking at a larger version of the blue sponge she'd lost in Khalki harbour. About the same size and shape as a human head, it was not the biggest she'd come across, but the Gift was much brighter than any sponge she'd ever seen, even underwater. Next to its intense colouring, the pendant in her pocket seemed a dull, dead thing. But like the smaller pendants, this one had been enclosed in a cage of copper wires, which seemed to be threaded through the sponge itself. Stray ends stuck out where they must have snapped off when the Colossus fell.

Aura shuddered, remembering her dream of the cave, and the feeling of helplessness and pain.

"You got to touch a wire," said one of the Moth girls, glancing at Aura's bandage. "Then, if it's working, it'll heal you."

Aura had almost forgotten her ankle. It wasn't hurting any more, but it was a good excuse. She took a deep breath and touched one of the wires. The Moths shielded their faces as the Gift blazed brilliant purple. Warmth flowed up Aura's arm. Her ankle prickled, and the final trace of discomfort disappeared. She closed her eyes as the rainbows surged through her head, wondering if she'd made a horrible mistake. But instead of the eye-power, another vision came, much clearer than the one she'd had underwater or in her dreams.

A great ship, with a strange eye design on its sail, leaps over the turquoise sea. On board, a man wearing a golden crown with a snake's head curling from his forehead sits under a fringed canopy. Slaves kneel at his feet, cooling him with feathered fans... She is inside a chest, peering out through a crack. Someone lifts the lid. There is the clink of something being moved aside, and an old man's face peers down at her...

Aura's stomach leapt into her mouth. He had extra lines around his eyes and more silver in his beard, but she'd know him anywhere.

"Father!" she breathed.

The vision rippled, and rainbows surrounded the man she'd last seen seven years ago. He peered closer at her, and his eyes widened.

"Father, can you can hear me?" she cried, her heart beating faster. "It's Aura! I'm on Rhodes. I'm speaking to you through Helios' Gift. Are you touching a god's pendant? One of the... er... blue sponges?"

At first she thought he hadn't heard. Then Leonidus' hand reached wonderingly towards her, and a tingle went down her spine.

"*Aura, darling…?*"

Her heart twisted. She tried to touch him, but her fingers closed on empty air. "Oh, Father, I've so much to tell you! But you mustn't come back to Rhodes! The chief priest wants to kill you!"

There was a short silence. Then, "*It's a bit late for that, my darling. I'm already on my way. This is King Ptolemy of Egypt's ship. He's bringing gold to Rhodes for the earthquake fund. We heard the Colossus of Helios fell. Is that right?*" His whisper was tense. He glanced up at the man under the canopy.

"Yes, it broke into five pieces, and the chief priest thinks you stole Helios' Gift, only the Moths did! Mother's here, too, and she's scared of it, but it sends me visions, and…" She didn't want to talk about the eye-power. "And it lets me talk to people through the pendants, like this."

"*Listen, Aura, this is important.*" Leonidus bent close to the chest. "*Does the Gift still have its wires in?*"

"Yes…"

"*Good. You must be very careful of it, Aura. The Gift's alive. Don't take its wires out, whatever you do, and keep it away from your mother. Bring it to the coast and meet me at the Invisible Village. Your Moth friends will know where that is. I'll get there as soon as I can.*"

"But the Moth leader's hurt…" The rainbows flickered, and darkness fell across her vision. "Father!" she cried.

"I'm sorry, my darling. I have to go now, or King Ptolemy will suspect this chest contains more than gold. Don't worry. The Gift will want you to bring it, so it'll help you. Be brave and look after your mother. I'll explain everything when we meet."

"Be careful, Father—!"

But the vision had gone.

Aura removed her hand from the wire, breathing hard. She eyed the Gift suspiciously. She wanted to believe she had spoken to her father on a ship sailing across the sea from Egypt, yet remembered how her mother had claimed the creature was tricky.

The Moths were staring at her. Some of them had their hands on their knives, but no one made a move. The telchine crouched at the back of the cave between Milo and his brother, her eyeless sockets fixed on Helios' Gift. They would all have heard Aura's half of the conversation.

"It's all right," Aura said, hoping she had understood correctly. "I think it'll heal your boss and the rest of you now, as long as we take it to the Invisible Village. My father's going to meet us there. He said it's alive, and I think it's in pain."

There were grumbles among the Moths. "Alive? In pain? What's she talkin' about?"

"...not takin' it nowhere till the boss wakes up...."

"...cheek of it, sayin' she'll take our healer to the Invisible Village!"

"...boss'll decide...."

The mutters fell silent as Timosthenes came across.

"This had better not be a trick, telchine-girl," he warned.

"It's not a trick, I promise! It let me speak to my father… he's on a ship, coming from Egypt. He said if we help the Gift, it'll help us."

Timosthenes chewed his lip. He looked at the unconscious Androcles, glanced at the cave mouth, and gave Aura a hard stare. He took a deep breath. "All right, see if you can make it heal him. Then we'll think what to do with it."

They all watched as Aura lifted Androcles' limp wrist and touched the Moth leader's finger to one of the wires sticking out of the Gift. There was a collective sigh of relief as blue sparks fizzled along the wire, haloing Androcles with rainbows. The gaping wound in his ribs closed, and the colour came back to his face. He moaned, clasped Aura's arm, and whispered, "Chariclea…?"

Aura blushed. Timosthenes pushed her aside and whispered in his leader's ear. Androcles closed his eyes on some inner pain as he learnt that Chariclea had been captured. Then he prodded his ribs to check they were healed and accepted Timosthenes' help to get to his feet.

The others cheered and stamped their feet so loudly, Androcles had to shush them.

Aura felt washed out and exhausted. As the Gift sent blue sparks along its wires to heal assorted broken arms and minor wounds, she unwound the bandage from her ankle. There was no sign of the cut she'd made during the earthquake. Not even a scar remained. She realized it must have been healing her all along, through the smaller pendants, whenever she'd used the eye-power or received a vision.

So many new questions whirled in her head, she didn't realize Timosthenes had finished reporting everything Androcles had missed, including her conversation with the Gift and her wish to take it to her father. A hush fell over the cave. All the Moths were looking at her.

Androcles raised an eyebrow. "You said you'd take our healer to the Invisible Village? Is this true, telchine-girl?"

Quickly, Aura explained. "It's not just a healer," she said. "It sends messages to the other statues. My father says it's dangerous. It can kill, as well as heal."

The protests that greeted these words fell silent when Androcles held up his hand. "I always thought that thing was weird. So it's alive, huh?"

Aura nodded. "So my father says, and I think he's right. I know it's been useful to you as a healer, but I think it was just helping you because it needed you to help it escape from the chief priest. Now it's realized you're not going to take it any further, it's a danger to you. It's already tried to make me use my evil eye on you. Please let me take it to the Invisible Village. None of you need come, if you can tell us which way to go. Milo and Electra can help me with my mother."

"Good idea," someone said. "Sooner we get rid of the telchines, the better! They're the ones the chief priest wants, ain't they? We'll be safer without 'em."

"You can't really be thinking of giving it to her, Boss?" Timosthenes said, scowling. "It's obvious she just wants the magic for herself. It would have killed us long before now, if it were going to. I've a better idea. Why don't we give the healer to the councillor, since that's what he's looking for, and trade it for Chariclea and the others? Then it can't make Aura use her evil eye on us, can it?"

"Better trade the telchines, too!" said another Moth. "That'll get both the chief priest and the councillor off our backs."

Aura stiffened. Out of the corner of her eye, she saw Milo step forward. "I won't let you give Aura back to the chief priest," he said.

"And Aura can use her evil eye without touching the Gift!" Electra said desperately. "I saw her kill two men in the Temple of Athene Ialysos. She burnt them to a cinder!"

Androcles laughed. "Is that so? The islanders are sticking up for each other, and one of 'em has the evil eye. We don't need that kind of trouble! Relax, telchine-girl. We're not goin' to give you back to the chief priest, and we're not goin' to give our healer back, either." He narrowed his eyes at Timosthenes. "But I don't like the sound of it sending messages. If it can send messages, what's to stop the chief priest and the council using it to spy on us? The telchine-woman's right – magic's tricky. We ought to find out more about it, before we try using it again."

Aura opened her mouth to tell him no one could hear any messages unless they were actually touching the blue sponges in the gods' pendants, then closed it again. A sheen of sweat formed as she eyed the Gift.

"But we can't simply tell you the way to the Invisible Village," Androcles went on. "No one can find it unless they've been there before. So we'll have to come with you and make sure our healer don't fall in the wrong hands on the way. It's not a bad idea at all. We can rest up there. Regroup, rearm ourselves, and make a plan. Then, when the time's right, we can take the coast road back to Rhodes City and rescue our friends. This valley'll soon be crawlin' with soldiers. The rest of the Sun God's crown'll keep – it ain't goin' nowhere in a hurry. But we got to move the gold we took last night before we set off. If the councillor starts questioning his prisoners, someone might talk."

There were horrified protests that any Moth would give away their hiding places. But Androcles held up his hand again. With a chilling reminder of the chief priest's words to Aura, he said, "Everyone has their breaking point. That's why we're goin' to the Invisible Village with the telchines. They won't think of lookin' for us there."

Aura wanted to snatch up Helios' Gift and run all the way to the coast so she would be there as soon as the ship from Egypt arrived. But the Moths needed time to move their gold, and she knew she wouldn't get far alone.

Androcles confirmed this when he sketched their route in the dirt of the cave, using a stick to show how he planned to avoid the roads the soldiers would be watching and cut across the hills. "We'll travel by night," he told them. "Rest up durin' the day. We can't risk leaving a trail by stealing stuff on the way, so everyone's got to carry what they need. Food and weapons only, no treasure. We leave at moonrise."

There were a few groans, but no one argued, not even Timosthenes. Now that the joy of their leader's miraculous recovery had worn off, the Moths were subdued. All of them had lost friends in the raid on Ialysos – either captured or dead – and the seriousness of their situation was starting to hit.

The waiting was terrible. While Androcles took a small force to move their stolen gold, the rest of them huddled round a lamp and shared a meal rationed out from supplies kept in the cave. They ate the food cold, because they could not risk the smoke from a fire being spotted from above. Aura's mother had to make do with a small, shrivelled sponge someone had brought along to clean people's wounds, which the amazed Moths watched her swallow whole. Afterwards, she clutched Aura's arm and whispered, "Aura, hungry I," until Aura wanted to cry.

She was hungry, too. Three olives and a crust of hard cheese had not been nearly enough to make up for all the energy she'd expended that day, and she felt light-headed and irritable. The rationing made her angry, even though she knew it made sense if they didn't know where their next meal was coming from. The thought of a night march through untracked hills did nothing to lift her mood, either. Androcles had given her a leather bag to carry the Gift, but she couldn't forget how it had tried to make her use her eye-power on the Moths. To be on the safe side, she put the pendant in the bag as well.

Electra shifted closer. "It really *is* a sponge, isn't it?" she whispered.

Aura recalled her conversation with Milo. "That's what I thought, at first. But normal sponges don't have its sort of powers. My mother wouldn't be frightened of a big sponge – she'd be too busy eating it."

Her attempt at a joke fell flat. Electra glanced at Aura's mother, who crouched miserably at the back of the cave as far as possible from Aura's bag.

"Does it act like a sponge when you cut it up?" the novice asked.

Aura frowned. "The wires, you mean? I suppose it must do, or it wouldn't have closed up around them so neatly. I think they hurt it."

Electra twisted her bony hands together. "What happens if you take a bit away?"

"What do you mean?"

Milo looked interested. "If you force a sponge through a net, it tries to reform itself, but only while it's still alive. When they dry out, they can't do it any more. And if you cut off a piece and take it away, they can't do much about that, either." The look he exchanged with his brother told Aura they'd done all these things. "Every diver tries sticking small sponges together to make bigger, more valuable ones. Only you can't do that because they know the other bits are from different sponges and refuse to seal up. Don't matter what you do – tie them together, sit on them, beat them flat, they won't have it."

"How do they know which bits are different?" Electra asked, impressed by the Khalki boy's knowledge.

"It doesn't matter how they know," Aura said, still irritable. "Helios' Gift isn't a sponge, I told you."

"Are you sure, though?" Milo treated Electra to his rare smile. "Sponges are weird creatures, when you think about it. My folks say some of them are supposed to be so old, they were living when Rhodes Island still belonged to the telchines, before it sank under the flood and rose again and Zeus gave it to Helios." He glanced at the Moths and lowered his voice. "Did you *really* contact your father through it, Aura? Or were you just making that up, so Androcles would give it to you?"

"I'm not a liar!" she snapped, and Milo's expression darkened. She looked at her mother, wishing they were alone so she could ask her about her father.

"So, if someone cut a bit off that Gift-thing, then it would still be alive?" Electra insisted.

Aura closed her eyes. "I don't know. Maybe. Father says the Gift's still alive, though I don't understand how. It must have been out of the water for ages, if it's been wired up to the Colossus ever since Chares built it."

"Fifty-six years," Milo said, nodding.

"And since it's a magic sponge, if they were kept apart, it might be able to talk to the pieces that were cut off?" Electra asked.

Milo frowned. "What are you getting at, priestess?"

Electra glanced at the bag again. "Aura said it sends the messages through the gods' pendants, and they're the same colour as the Gift – only duller because they're more dried out."

Aura's head spun. She wondered how she could have been so blind. It made perfect sense, and it would explain why her mother had been so afraid of the pendant in the sanctuary of Helios before she'd even seen the Gift.

"They're all part of Helios' Gift," she whispered. "The blue sponges my father collects, the one I found during the earthquake, the ones in the sanctuaries of Athene Khalkia and the one I stole from the statue of Helios in Rhodes – all of them... they're all pieces of the same creature! That must be how the Gift sends its power through the pendants, and why the chief priest wants it back so badly. He can't make more pendants without it! Oh Milo, don't you see? My father wasn't stealing the pendants from the temples – he was rescuing pieces of the Gift! He's not a traitor, after all!"

Milo grunted. "Depends whose point of view you take." He eyed the bag, obviously more interested in the creature it contained than in the question of Leonidus' innocence. "I wonder what happens if you put two of the pieces together? Does it reform itself like a sponge? And if it does, will it get more powerful as it grows bigger?"

Aura's stomach fluttered as she remembered the pendant. She scrabbled at the bag ties and peered in warily. But the little piece lay on top of the Gift. Glowing faintly, but separate still.

"I think the wires control its power in some way," she said. "That must be why my father didn't want me to take them out." What would happen when the wires were removed? She shivered and closed the bag on the blue glow.

Electra, however, was staring at the bag in awe. She clutched Aura's arm and whispered, "If the Gift's alive, and we get oracles through the gods' pendants, then maybe it wasn't always the chief priest's voice we heard on Khalki. Maybe the Gift is a *god*!"

Milo snorted, not noticing Aura's unease. "If that's true, I'll never be able to beat a sponge flat in the same way again!"

Cimon giggled and gave the bag a sly poke. "Wake up, god!"

Aura slapped his wrist and shifted the bag between her feet.

Electra gave the Khalki brothers an icy look. "I'm training to be an oracle-priestess. I know a lot more about gods than you do."

Milo smiled, teasing her. "Which god is it, then? Helios himself, maybe? Or Athene? No, I know... Aphrodite! She's supposed to have emerged from the surf, isn't she?"

Electra bit her lip. "Poseidon, of course. He lives under the sea. Tell him, Aura!"

By this time, both Milo and his brother were laughing, and so were some of the Moths who had overheard their conversation. Aura didn't know what to think. Could she have been right, from the start? Visions were supposed to come from the gods, and her mother had mentioned Poseidon. But when she'd used the pendants to talk to Electra, there had been no god or goddess involved, despite what Electra had thought at the time.

Before she could say anything, her mother shuffled forwards. "Danger, Aura!" she moaned. "Bad thing not play with!"

Aura caught the telchine's fluttering hands and sighed. "It's all right, Mother," she said. "I'm not going to touch it again, don't worry. I'll keep it safely in my bag until we get to the Invisible Village. Maybe Father will know what to do with it."

Chapter 9

DEMON POOL

ANDROCLES AND THE others returned at sunset, weary but triumphant, and there was a flurry of activity as the Moths divided their bundles and bags between them. It was a relief to be doing something, rather than sitting and worrying. Aura pushed all the talk of gods and oracles to the back of her mind. Think of it as a big sponge, she told herself. An unidentified sponge I'm taking to show Father. Thoughts of seeing her father again cheered her up, and she told herself the worst was over.

There wasn't much chatter as they climbed out of the valley using the steepest route. Even the Moths puffed for breath. Aura kept hold of her mother's hand, guiding her as best she could through the rocks, but she stumbled nearly as often as the blind telchine. The bag dragged at her shoulder, rubbing a blister under her tunic and making her mother flinch whenever it bumped her. The

Khalki boys and Electra were having a bad time of it, as well. But they struggled on without complaint. They knew they'd never have made it across such country in the dark on their own.

Towards dawn, they came to a road that snaked through the hills. Androcles sent Moths in both directions to check it out, and led the rest of them to a hollow between the rocks. Aura shrugged the bag off her shoulder in relief. But almost at once, Timosthenes came running back with news of a road block.

"Twenty men, Boss!" he reported. "They've overturned a cart in the pass, and they're watching the road from Ialysos. They've got catapults!"

Androcles grinned. "Then they think we're still up there. Good! Take two volunteers and work your way round that road block. Throw some rocks and make sure you let the soldiers see you running back towards Ialysos. When you've lost 'em, double back. Everyone else stay quiet. We'll cross the road further south and meet up at the Demon Pool." He looked at Aura, thoughtful. "They're serious this time. Since they can't know yet for sure we've got the Gift, they must want you two back pretty bad."

Aura turned cold as Timosthenes darted off with two of the Moth boys.

The rest of them shared out the extra bundles, crossed the road without incident, and pressed on into the hills on the other side. Soon they were in a wood with no obvious path. Androcles, however, seemed to know exactly where he was, and led them through the undergrowth to a glade where a spring gushed from moss-covered rocks to form a deep, dark pool. Timosthenes and his volunteers were there already, grinning triumphantly and teasing their friends for taking so long.

The Moths flopped down on its bank and plunged their faces into the water to drink. Milo lay on his back in the grass, arms spread to the sky, and closed his eyes with a sigh. Cimon collapsed beside him, complaining that his feet hurt. The telchine put on a spurt and stumbled forwards, taking them all by surprise. Aura lunged after her and grabbed her arm, worried her mother would fall in.

Electra smiled. "I expect she's thirsty. Careful, lady, there's a pool here. It looks very deep. Let me take your hand, that's right. Can you feel the water…?"

Aura needed a drink, as well. Her tongue felt like sand, and her head was spinning. But she couldn't risk dropping the Gift into the pool. She carried the bag to the trees and set it down carefully between the roots of an oak. Electra and Lindia were splashing each other. The telchine laughed as the water wet her hair. That should be me, Aura thought with a pang. Yet she hesitated to join them, unwilling to let the Gift out of her sight even for a moment.

The other Moths had broken open their bundles of food and were arguing over the best way to get to the Invisible Village. Androcles drew another map in the mud. Milo crouched over it, interested, asking questions. The village seemed to have got its name because, before any of them were born, the whole population had vanished and never been seen again. People were afraid to live in it after that, so the village had been abandoned. The houses had gradually disappeared in the undergrowth, and the paths to it had become so overgrown that no one remembered where they were. But it was said that if you needed a place to hide, you'd find the original village and be safe from the eyes of the world.

Some of the Moths laughed nervously. Others stared at the shadows under the trees. A girl asked how the people who hid in the Invisible Village got back to the world again, and Androcles said they'd worry about that when they got there.

Aura shivered. She wondered how close they were to the sea, and how her father knew about the village. Might he be there already? She glanced at the bag. She longed to contact him again, but didn't want to put him in danger.

"You go to your mother, telchine-girl," Timosthenes said, making her jump. "No one's going to make off with your magic sponge, don't worry. This is a haunted place. Not many people come here. I'll watch it for you."

Aura gave him a grateful smile, and joined her mother and Electra by the pool. Sunlight cast bronze beams across the surface, concealing the depths as she satisfied her thirst. The Moths were still arguing about the Invisible Village. The telchine dangled her webbed feet in the water and splashed in delight.

"Why are you so frightened of Helios' Gift, Mother?" Aura asked softly.

Her mother's feet stilled. She did not answer.

"It's got something to do with you losing your eyes, hasn't it?" Aura insisted. "Was it something to do with your eye-power?"

The telchine hissed. "Aura not questions ask!"

Electra frowned. "You need to tell us, lady, so Aura knows the dangers. She has the eye-power, too. You don't want the same thing to happen to her, do you?"

The telchine's rolls of sea-scented flesh trembled. "Aura bad thing away from stay! Aura eye-power not use again!"

Electra began to say it wasn't as simple as that. But Aura caught her mother's hand and held it tightly, remembering how that same hand had slapped her legs when she'd been a child back on Alimia.

"You're tying to protect me, aren't you, Mother?" she whispered, finally understanding the reason for what had seemed an unfair punishment at the time. "You didn't want me to learn how to use the eye-power, because you were afraid the Gift would hurt me, like it hurt you. But I'm up-grown now, and I need to use it so I can stay in contact with Father. He's going to meet us soon with some pieces of the Gift he's rescued. But the soldiers are still hunting us, so I might need to use my eye-power again to help us stay free. Please tell us what happened. I'm not a little girl any more."

The telchine went very still.

"Lady?" Electra said, glancing at Aura. "Don't you want to see Leonidus again? Is that it? Did he have something to do with your losing your eyes?"

"Lindia love Leonidus," the telchine whispered. "When Lindia up-grow, bad thing make Lindia kill humans. But Lindia not hurt Leonidus, never, ever!"

Aura exchanged another glance with Electra. "Do you mean the Gift tried to make you use the eye-power on my *father*?" she whispered, thinking of how it had almost made her use the power on the Moths in the cave. "But why? What happened?"

But her mother would say no more. She hugged herself and started to sing softly, rocking back and forth, her blind face turned to the pool.

Aura sighed. She knew it was pointless talking to her mother when she got upset like that. She looked at the bag containing the Gift, and saw Timosthenes jump guiltily away from it. She ought to check it had survived the journey.

Leaving Electra to look after her mother, she untied the cord and peered inside. The Gift was glowing faintly, but she couldn't see the little pendant. Her heart thudded as she thought of what Milo had said about sponges reforming. She reached into the bag and felt around. With some relief, she found the pendant had slipped to the bottom – and as she did so her hand brushed a wire.

Rainbows glimmered in her head. She closed her eyes and whispered, "Father? Is that you? Are you still on the ship?"

But there was no reply, just a hissing in her head. She tried to open herself to a vision, but received only a jumble of images.

Glittering gold and jewels, like she'd seen in the temple sanctuaries... clouds of incense... burning torches...

A loud SPLASH jerked her back. Electra stood beside the pool, her hands over her mouth and the front of her robe soaked, staring at a ring of dying ripples. There was no sign of Aura's mother.

Aura abandoned the Gift and rushed to the pool, her head still spinning from the half-visions. "Mother, *no*! I'm sorry I upset you! Please come back!"

Milo was already dragging his tunic over his head in preparation to dive. Androcles seized the boy's arm. "I wouldn't, if I were you. That's not called the Demon Pool for nothin', you know. It's supposed to be haunted by water-demons. They lure people down to their world, where time stands still. If you ever find your way back, years have passed and your family and friends are all dead."

"Don't be so stupid! That's my mother in there, and she's blind!" Aura pushed the boys aside, her stomach jumping with anxiety. Before anyone could stop her, she threw herself into the pool.

She dived through trailing weed into the murk. It was not like the sea. She could see nothing beyond her fingertips, and it was *cold*. She swam fast, partly to keep warm, partly in fear of losing her mother, her body twisting to investigate shadows that turned out to be floating clumps of weed. Her air ran out. Praying it would work for her a second time, she changed to water-breathing. It was easier than before, because this time she was expecting the coldness in her lungs. What had made her mother dive in? Had she thought she'd find sponges to eat down here?

Aura went deeper. The water was darker and colder than any she had ever swum in before. Not having to surface for air, she searched and searched until she could no longer feel her fingers and toes. She kept thinking she saw things from the corners of her eyes – glimmers of rainbows, strange lights in the gloom – but they vanished as soon as she turned her head. Finally, afraid of getting cramp, she headed back up.

Firelight glimmered above. Night had fallen while she'd been underwater. Her stomach gave an uneasy turn as she remembered what Androcles had told them about the legend. She must have been in the pool ages, yet it hadn't felt that long. Hoping she wouldn't find her mother, Electra and the Moths all dead, she kicked for the surface.

She choked as her lungs emptied of water and took their first breath of air, then froze as a scream split the darkness. She trod water and blinked round in confusion. Torches flared through the trees. Everywhere she looked, people were running. Somewhere in the wood, a girl screamed again. Men's voices called to one another:

"There goes another one!"

"...cut them off at the road!"

"...curse this wood – it's like chasing shadows!"

At first, Aura couldn't think what was happening. Then she saw the soldiers who had raided Ialysos, chasing the Moths with their torches and spears. She twisted round in despair and looked for the tree where she'd left her bag, but couldn't see the Gift.

A shout rang out as one of the soldiers spotted her. Several men ran towards the pool. Heart pounding, Aura ducked back underwater. She had no time to take a proper breath, but this actually made the change to water-breathing easier. She clung on to a weed rope, far enough down that the men wouldn't see her, and stared up at the rippling torchlight, terrified in case her mother surfaced while they were searching.

The soldiers poked the reeds with their spears. They peered into the depths, shook their heads and moved away. They were still in the clearing, though. There seemed to be a group of captives, huddled against the rocks, some of them groaning from wounds. Aura dared not go nearer to the surface in case the soldiers spotted her again.

Was Electra captured? Androcles? The Khalki boys? At least they couldn't get their hands on her mother, if she was still in the pool... Aura felt torn. Half of her was desperate to dive back down and continue the search; the other half wanted to help her friends. Common sense said there were too many men. She had no weapon, no pendant, and getting herself captured wasn't going to help anyone.

Undecided, she clung to the weed with her scarred fingers. She wondered if the soldiers intended to make camp here. The thought of having to stay under the black water all night made her shiver. But it seemed they had no wish to hang around the haunted waters. After some discussion, they roped their captives together and marched them off into the wood. Two of them stayed for a final poke around the reeds, before jogging after the others.

Aura counted to a hundred to make sure they weren't coming back. Then she surfaced, spluttering and coughing. She swam to the bank, grasped a tree root, and hauled herself out. Shivering violently, she stumbled to the place where she'd left the Gift and searched through the undergrowth. Without the torches, it was very dark under the trees. Behind her, the Demon Pool looked like a hole in the ground.

She was about to check the neighbouring trees in the hope she'd remembered wrongly, when a quiet voice behind her said, "Been swimming, have you, telchine-girl? Find anything interesting?"

She whirled in alarm as a man wearing a dark cloak stepped out of the shadows and dropped his hood. The silver in his hair and beard glimmered in the starlight.

It was Councillor Iamus.

Aura's first instinct was to run. Let Councillor Iamus take the Gift – and good luck to him. She was almost certain the strange creature had made her mother dive into the pool. But if she let him take the Gift, she'd lose her only contact with her father.

The councillor smiled and spread his hands to show he wasn't carrying a weapon. "Relax, telchine-girl. You're under no threat, so you don't have to use your evil eye on me. I sent the soldiers on ahead with the captives. You don't seem to have found Helios' Gift down there, after all – a pity, but that's not the only reason I'm here. I wanted a word with you in private."

"Don't touch me!" Aura said, backing against a tree. "You ordered me chained on your ship. And then your horrid chief priest had my mother brought to Rhodes, and now I've lost her in the Demon Pool!"

"Lost your mother?" The councillor raised an eyebrow. "I doubt that, somehow. The Moths insisted both you and your mother had drowned. But when my men claimed they'd seen a nymph, I knew you'd be back. Telchines don't drown in a little bit of water like that. I expect she's still down there somewhere, hiding."

He didn't seem worried about her mother. Aura darted suspicious looks at the undergrowth. She didn't trust him. He might have kept some soldiers lying in wait. They would be wary of her eye-power, not realizing she couldn't use it without a pendant to contact the Gift. The sensible thing would be to run before they found out.

"If you're thinking of running off," the councillor said, as if he could read her thoughts, "I shan't try to stop you. I'll find you and your friends again eventually. But if you help me, I might be able to help you. The chief priest—" He must have noticed her stiffen, for he added, "Don't worry, he's not here. That stone you threw at him from the wall during your escape cracked his skull. He has the best physicians Rhodes can offer, so he'll live. But his temporary incapacity has given me an opportunity to investigate the matter of this missing Helios' Gift without him breathing down my neck. Xenophon, of course, wants you brought back to the city at once with Helios' Gift when we recover it. But since some of the Moths seem to have eluded us again, I think he'll believe me if I tell him you escaped as well."

Aura glanced behind her, only half listening. *When we recover it*. He didn't have the Gift, after all.

"You might not be aware of this," the councillor continued, "but a very important visitor is on his way to Rhodes with Egyptian gold for the rebuilding of our Colossus of Helios and the restoration of our damaged towns and temples. Normally, the Council would accept his offer without question, and of course everyone wants to see their Sun God stand tall and proud again. Public opinion is a powerful thing, and we on the Council ignore it at our peril. But if we rebuild our Colossus of Helios, even King Ptolemy's gold will not go very far towards other, more pressing projects. Another reason for my caution is that the chief priest seems curiously reluctant to raise his Colossus without the Gift, and I'm starting to wonder quite why."

He gave her a quizzical look. Aura said nothing.

"I was too young to remember the Colossus being built," the councillor went on in a conversational tone. "But according to Xenophon, Helios' Gift was part of a sacrifice to give the statue strength. I assumed it was the heart of a bull or a horse. Then, later, I wondered if it might have been the heart of a man. Unlike the little pendants the gods wear, the Gift was always kept away from people, and only priests were allowed in to touch it. There is some mystery surrounding the death of its architect, Chares of Lindos, and I wondered if old Xenophon might have decided the blood of its creator would help make the Colossus strong. There's a precedent for such sacrifices in the ancient texts, and it's exactly the sort of thing Xenophon might do."

Aura stared at him, remembering how the soldiers who had escorted her to the Temple of Helios claimed her grandfather, Chares, had killed himself. She shivered. Her wet hair clung to her like waterweed, and she was aware of her tunic sticking to all the plumpest parts of her body. But she was pretty sure the Gift was not anyone's heart.

The councillor regarded her thoughtfully. "Yet it seems this Helios' Gift is much stranger than any sacrifice," he said. "As for the reason Xenophon wants *you* returned so badly, I've been doing some checking, and it seems your absent father Leonidus was Chares of Lindos' son. Most interesting, don't you think?" He watched for a reaction, and seemed disappointed by her lack of surprise. "This puts things into perspective. So talk to me, Aura. Tell me if the rumours are true. Do you telchines have some kind of connection with this Gift?"

Aura eyed the trees. Exactly what had the captured Moths told him? "I... yes, we do."

The councillor sighed. "Ah. Then I assume that means you already know about the messages, and the way it controls the pendants the gods wear?"

Aura nodded warily.

"It can kill, too, or so the priests of Helios claim," the councillor said. "Apparently, the priests who were inside the Colossus when it fell were found burnt to death. So I think we've established it's a thing of power. That probably explains why old Xenophon wants it back so badly. What else do you know about it? Do you think it might, for example, be able to cause earthquakes?"

"Earthquakes?" Aura repeated, her stomach fluttering.

"Obviously, you don't know," the Councillor said with an impatient flick of his hand. "But maybe you can find out for me. I expect your grandfather told your father its secrets before he died. Let me explain something to you, Aura. Rhodes remains independent only because she maintains good relationships with the various powers of the civilized world. Rome, Egypt, Greece, Macedonia, Anatolia, Persia… we are caught in the middle of them all when it comes to war, so I'm sure you can see it's in our best interests to maintain peace. I wouldn't expect an uneducated sponge diver to understand the finer politics, but believe me when I say an ambitious man like Xenophon with a powerful enough weapon, as this Helios' Gift seems to be, could destroy our island. I'll have the Gift safe very shortly. In the meantime, if you can find out for me exactly what it's capable of, you'll not only be helping the Council – you'll be helping your family and friends, as well."

It was too much on top of her recent loss. The only thing Aura understood was that, for some reason she didn't quite follow, the councillor was letting her go.

She backed away from him, shaking her head. "I don't know anything about earthquakes," she said. "I just want my mother back, and my father to be safe. I want to go *home*."

The councillor regarded her coolly. "Find out for me, telchine-girl. Talk to your father, and your mother, too, when she comes out of that pool. I've persuaded the Council that before we agree to rebuild the Colossus of Helios it would be wise to ask the advice of the oracle at Lindos. The public will accept what the oracle says, so the Council risks no disfavour from Helios' priests if the answer is no. As soon as King Ptolemy arrives, we'll be taking him there. You can meet me at Lindos, safely out of earshot of the priests of Helios. I promise to protect your family if you co-operate with me. Meanwhile, I'll keep the chief priest off your trail as long as I can." He backed away through the trees, watching her warily until the darkness swallowed him.

When he'd gone, the fear caught up with Aura like a wave breaking over her head. She stumbled back to the pool, calling for her mother, although she knew the telchine wouldn't hear her underwater. But before she could reach the pool, someone dropped from the treetops, put a hand over her mouth and pulled her to the ground.

She struggled in panic and managed a muffled scream.

"Shh, you idiot!" said a familiar voice. "Do you want the soldiers to come back?" Milo's dark eyes peered down at her. She went limp with relief.

The Khalki boy rolled off her. Aura climbed to her feet and brushed herself off, her embarrassment mixed with unexpected relief. "Milo… you escaped."

"No thanks to you!" He gave her an unreadable look. "What did you think you were trying to do, diving into the Demon Pool like that? You were down there ages! I know you've got a sponge diver's lungs, but I honestly thought you'd drowned. I was about to dive in after you, no matter what Androcles might say about demons, but then the soldiers came and we had to hide. I've been up that tree for ages, waiting for you to surface!" He grimaced. "They caught some of the Moths and questioned them. But they obviously didn't tell the councillor much. Why did he let you go?"

He'd seen the whole thing, Aura realized. She shook her head. She hardly understood herself. "I don't think he's working with the chief priest. He talked about keeping the Gift safe. He hasn't got it yet, but he seems to think he's going to find it soon. He wants me to meet him at Lindos when I've had a chance to ask Father more about its powers. He already knows about the messages and telchines having a connection with it, but he doesn't seem to realize the gods' pendants are pieces of it. Maybe I should have told him..." Her teeth chattered again.

"No, you shouldn't!" Milo gripped her arm. "Don't tell him anything! Don't worry. Electra's safe with the others. When the soldiers went, I volunteered to come back and wait for you. Timosthenes says they're taking their captives to the coast road, but they didn't catch us all."

"Milo, wait! My mother's still in the pool. We can't just leave her down there. And now the Gift's missing, too..."

Milo smiled. "You needn't worry about that. Electra grabbed your bag when the soldiers came. She's quick when she wants to be, I'll give her that." He glanced back at the pool, and his tone turned serious again. "I know you're missing your mother, Aura, but she must have her reasons. No one forced her to jump in, did they? She'll be all right. She'll come out when she's ready to. At least you know where she is. We can't hang around here any longer. The soldiers might come back. Come on, this way."

Aura sighed, knowing he spoke the truth. Vowing to return for her mother as soon as it was safe, she followed the Khalki boy into the woods.

Chapter 10

BETRAYAL

MILO LED THE way through dark trees to a small cave. Five boys and four girls, even dirtier and more unkempt than before, crouched in the shadows around a flickering torch. Androcles was waving his fist and talking fast. He seemed to be trying to cheer the others up, but no one was smiling. Electra knelt at the edge of the group, crying quietly and trying to hide it. Her black hair was a tangled mess and she had a nasty scratch on one cheek.

Aura trod on a twig, and everyone jumped. In the blink of an eye, the torch was extinguished and a drawn dagger appeared in Androcles' hand. Cimon rushed to his brother, wrapped his arms around his waist, and buried his face against his chest. The others stared at Aura as if she were a ghost.

The Moths searched the wood with frightened eyes, as if they expected soldiers to emerge from the darkness behind the newcomers. Then Electra gave a cry and rushed across to grasp Aura's hands. "I thought you'd *drowned*!" she sobbed. "Oh Aura, don't ever frighten me like that again!" She squeezed Aura's fingers so tightly, they hurt nearly as much as when she'd cut off her webs.

She wriggled free, and Electra sniffed and picked up the bag with the Gift in it with a tight smile. "I rescued the god. We can't let the chief priest wire it back to his Colossus and pretend to be an oracle again! Androcles thinks someone must have betrayed us, because the soldiers knew exactly where we were."

Aura remembered the way Timosthenes had jumped away from the bag before her mother had dived in the pool. She glanced at the blond boy and shook her head. No. Even if Timosthenes knew how to use the Gift to send a message, he was Androcles' second in command. He wouldn't have betrayed them to the councillor. More likely, one of Xenophon's priests had been in a temple sanctuary when she'd tried to contact her father, and heard her through a god's pendant.

"Take it, Aura," Electra urged. "I can't carry the god. I'm not worthy."

Nor am I, Aura wanted to say.

Just in case, she kept her face turned away from her friends as she took the bag. But there were no rainbows in her head. She fingered the ties uneasily, wanting to look inside, yet afraid to touch the Gift after what had happened last time.

In a subdued mood, the Moths lit another fire in the back of the cave and huddled close to the flames to plan what they were going to do next. It was clear they had been badly frightened by the attack at the pool. Two more Moth boys joined them during the night, having fled deep into the woods and worked their way back using owl hoots to find their friends. With Aura and Milo, that made thirteen. A small, sad number compared to the high-spirited camp she remembered at Ialysos.

"The question is, does the councillor know we're goin' to the Invisible Village?" Androcles said. "It might have been a lucky guess we'd be at the Demon Pool."

"He knows we're on our way to meet Aura's father," Milo said, looking at her.

So Aura had to explain about her interview with Councillor Iamus, and why he'd let her go. Timosthenes nodded, but the other Moths gave her suspicious looks. She didn't blame them. Even Electra frowned.

"Of course it wasn't luck," Timosthenes said. "It's obvious they found out we were on our way to the coast and set a trap for us. I say we should catch them off guard and do what they least expect. I'll take Aura and the Gift on to the Invisible Village, while you take the others back to Ialysos. I know where it is – my father took me there once when I was little. There's no need for us all to be in danger." There were murmurs of agreement, and an argument began over which route would be safest.

Aura closed her eyes. She wondered if it was safe to go back to the pool yet. The Moths seemed to have no intention of returning there.

"No," Androcles said firmly. "We're not going back to Ialysos until we've rescued our friends. The councillor will never find the Invisible Village. And if this King Ptolemy has brought a shipload of Egyptian gold to rebuild the Colossus, everyone'll be distracted by that. Aura can help us with her evil eye."

"We might even get our hands on some of that Egyptian gold, while we're at it!" one of the Moth girls suggested, and there was a smattering of laughter as this raised their spirits.

Timosthenes pulled a face as the other Moths offered suggestions for stealing the gold. Androcles let them talk, staring thoughtfully out into the night. The cave grew noisy as they hatched ever more daring plans to rescue their friends, capture King Ptolemy's ship with the gold on board, and sail it to a deserted island, where they'd live happily ever after without any adults to order them about.

Quietly, Aura untied the cord and reached into the bag. The Gift glimmered as she touched a wire. She closed her eyes, ready to break the contact the moment she had another vision of a temple sanctuary, but this time there was nothing at all.

"Father?" she whispered, trying to summon an image of the ship she'd seen. "Father, can you hear me?"

Nothing.

"Mother? I'm sorry I upset you. Please come out of the pool."

Nothing.

She clenched her fists, dragged the Gift out of the bag by its wires, and slammed it against the rock in frustration. "Let me speak to my family!" she shouted, glaring at the creature. "Don't just ignore me!"

"No, Aura!" Electra gasped. "Poseidon will punish you—"

The Gift flared intense blue, lighting up the night. Rainbows invaded Aura's head. Dust showered from the roof of the cave as the rock trembled. She staggered to her feet in a mixture of triumph and alarm, her heart beating wildly, blinded by the sudden light. Milo's arms caught her. He guided her towards the entrance, bumped by the Moths, who had also scrambled to their feet when the earth shook.

Aura clung to the Gift, knowing she should drop it and break the contact, but needing to find out what had happened to her family. She closed her eyes again. "Help me!" she hissed.

"Steady, Aura," Milo whispered, mistaking her plea for fear. "It's all right. It's only a little tremor. I don't think the roof's going to fall on us. Look – you're safe, see?"

She shook her head. The rainbows were fierce and bright. She knew with dreadful certainty that the moment she opened her eyes, someone would get hurt.

"Take me outside," she said through gritted teeth. "Please Milo... just do it."

She heard whispers and mutters from the Moths, and a frightened question from Electra. Then Milo's strong arms guided her through them, and she felt the night breeze lift her hair. Leaves brushed her face as he guided her into the trees. She smelled the mandrake flowers and breathed a little easier.

"Leave me here," she said. "Go back and get the others out into the open, but not near any trees, and keep them away from me."

"I'm not leaving you here in this state, don't be silly! The soldiers might come back. What's wrong? Come on, Aura, you can tell me. I won't pass it on. Sponge divers' code, remember?"

"I've got to talk to the Gift. I'm safe if the soldiers come – I've got my eye-power. But the others are in danger. Trust me, you have to get them out of that cave. *Go*, Milo!"

Reluctantly, he released her. She heard him move back through the undergrowth the way they had come. She knelt and pressed her face to the ground, holding in the rainbows. "Show me where my mother went!" she said through gritted teeth.

But Electra must be right. She'd made the creature angry. She clenched her fists as the rainbows brightened. The power built up, more and more painfully, pressing against the inside of her skull. She could hold it back no longer.

She opened her eyes.

With a deep groan, the earth cracked beneath her hands and knees.

A tree crashed in the darkness nearby, its roots torn from the ground. She heard screams as, with a great tumbling of rocks, the cave they had been sheltering in collapsed.

Aura straightened. The Gift lay in the leaves, dull now under the stars. She felt numb. The Moths gathered round her, silent. Milo held his sobbing brother under one arm. Androcles shook dust from his hair, his lips pressed tight.

Electra bit her lip. "You shouldn't have done that, Aura," she said. "Poseidon got angry. He shook the earth to punish us."

"Two injured, Boss," Timosthenes reported, glaring at Aura. "Good job the Khalki boy got the rest clear when he did, or we'd all be buried alive back there."

The Moths gave Milo grateful looks. Thankfully, they seemed no readier to believe Electra's words than they had been before, when she'd claimed their "healer" was a god. The last thing they were going to do was blame Aura for a brief tremor nothing like as bad as the one that had toppled the Sun God. Yet she couldn't stop thinking of the councillor's words. *Do you think it might be able to cause earthquakes?*

She hugged herself miserably. Two injured. One boy had a broken leg, and blood was running down the other's face from a wound on his head. It could have been worse. It could have been a lot better. Why, oh why, had she been so stupid?

"The telchine-girl obviously can't control her magic," Timosthenes said, still glaring at her. "She'll be worse than useless on a raid. Please let me take her to the Invisible Village, Boss, while you stay here with the injured."

Androcles scowled. "I told you before, we stick together, 'specially now."

The injured boys agreed, and the one with the broken leg hauled himself to his feet. Using a branch for support, he hopped across the clearing and snatched one of the slings to demonstrate how well he could throw a stone. Timosthenes told him not to be so stupid, and how on earth did he think he was going to hop all the way to the coast like that? The boy who had been hit on the head could walk fine, but his vision was blurred and he couldn't throw straight. When one of the girls joked that the two injured Moths made a whole Moth between them, and Timosthenes muttered that the only sensible thing was to split up, Androcles lost his temper and yelled at them all to shut up so he could think what to do.

Throughout this, Aura had been trying to work up the courage to touch the Gift again. She had just about convinced herself that it was unlikely to make her use the eye-power so soon, when Timosthenes seized her hair.

"I don't know what you're up to, telchine," he hissed. "But if you try anything like that trick back at the cave again, you and your Khalki friends are dead."

Aura tugged free, impatient. Didn't he understand they had more important things to worry about now? She reminded him that she was only half telchine and couldn't always make the Gift do what she wanted, and Timosthenes' expression turned ugly. He clenched his fist. But she never found out if he would have hit her, because Milo punched him first.

The two boys rolled in the leaves through patches of starlight, scratching and biting like animals. Cimon shouted encouragement to his brother, while Androcles yelled at them to grow up. Electra widened her eyes at Aura. "Do something!" she said. "Or the soldiers will hear." The Moths tried to separate Timosthenes and Milo, but someone got hit by mistake, and soon several others had joined in.

Aura did the only thing she could think of. She snatched the Gift out of the leaves and reached for the rainbows. The contact was almost as fierce as before, but this time she had more control. She checked no one was near enough to get hurt, and let the eye-power free. Blue lightning struck the rocks blocking the cave mouth. Stone chips flew. The noise came a fraction later, a crack like thunder.

The Moths broke off their brawl to stare at her, very quiet. The two original fighters rolled apart and glared at each other. At first, they didn't notice Aura standing in the shadows with fists clenched, panting. Milo had a cut over his eye, and Timosthenes' lip was bleeding. For a horrible moment, Aura thought they were going to continue the fight. Then Milo sighed and helped the blond boy up.

Androcles shook his head. "That was *stupid*," he said, scowling at them all in turn. He considered the rubble in the cave, the fallen tree, and the two injured boys. "Right, we need a stretcher for our friend with the broken leg. You and you, carry it." He pointed to two strong-looking boys and stamped on the earth to check it was solid again. "You, telchine-girl, make yourself useful and see if you can persuade that Gift thing to heal the injured. We're goin' to keep to the plan and hole up at the Invisible Village till we're strong again. We can see if Aura's father's got any bright ideas when he arrives. Meanwhile, everyone collect some of them stones, keep your slings handy an' follow me. Anyone who starts another fight, uses their evil eye, or says another *word* before we reach the coast, is no longer a Moth and will be left to fend for themselves. Understand?" His gaze lingered on Timosthenes.

The others nodded, avoiding one another's eyes.

While the bearers made a stretcher out of two branches and a cloak for their injured friend, the rest of the Moths went to rummage through the rubble for the right-sized stones. There was a quiet gathering-up of clothing and weapons. The other injured boy tied a rag around his head to keep the blood out of his eyes. Aura carried the Gift across without much hope, and wasn't really surprised when it refused to heal them. She put the creature back in the bag with the pendant, and watched Electra tie a splint to the Moth boy's broken leg. Androcles fixed them all with a final glare, before leading the way carefully through the night.

Having difficulty seeing where she was going on the dark path, Aura ended up at the back with the stretcher bearers and Electra. Timosthenes darted her hostile glances, but seemed wary after her latest display of eye-power and kept his distance. There was no breath for talking, and little energy to spare for arguments. As it began to get light, Androcles cut a stick to beat the undergrowth aside so they could go faster. The others followed in silence, darting frightened glances at the shadows around them, which were even more unsettling than when it had been fully dark.

The trek through the ghostly half-light seemed endless. Twigs snagged on Aura's clothes and the Gift caused her back to ache. She began to wonder if the Night Moth leader had lost his way. Then, all of a sudden, they emerged from the trees at the top of a cliff and stopped, breathless.

The sea sparkled beneath them, colourful in the sunrise. On the horizon the coastline of Anatolia made a purple smudge against the huge red sun. Although they were on the wrong side of Rhodes to see her home, something tugged at Aura's heart.

"Aura?"

A touch on her arm startled her. "You were

dreaming," Electra said with a smile. "You nearly went over the edge. Androcles says the Invisible Village is down there. Apparently, before the earthquake, the wood continued down this slope."

Aura looked where she was pointing and saw a steep face covered in loose shale and the wreckage of trees, strewn with boulders. There seemed to be a ledge about halfway down, beyond which the cliff fell away steeply to the sea. A deserted pebble beach was just visible at the bottom. Seabirds swooped below them to their nests in the rocks, showing how high they were. Her heart sank. She hoped Androcles would not expect her to climb down there. The Moths were already scampering across the slope, collecting more stones to use as missiles for their slings. They'd wasted quite a few on route, slinging at shadows in the wood.

But after scouting along the cliff top, Androcles beckoned them over to a precipitous path that led diagonally down the slope to the ledge. The Moths carrying the stretcher went first, picking their way down slowly and carefully. Timosthenes followed, glancing over his shoulder. He had hardly spoken since the fight, and Aura was glad Androcles hadn't let him take her here alone. She watched Milo helping his brother on the steep places. He caught her looking and winked. She felt warm inside, remembering how he'd protected her when Timosthenes had been going to hit her. But that might have been because he needed the Gift to heal his father, and she was the only one who could make it work… sometimes make it work. She shook her head, annoyed the Khalki boy could confuse her so much.

"What's wrong?" Electra said. "Has the god spoken to you again?"

Aura shook her head and whispered, "Electra, do you know where we are?"

"Somewhere on the coast between Rhodes City and Lindos, I think. There's a town along here where old people go to get rid of their aches and pains, but we're quite a way south of that, I think."

"No, I mean this Invisible Village… do you know anything about it? That story the Moths told us about the people disappearing sounds strange."

"Probably just a ruin," Electra said with a shrug. "There are loads of abandoned villages on Rhodes. Look at Ialysos – the whole population went to live in Rhodes City because they thought it was a better place. Why do you ask, anyway?"

"I was just wondering how my father knows about it. Androcles said no one could find this place unless they'd been here before, didn't he? That means my father must have been here at least once, and if the chief priest was hunting him that was probably before he left Rhodes and came to Alimia and met my mother, maybe before the people who lived here disappeared." She shook her head. "Oh, I don't know! I just wish my mother hadn't gone. There's still so much I want to ask her. I never really got a chance."

Electra bit her lip and put her arms around her. "Oh, Aura. I'm sorry! I know I should have tried to stop your mother jumping in that pool, but it all happened so fast—"

"You couldn't have stopped her," Aura said quickly, giving the novice's hand a squeeze. "And you saved the Gift from the soldiers. I'm glad you're with me. You're the only one who really understands what it's like to hear words through it."

Electra gave her a fleeting smile. "Oracles often don't make much sense. At least your mother's safe from the soldiers now. We'd better go down. Androcles is waving to us."

Aura didn't mention her strange feeling about this place, which grew stronger as they descended. They had no breath for talking as they negotiated the steep path, clutching hands. Her bag bumped against the rock face and snagged on broken branches. More than once she slipped, kicking shale over the edge of the path in a heart-thudding scramble to keep her balance. The Moths were already down safely. Aura could hear them whooping in triumph as they ran along the ledge to explore the village. Timosthenes hurried on ahead to check it out.

"Ruins, just like I told you," Electra said, squinting down. "They look like they go right into the cliff – must be a sort of cavern."

Red light bathed the slope. The sun was in their eyes as they came to the first overgrown wall. The boy with

the broken leg was sitting up on his stretcher, panting as if he had walked down himself.

"That was *scary*," he said with a grin, as they joined him. "I thought they were goin' to drop me over the edge. This place certainly ain't obvious! Even if it ain't the Invisible Village, we can hide out here for a while—" He broke off, staring at the shadows under the cliff where Timosthenes had gone. He whispered, "Did you see something move in there?"

Aura stiffened, the hairs on the back of her neck prickling. Even as Electra said, "Ghosts, maybe…" there was a shout from further along the ledge where the Moths had gone exploring, and Timosthenes came running back, waving his arms.

"It's a trap!" he yelled. "Everyone back up the cliff!"

Soldiers emerged from behind the walls with drawn swords. The boy with the broken leg paled. The others scattered back up the slope on all fours. Stones rattled down as they tugged out their slings and tried to gain enough of a foothold to aim properly. With trembling hands, Electra picked up one end of the stretcher. She looked frightened, but determined. "Come on, Aura!" she said. "We can't just leave him here!"

But even as Aura picked up the other end, she knew it was hopeless. More soldiers blocked the path they'd used to get down to the village, and the rock fall was too steep to climb, even for the agile Moths. The cavern was a dead end. On their other side was the vertical cliff.

Councillor Iamus rode out of the shadows on a black horse and held out his hand. "Give me the Gift, telchine-girl," he said.

Aura shook her head, tears in her eyes. "I have to take it to my father. I thought you said you wanted me to find out more about it for you?"

"You don't need to keep the Gift for that. Give it to me, and you and your priestess friend can go free to find out what you need to. The others come with us. We can discuss their fate when you meet me in Lindos with the information."

"Not likely!" yelled Androcles from halfway up the slope, and a stone bounced off the wall in front of Aura. The horse whipped round, nearly unseating its rider. Councillor Iamus cursed under his breath and shouted orders to his men, who sorted themselves out with chilling professionalism… two up the slope after Androcles, two to carry the boy on the stretcher, four to guard the Moths they had already caught, another two to block the path. Androcles was dragged down, struggling furiously, and made to kneel with a sword across his throat. Timosthenes clenched his fists, helpless. The remaining Moths slid down the slope on their backsides to help their boss, yelling and bringing down an avalanche of shale and dust.

"It's all going wrong!" Electra cried, her eyes filling with tears. "Androcles was right about us being betrayed – someone must have told the councillor we were bringing the Gift here! Aura, do something. Use your evil eye!"

Trembling, Aura opened the bag and grabbed a wire. She tensed. But the rainbows did not come, not even a whisper. She frowned at the Gift, confused.

The councillor had regained control of his horse. He smiled and walked it slowly across to where the two girls crouched. Aura looked round desperately. She couldn't see what had happened to Milo or his brother.

She grabbed Electra's hand and dragged her away from the horse. "Help us!" she shouted at the Gift. "Do you want the chief priest to wire you back in that pendant on his Colossus?"

The Gift stayed dull.

"What's wrong?" Electra gasped. "Why isn't your evil eye working? Quick, Aura!"

Two soldiers were creeping closer to cut off their escape. Aura took a deep breath and held the bag over the edge of the cliff. "Don't come any closer, or I'll drop it!" she threatened.

Councillor Iamus signalled the soldiers back. "Be sensible, telchine-girl," he said quietly. "I'm not going to give it back to Xenophon, am I? I'll keep it safe until we know more about its powers…"

The horse came forward another step, and blue light spilled out of Aura's bag. The councillor sucked in his breath and reined the animal back to safety. At last, Aura's head filled with rainbows – but too late. Electra screamed and grabbed her hand as a crack zigzagged like lightning towards their feet.

Aura staggered. A piece of the ledge crumbled under her weight and went bouncing away down the cliff. Electra screamed again as the rock beneath their feet vanished, leaving them standing on air.

Out of the corner of her eye, she saw Electra's arms waving wildly as if the novice were trying to fly. The councillor shouted something, and the soldiers ran to the edge. Aura closed her eyes, at last realizing the true extent of the creature's trickery. *We're going to die*, she thought. *It'll be safe in the sea, but we're going to smash our skulls on the rocks down there, and—*

Rainbows blazed.

The shouting above cut off as if someone had slammed a door, and there was only the wind blowing in her ears.

She didn't remember landing. The next thing she knew, she was rolling through soft sand. A gasp nearby told her Electra was alive, too. She risked a peep. Sea, sky, and red sun whirled around her. Then the slope levelled out, and she rolled up hard against the wall of a hut that had not been there before. She still had hold of the bag. Inside, the Gift was shining brighter than ever before, rainbow colours rippling along the wires beneath its blue flesh. The pendant had fallen out and lay nearby, glowing just as fiercely. Aura scooped it up, shivering and gasping for breath.

"What happened?" the novice whispered. "Did the Gift save us? I'm bruised all over, and my ears feel funny. Oh Aura, I thought we were dead!" She sat up and blinked around in confusion. "Where are we? Where did these huts come from? What happened to the Moths? Aura… where's the Invisible Village gone?"

Aura got shakily to her knees and looked up. There was no sign of Councillor Iamus or the soldiers who had been peering over the cliff. There were no men that she could see, no captive Moths, and – like Electra had said – no sign of the ruins or the ledge they'd fallen from. The cliff rose up, vertical and white, to the trees at the top, which stood tall against the sky as if there had never been an earthquake.

She turned her head very slowly. The sea was still there, sparkling in the early sunlight. But two boats were drawn up on the beach, laden with sponges. The hut that had broken their fall was part of a village that had definitely not been here before. Strings of shells chimed at every door, and the round walls were decorated with treasures from the deep that Aura, in her confusion, could not identify. As she stared, wondering how an entire village could have been so well hidden from above, massive creatures with webbed fingers and floating silver hair emerged with slow grace from the huts and gathered round them, silent and eerie against the red sun. With them came the wild scent of the sea.

I've hit my head and this is a dream, she thought. But she ached far too much for it to be a dream, and Electra was in it, too. Also, she knew that scent better than she knew her own heart.

The novice pushed a cold hand into hers. "Aura," she breathed, blinking at the huge creatures surrounding them. "Who are *they*?"

"Telchines," Aura whispered back, tightening her grip in excitement and more than a little fear. "I think we've found my mother's people."

PART 2

TELCHINE WORLD

To you, O Poseidon,
the children of Rhodes
return this Gift under the waves,
after they have been shipwrecked by
war and used its power to protect
themselves from the enemy.

Chapter 11

INVISIBLE VILLAGE

STUNNED BY THE FALL, Aura had just enough wit to push the bag containing the Gift behind her. She slipped the pendant under her tunic as a plump telchine boy knelt at their feet, poked their toes and counted under his breath. A woman with yellow eyes and ankle-length hair shooed him away. She gazed down at them, hands on hips. Her fingers had thick green webs like the boy's. Although she looked old, she carried herself upright with the same solid grace as the rest of her people. The other telchines hung back, staring and whispering, every one of them massive and silver-haired.

The old woman grunted. "A human and a half-breed! How strange. No one's come through the Barrier since Lindia stole Poseidon's Gift and took it into the human world. How did you get through, I wonder?"

She spoke Greek much better than her mother, Aura thought, too dazed to make much sense of the actual words. Barrier? *Poseidon's* Gift? Lin...? She sat up straight, her skin prickling. "My mother's name is Lindia!" she said, looking at the ring of telchine faces in growing excitement. "Is she here? Is this where she came?"

Electra squeezed against her and clutched her arm. "Don't look at them, Aura, or they'll use their evil eyes on us!"

"But she knows my mother! Maybe she knew her before she went to Alimia and married Father... Is that the Lindia you mean?" she asked the telchines, still hopeful. "The one who married Leonidus, son of Chares the sculptor?"

The boy opened his mouth to say something, but the old woman put a finger to her lips. She studied Aura more carefully. "Ah, I see now. Breeding with the human is just the sort of thing Lindia would have done. So, you're Lindia's daughter, are you, Half-and-Half? That no doubt explains how you knew about this place. Where's Lindia now?" She glanced up the cliff, as if she expected Aura's mother to come tumbling down after them at any moment.

"She dived into the Demon Pool," Aura whispered. It still had the power to bring tears to her eyes.

The telchine frowned. "She must be trying to get back to the grotto through the underwater tunnels. I *thought* I sensed Poseidon's Gift close by! Is that it, in your bag?"

Her expression grew eager. She loomed over them, her hair brushing Aura's knees. The other telchines shuffled closer, their yellow eyes gleaming.

"Don't let her have it," Electra whispered.

"Come on, Half-and-Half," the old telchine said, growing impatient. "I need to check it hasn't been damaged. I expect Lindia sent you here with it because she was too afraid to come herself, though I can't think why she told you to jump off the cliff like that. There's a perfectly good path."

Aura's stomach fluttered as she remembered why they had been on the cliff in the first place. She scrambled to her feet. "We have to get back! Our friends are in trouble up there. And you've got it wrong. This is Helios' Gift, not Poseidon's." She hugged the bag and stared up the sheer rock face. How had they survived that fall?

The old telchine nodded slowly. "I've heard humans call it that – Helios' Gift. But to us it will always be Poseidon's Gift. Long before the humans stole it from us, Poseidon gave it to us so we could defend ourselves when we were attacked and heal our wounded. Later, when Helios created the Barrier between the human and telchine worlds, we used the Gift to communicate through the thin places. This village is one of those places where our worlds touch. Perhaps now you understand where you are?"

"We're in another *world*, Aura!" Electra breathed. "Priestess Themis always said the telchines vanished too suddenly for them all to be dead. Oh, this is so strange…" She giggled nervously. "At least the chief priest can't get hold of the god now and hang it back around the neck of his Colossus!"

Another world… Aura knew she ought to be more frightened, but at that moment the Barrier between worlds seemed merely another hurdle separating her from her family.

Uneasy, she looked at the village and the sponge boats. "We can't stay here. When the ship from Egypt arrives, Father will be expecting to meet us in the human world… if he can't find us, he'll go back to Alimia to look for us there. He'll find the message you said those men left in our hut, and go to Rhodes City after us, and then Chief Priest Xenophon will kill him!"

The telchines let out a collective hiss at the mention of Xenophon's name, making Electra flinch.

Then the old woman said in a soothing, sing-song voice, "Poor child, Half-and-Half. Shamefully thin, too. You've not had an easy time of it, I can tell. I understand your anxiety. We have heard the name of Xenophon before. But we can't let you go back through the Barrier with Poseidon's Gift. We've already lost it once, thanks to Lindia. We're not going to lose it so easily again. I'm sorry." She took the bag from Aura's numb fingers.

Electra paled. "Are we your prisoners, then?"

The telchine looked into the bag and frowned at the wires. "Don't be afraid. You wear the robe of Athene, whose priestesses have always listened to the voices of the gods, and the Half-and-Half's mother is my daughter. You've brought us the means of our salvation, which we thought lost forever. We won't hurt you. But we need to decide how best to proceed. The first thing we need to establish is whether the Gift has been damaged by its stay in the human world, which from the look of it I fear it might have been. If we can't heal it, then we may have to face the fact that we can no longer hide from the humans and prepare ourselves for war. The Barrier was disturbed when Lindia took the Gift through it. Many humans fell through the holes. We managed to contain the problem – they were simple villagers, who weren't looking to harm us. But it's only a matter of time before someone like your chief priest discovers how to bring an army through to wipe us out."

She turned with a slow grace, pushed her silver hair over her shoulders, and carried the Gift into one of the huts. Gently but firmly, the other telchines led Aura and Electra in the opposite direction to the beach. They placed a piece of driftwood at the centre of a hollow in the shingle so that they could sit.

Aura tried to think. The story of the villagers who had fallen through the holes in the Barrier tied in with what the Moths had told them about the population of the Invisible Village disappearing. She was afraid to ask what had happened to those people. The driftwood seemed to be part of a wrecked ship. The piece she sat upon bore the fading paint of a sea-eye. They could run, she supposed. If the telchines were as slow and clumsy on land as her mother, they might get away. But where could they run to, without the Gift to take them back to their own world? Milo and the others must think she and Electra were dead. If they tried to break into the hut where the old telchine had taken the Gift, they'd only be caught. It seemed best to play along until they had discovered more about this place.

While the adults built a bank of pebbles around the hollow, the boy crept across. He gave them a hesitant grin. "I'm Phaethon," he said, and pointed to the hut where the old woman had gone. "The Old One is called Rhode."

"Rhode?" said Electra, curiosity overcoming her fear. "Like the island, you mean?"

The boy's grin widened. "Exactly! She's very old, you know. The oldest of us all."

Aura frowned. She counted twenty telchines sitting around the edge of the hollow, casting them watchful looks. About as many others moved slowly around the village. Could the old woman, Rhode, really be her grandmother?

"Where did you learn such good Greek?" she asked, in an attempt to take her mind off what might be happening in the human world. "My mother... Lindia, I mean... could never pick it up properly."

Phaethon gave her a peculiar look. "You're speaking the old language."

Aura blinked. "But I could never learn Mother's language. I tried, believe me." She looked at Electra. "You must be speaking Greek! Electra can understand you, too."

"It's Poseidon's Gift, letting us understand each other." Phaethon's shrug dismissed this as unimportant. "Old One Rhode said it could do that, before your mother stole it and took it into the human world. Humans used to come to the grotto under Lindos to ask us things, and Cousin Lindia and Great Aunt Kamira told them all sorts of stuff to scare them away from Rhodes. Must have been funny, but I wasn't born then. I've heard all the best stories, though. Apparently, humans are stupid enough to believe in talking rocks. They call them oracles, and believe they are the gods speaking to them. So, of course, they thought Great Aunt Kamira and Cousin Lindia were goddesses giving the oracle through the rock, which meant they believed everything they said."

"But that's sacrilege!" Electra said. Then she blushed, obviously remembering how she'd been fooled by Athene Khalkia's pendant. "That's as bad as the chief priest pretending to be the voice of the goddess. Maybe your mother told the chief priest how to use the Gift, Aura, and that's why Poseidon punished her?"

Aura stiffened. "My mother would never have done a thing like that!"

Phaethon, of course, wanted to know how Poseidon had punished his cousin, but Aura hardly heard Electra's explanation of how they thought her mother had been blinded by the Gift when she'd refused to use her eye-power on Leonidus. "Who gives the oracle in the grotto now?" she asked, turning cold as she remembered what Councillor Iamus had said about asking the oracle's advice.

"No one goes to the ancient grotto any more, silly," Electra said. "They go up to the Temple of Athene on the Acropolis in Lindos. The priestess breathes smoke so she can pass on the word of the goddess, and..."

She broke off as she realized what this meant.

"...And the chief priest sends messages to the pendant worn by the statue of Athene Lindia," Aura finished for her. "Which means when the Council takes the Egyptian king to Lindos to ask the oracle's advice, all the chief priest has to do is tell them to rebuild it!"

"Except he can't, because we've got the Gift," Electra said. "Anyway, didn't you say Councillor Iamus knows about the messages? Surely he won't fall for a trick like that."

Aura wasn't so sure. Could the councillor be working with the chief priest, after all? Or did he believe the goddess would speak truly, if the chief priest didn't have the Gift to send false messages to the pendants?

She shifted uncomfortably on the driftwood as Rhode emerged from the hut. The telchine walked slowly and with dignity, blue light rippling under her skin. The other telchines stopped talking. Phaethon took one look at the Old One's glowing skin and scrambled away from them. Aura's heart beat faster as she remembered how Milo had said her skin lit up when she used the eye-power.

But Rhode blinked, and the blue light faded. "I have taken the humans' cruel wires out of Poseidon's Gift," she said softly. "And the god has spoken to me."

The telchines gave a collective sigh.

"The Gift is smaller than it used to be. The humans have cut many pieces off it."

There were gasps of horror. The telchines turned accusing yellow stares on Aura and Electra.

"But the god has told me humans cannot use the Gift as we do, by digesting morsels of its flesh. They need to touch it to access its powers, which is why they cut off so many pieces in an attempt to spread its power through their world."

The telchines *ate* pieces of the Gift…? That seemed worse than cutting pieces off it to put in the gods' pendants. Aura couldn't help feeling a bit sorry for the creature. No matter which world it was in, someone wanted to hurt it.

Then she remembered her father's warning.

"But you can't take the wires out!" she cried, leaping to her feet. "Father said it's dangerous. He's coming to meet me here. At least, he's coming to the Invisible Village in our world… I mean, in his world…" She shook her head, no longer sure which world she could call her own.

"It is as the Half-and-Half says," Rhode said, looking hard at her. "The human Leonidus is bringing the missing pieces back to the place known as the Invisible Village in the human world. I'm not sure what his intentions are.

But I think he must have told his daughter not to remove the wires from the Gift because he was afraid that it would gain enough power to take her and her mother through the Barrier without him. Leonidus knows that returning its missing pieces will make it more powerful. Possibly he intends to try crossing the Barrier himself."

The others fidgeted uneasily.

Rhode continued, "We need to heal Poseidon's Gift as soon as possible, and we must make certain it does not fall into human hands again. When the human Leonidus comes, Half-andHalf Aura can be our go-between. In the meantime, each of us must recharge our power in case of trouble. Kamira, sort out some food for our guests. Phaethon, come with me. Lookouts to their posts, and stay alert. The rest of you, watch our guests. Half-and-Half Aura and Priestess Electra, please understand that if you leave this hollow without permission, we'll be forced to treat you as enemies."

Phaethon left the hollow and followed Rhode back to the hut. One of the women frowned at Aura and Electra, stamped off down the beach and dived into the sea. Four others went off to the lookout points. That left fifteen telchines guarding them. Although they seemed not to pay much attention to their prisoners, the occasional flash of a yellow eye was enough to convince them an escape attempt would be pointless.

Electra shifted closer to Aura. "I'm frightened, Aura."

"They haven't hurt us yet," she whispered back. "I think they're more frightened of us than we are of them.

Don't worry, if the worst happens I've still got this." She showed the novice the pendant under her tunic.

Electra's eyes widened. But they had no time to plan anything, because Phaethon returned with a platter bearing wafer-thin slivers of what could only have been the Gift. Each telchine bowed its head with great reverence before devouring the morsels. Almost at once, the telchines' skin began to glow a faint blue. When the ritual was over the telchines tucked into sponges from their boat. Then Kamira returned carrying two raw fish, which she plonked in Aura and Electra's laps.

"Eat," she said. "Lindia did a bad thing, but we don't starve our guests."

"It's not their fault, Great Aunt," Phaethon said. "They brought Poseidon's Gift back to us, didn't they?"

"It remains to be seen whose side they're on," Kamira said stiffly, and marched off to join Rhode in the hut.

Phaethon took a huge bite of his sponge and spoke with his mouth full. "Great Aunt Kamira still hasn't forgiven your mother. I'm sorry. Why aren't you eating? I thought humans liked fish."

Electra gave her fish a doubtful look, but the last time either of them had eaten a decent meal was back on Khalki. When Aura helped her break off the head and pull out the spine, she screwed up her nose and chewed the raw flesh.

"Eat it all," Aura whispered. "It's good. You need to keep up your strength."

Electra nodded and forced the mouthful down. As they ate, Aura listened to the telchines arguing about what they should do once the Gift was whole again. The younger ones seemed to favour taking it straight through the Barrier to Rhodes City and driving out the humans, once and for all, with their eye-power. The older ones said there weren't enough of them for an all-out attack, and the humans would kill them the moment they crossed the Barrier. They were the wronged people in this war, so they could trust Poseidon to look after them. Most seemed to want to wait, like their Old One, until they found out if the Barrier was strong enough to keep them safe, as it had before.

Aura couldn't stop thinking of her father, waiting for her in the human world. She wondered if the pendant would let her speak to him across the Barrier. But now Phaethon had crept back into the hollow, and Electra was asking him why telchines hated humans so much and how the Barrier had got built in the first place. She moved her hand away from the pendant with a sigh. The novice was right. The more they could discover about this world of telchines, the easier it would be to find a way to get back to their own.

"That's a long story," Phaethon said. "It all goes back to the beginning, when this island belonged to the telchines. No humans lived on Rhodes until after the great flood, when the island rose from the sea. Then Zeus took it away from Poseidon, and gave it to the Sun God Helios. Helios drove his chariot down from the sky to inspect his new land, and fell in love with a young telchine girl named Rhode, who was Poseidon's daughter born under the waves. He named the island after her."

"We have that legend, too!" Electra said. She glanced at the hut and whispered in awe, "Aura! Do you think their Old One could be the same Rhode as in the legend?"

"Don't be silly," Aura said. "They probably re-use names, like everyone else. Rhode said she was my grandmother. She's not *that* old!"

Phaethon frowned. "Stop interrupting, or I'll forget the rest of the story. Where was I? Oh, yes... After coupling with the god, Rhode gave birth to seven daughters and seven sons, who ruled the island after Helios returned to driving his sun chariot across the sky. These children of Helios built fine temples and cities and brought up their children to breathe air. They traded with other human races from across the sea, who hunted telchines like fish, calling them sea-demons. They married humans and forgot the old stories. But Rhode's telchine family did not forget the island had originally belonged to them. They prayed to Poseidon to help them drive out Helios' children. Poseidon took pity on them and sent them his Gift so they could heal their wounded and defend themselves with eye-power. That was how the war between the telchines and humans began."

"That's sad," Electra said. "Wasn't there enough room on Rhodes for both races?"

"I suppose there was at first," Phaethon said. "But you humans breed much faster than us. Old One Rhode says they'd have wiped us out, if Helios hadn't stepped in and created the Barrier between the telchine world and the human world. Although the humans were his children, he remembered how he had loved Rhode. He didn't want to see either race hurt, so he made the Barrier to keep us from fighting each other. We took the Gift to the grotto at Lindos, which is one of the thin places where the worlds touch, so we could keep an eye on what the humans were doing. It allowed us to speak to each other across the Barrier. But because we kept the Gift on our side, we controlled the contact so the humans couldn't see us, only hear us. Eventually, after Great Aunt Kamira and Cousin Lindia had told them so many things to frighten them away, the ancient oracle got a reputation for giving unpopular advice, and humans stopped coming. I suppose that's when they started going to your Temple of Athene instead. In the end, only the most desperate came down to the grotto to ask the ancient goddess for help. The last of these was a boy called Leonidus. That was when Cousin Lindia stole Poseidon's Gift from us and took it through the Barrier into the human world."

"My father," Aura whispered, trying to imagine the man she loved as a boy. "That still doesn't explain why my mother stole the Gift and took it through the Barrier. She must have had a good reason."

Phaethon shrugged. "We don't know why she did it. Didn't she tell you?"

"She never spoke about the time before she lost her eyes, and I never knew the Gift existed until I saw it in the Moth's cave, though I saw pieces of it in the gods' pendants, and it sent me visions before then. Also, I think it healed my ankle and—"

She bit the words off just in time. It was best if the telchines didn't realize just yet that she could use the eye-power.

Phaethon considered her with his head on one side. "Why didn't your mother come back with you? Was she really scared of us, like the Old One said? We wouldn't hurt her, you know. Great Aunt Kamira's only angry because she got in trouble for letting her take the Gift through the Barrier. Cousin Lindia was only about your age when she left us."

Aura smiled. It wasn't so difficult to imagine her mother as a girl, since she still acted like one. "Please help us get home," she said. "I've brought your Gift back, so you'll be safe if you stay here. But my father's still in danger in the human world, and my mother's lost in the Demon Pool. I have to go back and find them before the chief priest does."

"The Old One says you have to stay. If we let you go back to your own world, you'll bring other humans here to kill us all."

"No we won't! I promise. We only got through your Barrier because the Gift *brought* us through. Humans don't want to invade your world. I don't think the chief priest and the councillor even know about this place."

"They'll find out if you go back, and then they'll come here to steal the Gift again. Humans have been trying to wipe us out for ages. We have to defend ourselves." Phaethon set his jaw, as if repeating something he'd been told, rather than believed himself.

"But Aura's right – you'll be safe if you stay behind your Barrier and keep your Gift here," Electra said. "I had no idea your world existed! Nor did Aura, and she's half telchine. Poseidon wouldn't want you to fight, would he? And from the sound of it, Helios doesn't want his humans to fight, either. I thought you said he made the Barrier to *stop* the war? Surely Poseidon wouldn't have let him do that, if it meant you'd be in danger?"

Phaethon frowned. He looked a bit confused and Aura's hopes raised. Maybe he'd help them, after all. But Kamira called to the boy and he climbed out of the hollow in obvious relief.

"You have to stay," he said again. "Then you'll be safe, too."

The sun climbed higher and the day grew warm. Despite the strangeness of being in another world, the two girls dozed against the driftwood, worn out with the tension of the past few days. Finally, the Old One emerged from the hut, carrying the Gift on the same platter Phaethon had used to serve the slices earlier. A solemn procession of telchines followed her. Aura sat up with a shiver. With the wires removed, the Gift glowed brighter than ever. Rainbows flickered in the air around it, and patches of darkness danced in the sky above it.

Rhode carried the Gift into the hollow and set it down carefully at Aura's feet. The telchines shuffled closer, their yellow eyes fixed on her. Aura stiffened. Would the creature take them back through the Barrier if she asked it to, or refuse to help her, like when she'd needed the eye-power on the cliff?

"I know what you're thinking, Half-and-Half," the Old One said. "We've debated whether we should trust you to do this, but we seem to be having some trouble communicating with your father through the Barrier. We're hoping you might have more success, since you are half human." She glanced at Kamira, who folded her arms. "I think you've no more wish to see Poseidon's Gift wired back up in the chief priest's Colossus than we do. Am I right?"

Aura nodded. She wet her lips. The holes in the sky had stars in them. She could see patches of beach and black sea through them. Was it night already in the human world?

The Old One saw her confusion and smiled. "Yes, that's the human world you can see through the Barrier. And yes, time runs faster there – which is why we don't have as much of it as we'd like to convince you to help us. But I promise that once the Gift is restored, we'll bring

Lindia home and care for her as best we can. She was very young when she took the Gift, and Phaethon's told us what you said about her eyes. We've decided her stay in the human world has been punishment enough."

"What about me?" Aura whispered.

"You're my granddaughter. If you want to stay with us, you'll be welcome as well."

Aura blinked. That wasn't quite what she'd meant. "And Father?" she said.

"We first have to determine why Leonidus is bringing the missing pieces of the Gift back to Rhodes, and what he intends to do with them. That's why we need you to contact him for us, so we can negotiate their transfer across the Barrier. The vision I received was puzzling."

Aura stared at the patches of dark sea, her heart thudding afresh. "Have you seen him, then? Has his ship arrived?"

The Old One glanced at the others. "We think the Egyptian ship has arrived, yes. But I don't seem able to make him hear us. It might be because he is human, and the Gift is not yet powerful enough to allow us to communicate across the Barrier as it used to do. Or there could have been some trouble—"

She didn't finish. Aura slammed her hands to the Gift, terrified the chief priest had already killed Leonidus.

"Father!" she called. "Father! Can you hear me?"

The rainbows flared, showing her the same chest as before, but this time the lid was shut and she could see nothing except *a crack of faint starlight... dark legs running past... a spray of seawater... a confusion of bodies struggling out on deck...*

Fear and worry for her father tied Aura's stomach into knots. She wasn't sure what happened next, only that her need to be with him grew so powerful that she felt it reach out across the Barrier. The holes in the sky widened, and she found a ragged patch of night right in front of her. The rainbows flared again. A blue flash blinded her – and one of the telchines on lookout duty shouted:

"Ship! *Human* ship!"

Old One Rhode squinted at the sea, let out a curse and seized Aura's arm. She signalled the others to take the Gift back to the hut. Her eyes were hard. "What do you think you're doing, Half-and-Half Aura? You brought the humans through the Barrier! I meant you to contact them, not bring them here! Who's on that ship? Is it your father? Tell me!"

In the sunlight of the telchine world, the ship's prow dazzled gold. It had two masts and a double bank of oars. Telchines ran down the beach to meet it, their webbed feet slipping on the shingle. They splashed into the water and dived. Aura saw streams of bubbles heading for its oars, and her stomach fluttered. Rhode's grip was fierce. Blue light rippled once more under her skin.

Electra paled. "Don't hurt her, Lady Rhode, please! She didn't mean to do it."

"Who comes?" Rhode insisted, the light under her skin brightening.

"My father," Aura whispered, hoping it was true.

She stared at the flapping sails, her stomach doing strange things. Whoever was on board had no idea how to sail the ship. A few oars worked out of time, splashing ineffectually. Seeing the bubbles approaching through the water, someone made an attempt to turn the vessel, and wind briefly filled one of the sails to reveal a bold eye design, black on red.

"Do you think it's King Ptolemy and the Council on their way to Lindos to consult the oracle?" Electra whispered.

Aura caught her breath. She hadn't thought of that. What if the Moths were still captive, and the councillor was in charge, taking his prisoners to Lindos to make sure Aura brought him the information he wanted? If so, she'd just brought the very army the telchines feared through the Barrier to wipe them out. She felt a bit sick.

The telchines must have thought the ship was bringing an army, too, and reacted with the fierceness of cornered animals. Aura saw their hands break the surface and grasp the oars. Blue lightning crackled as they directed their eye-power at the deck. Screams sounded across the water as the humans on board took cover. But the telchines heaved on the oars, flipping bodies over the side into the sea. Webbed hands grabbed their victims and pulled them under to subdue them, until the water around the ship churned with bubbles.

Amidst this horrifying spectacle, all Aura could think was at least the telchines hadn't killed anyone yet, and their captives looked too small to be her father.

Then Electra gasped, "It's the Moths, Aura! You have to stop the fight, Lady Rhode! They haven't come to destroy your village. They're children, not soldiers! Most of them were slaves, or ran away from their families because they were being mistreated. They helped us. They're our friends."

Rhode frowned at the novice. "Expect me to believe that?"

Aura pulled herself together. "It's true! They helped me and my mother escape the chief priest. They're the ones who rescued Helios' Gift... I mean, Poseidon's Gift... from the Colossus in the first place. I think they've stolen that ship."

Her mind raced, trying to catch up with what she could see. Rhode had said time passed faster in the human world, even as it had while she'd been in the Demon Pool – how much faster? Obviously long enough for the Moths to escape and steal the Egyptian ship, as they'd planned. Whatever had happened, it was here with her father's chest on board containing the missing pieces of the Gift. Surely Leonidus wouldn't have left that behind willingly?

The ship drifted, crewless, turning with the tide. A few of the Moths slung stones from the deck at the telchines, trying to help their friends, but were driven back by sizzling bolts of eye-power. Some dived in, only to be pulled under as well. The distance was too great to recognize individuals, but Aura felt sure she saw Timosthenes' blond hair in the sea, and Chariclea clinging to the rigging, yelling advice.

"Please, Old One," she said, still searching desperately for her father. "At least give them a chance! If you save the Moths' lives, I promise I'll help you get the rest of your Gift back."

Rhode considered her. She watched several more Moths dragged under the water. Then she pressed her lips together and jerked her head at Phaethon. "Go tell the others to bring the young ones ashore alive. Tell them to kill any soldiers they find on board, and secure any other adults. They're to save the ship. We might be able to use it."

Phaethon raced to the sea. He entered the water with barely a ripple and disappeared from sight.

Aura sank down on the pebbles, shaking. "Thank you, Old One," she whispered.

They watched in silence as the Moths were dragged, half-drowned, to the beach and laid on the shingle. Some struggled to their knees and retched up water, shivering and blinking at the telchines in confusion and fear. Androcles, after coughing himself to life, crawled across and put his arms around Chariclea. Seeing Aura and Electra with the Old One, his eyes narrowed. Timosthenes lay pale and still, while a girl pinched his nose and breathed into his mouth. The Moths had been disarmed while they were helpless under the water. A few had scratches and bruises, but none seemed to be badly hurt. A collection of knives, daggers and slings was taken to one of the huts at the edge of the village. Aura's anxious gaze passed over the captives and finally found Milo, cradling his brother in his arms. The relief made her knees weak.

Phaethon returned, dripping and breathless, with seaweed caught in his hair. He parted his cupped hands to reveal a god's pendant, glowing brightly. "Great Aunt Kamira said to bring this to you, Old One, but it isn't the only piece. There's a chest full of them! And there's a human man on board, demanding to see his daughter." He winked at Aura. "He says he knows Cousin Lindia."

Aura's heart lifted.

She didn't care that Chariclea and some of the other Moths were glaring at her as if she had betrayed them, didn't care that Milo was giving her another of his unreadable looks, nor that they were captives in the wrong world. She had eyes only for the man with a lot more grey in his hair than she remembered, being hustled out of the sea by the telchines, with his hands bound behind him.

"Father," she whispered. "Oh, Father!"

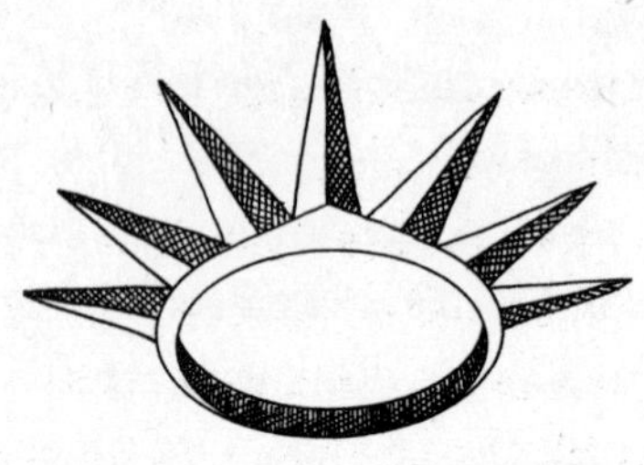

Chapter 12

REUNION

IT WAS NOT quite the reunion Aura had hoped for. The telchines escorted Leonidus to the driftwood and sat him down. He seemed dazed from his journey through the Barrier and did not resist. He blinked at the huts, the exhausted Moths, Rhode holding the glowing fragment of the Gift... His gaze stopped at Aura, and he went very still. He looked her over carefully. Satisfied she was unharmed, he gave her a small, sad smile.

"I'm sorry, my darling. I should have warned you this might happen. I guess we're in Lindia's world? It's a lot more like ours than I thought it would be... except for the telchines, of course." He smiled again. "To think I've lived to see the real Invisible Village!"

Aura trembled. She wanted to rush to him, fling her arms around his neck, and curl up on his lap like she used to do when she was small. But Rhode's fingers, digging into her arm, held her back.

"Do not mock us, human!" she snapped. At her signal, one of the male telchines hit Leonidus across the face. The slap from his webbed hand echoed up the cliff. Leonidus, unable to regain his balance with his hands tied, fell off the driftwood with a grunt of pain.

"Don't you dare hurt him!" Aura wrenched her arm free and glared at the Old One. Before she had time to think what she was doing, she had pulled out the pendant of Helios Rhodos and reached for the eye-power.

Rainbows filled her head, fiercer than when she'd been in the human world. But the pendant in Rhode's hand brightened as well, and the old telchine's skin began to shine. Her yellow eyes locked with Aura's, furious. "Is this what your promise is worth, Half-and-Half?" she hissed. Aura's stomach fluttered, but she did not look away. The beach between them shimmered with sheets of coloured light. The other telchines stiffened. They closed around Aura, their skin flickering blue.

Kamira whispered, "Stop her, someone. She doesn't know what she's doing."

Electra squeezed through the ring of telchines and seized Aura's arm. "No!" she cried. "No, Aura, don't! If you use your evil eye on the Old One, they'll kill us all!"

Aura clenched her fists. The pendant was the only way she had left of accessing the Gift's power, but she knew the novice was right. And it was frightening how easily the power had come to her, almost as if the Gift wanted her to defy the telchines. With a supreme effort, she closed her eyes. Through her lids, the light faded to orange, then red, then dull purple. She risked a peep through her lashes. Rhode was still shining, but the light under the others' skin had died when they realized she wasn't going to fight them. The Moths, who had broken off their muttering to watch, sighed in disappointment as Aura bowed her head and surrendered her pendant to the Old One. Chariclea scowled. Milo picked seaweed out of his brother's hair and gave her another of his unreadable looks.

Probably thinks I'm a coward, she thought. She avoided the Khalki boy's gaze, unable to deal with that sort of complication just now.

Leonidus grimaced as his captors helped him up. "I wasn't laughing at you, Old One. I don't blame you for not trusting me, but please believe me when I say I'm not your enemy. We need to talk."

"What is there to talk about, human?" Rhode said. "It's simple. We have Poseidon's Gift back at last, and you've brought some of the missing pieces your priests cut off it. Since we can't seem to trust Helios' Barrier any more, we'll heal the Gift and use it to drive the humans from our island for good, as we should have done right at the start."

Leonidus shook his head at her. "Have you any idea how many humans are living on Rhodes these days?"

"They've multiplied many times over since the Barrier separated our worlds, I know. But we've got our Gift back now. Poseidon will help us."

Kamira and some of the other telchines nodded, eager.

"You expect the gods to intervene, after all this time? Isn't that a bit optimistic?"

"Poseidon brought the Half-and-Half to us. Isn't that a sign of his favour?"

Leonidus looked at Aura. "Seems to me my daughter isn't too pleased to be here."

Rhode dismissed this with a flick of her fingers. "The Half-and-Half will choose the right side when the time comes. She's naturally confused, being brought up in the human world. She knew nothing whatsoever about telchine history! That was your doing, I suppose, but how did you stop Lindia from teaching her about Poseidon's Gift?"

"Stop Lindia teaching her?" Leonidus smiled sadly. "It seems there are things you don't understand about *your* daughter, Old One. How about you untie me, and we discuss our situation like civilized beings? Where is Aura's mother, anyway?" He looked at the huts. "Is she your prisoner, too?"

"She went to the grotto through the underwater tunnels," Rhode said. "It seems she was too afraid to accompany her daughter through the Barrier and face us."

"Ah." Leonidus bowed his head. "You know she's blind now?"

"So we heard," Rhode said. "I gather that was your fault, too." Then she sighed. "All right, since you're here, we'll listen to what you have to say. There are still some things I don't understand. Like how you persuaded Lindia to take Poseidon's Gift into the human world in the first place, and what happened that she let it burn out her eyes rather than use her eye-power."

The telchines did not trust Leonidus enough to untie his hands, but they let him sit beside Aura on the driftwood. Besides the new grey in his hair and beard, he'd picked up a scar on his thigh. But he had the same strength she remembered, and a quiet determination lurked in his dark eyes.

"She did it for love," he said softly.

There was a hush. Even the Moths, who had started making whispered plans to escape, shut up as Aura's father told his story.

Councillor Iamus had been horribly right about the priests of Helios practising human sacrifice. When the Colossus of Helios was nearly finished, they sent Chares' body home to his family, claiming he'd killed himself because he had discovered an error in his calculations that would make the statue unstable in earthquakes. But when the body was prepared for burial, it was found to be missing its heart. Leonidus was only ten at the time. He ran at once to the grotto and tearfully begged the ancient oracle to help him.

"Lindia said if the priests had taken out his heart, all we had to do was touch him with the Gift before his body rotted, and Poseidon would grow him a new one," Leonidus explained. "I couldn't carry my father's body to the grotto, so she brought the Gift into the human world to help me heal him. We were crazy, I suppose. I never stopped to consider what people would think when a dead man suddenly came alive again, and Lindia never considered what would happen to the Barrier when she brought the Gift through it. She was much younger than I'd imagined. But the magic worked fine. That night, we sneaked into the room in my house where my father was laid out for mourning, unwrapped the linen from his body, and brought him back to life."

The Moths exchanged sceptical glances. But the telchines didn't seem very surprised. Aura remembered how even the damaged, wire-bound Gift had healed Androcles' fatal wound back at Ialysos, and shivered.

"So what happened to make her go blind?" Kamira demanded.

Leonidus closed his eyes, as if the memory was too much to bear. "Mother had a screaming fit and summoned the priests. They made me tell them what we'd done, and dragged Chares off to their temple. Then they tried to take the Gift. Lindia used her eye-power on them. Their bodies caught fire, and they fell down dead."

"Good for Lindia!" said Kamira. Several other telchines nodded, looking grim.

Rhode held up a hand. "Let the human continue."

Leonidus went on quietly, "Their leader, a young priest called Xenophon, threw his cloak over Lindia's head and pushed her down the stairs. She fell badly. When I tried to help her, she must have thought I was an enemy as well, because her skin lit up blue, like it had when she killed the priests. I thought she was going to kill me in the same way, with her magic. But she yelled in horror, slammed her hands to her eyes and closed them tight. Xenophon got away with the Gift. Lindia fled back to the sea and disappeared. Shortly after that, Xenophon started distributing pendants to the temples with pieces of the Gift inside, saying they were gifts from Helios and would heal people. He told Mother that Chares had been cursed by the sea-demon, and ordered his body burnt so he couldn't come back to life again. No one believed my story of the goddess and her magic sponge. I was only ten. They said I was making things up because I was so upset about my father's 'suicide', and of course the priests of Helios denied everything. Many years passed before I realized they were hiding something from me and set out to look for Lindia. When I eventually found her on Alimia, she didn't have eyes any more."

The telchines were silent. Aura sat very still. She knew the rest.

Her father had set out to recover the Gift from the priests so Lindia could go home to her people. Everywhere there was an oracle, everywhere it was claimed statues spoke to priests and priestesses, he had paid a visit disguised as a pilgrim. Wherever he found a piece of the Gift wired into a god's pendant, he rescued it and left a common blue sponge in its place. He hid the pieces he'd collected in an underwater cave off the coast of Alimia, while he travelled to find more. But it was slow work, and meanwhile Lindia gave birth to a daughter...

At last, her father looked up. "I'm sorry, my darling. It wasn't very fair on you, was it?"

"You should have told me about the telchine world, and how the Gift blinded Mother!" she shouted, springing to her feet. "Why didn't you *tell* me?"

Aura's cheeks were hot. Everyone was looking at her.

Leonidus looked to be in pain. "You were half human," he said. "You couldn't digest sponges like a telchine. There was no evidence you would grow up to have telchine powers like your mother. You were happy sponge diving. I thought there would be plenty of time to tell you, once I'd managed to collect enough pieces of the Gift to send your mother home."

Aura bit her lip and nodded, trying hard to understand.

Meanwhile, Rhode considered the pendants she held – the one she'd confiscated from Aura, and the one Phaethon had brought her from the ship. "How many of these pieces did you bring through the Barrier?"

"Not all," Leonidus said. "These are just the ones I've been dragging round the Mediterranean. There are still some in my underwater hideout at Alimia, if the earthquake hasn't damaged it."

Aura realized the message system must be a lot bigger than they'd thought. "I'm afraid it might have done, Father," she whispered, remembering the first piece of the Gift she'd found.

"Sit down, Half-and-Half," Rhode said. "We need to think about this."

Aura sat numbly and stared out to sea. Electra put an arm around her shoulders, whispering words of comfort. Meanwhile, Rhode interrogated Leonidus as to what had been happening during the past few days in the human world, about their escape from custody and what the chief priest was planning. Aura couldn't take it in. She was still trying to get her head around the story Leonidus had told them.

The Gift had healed her grandfather Chares by giving him a new heart, but everyone thought he was cursed and so he'd been burnt alive. And then it had tried to make her mother kill the boy she loved, just as it had tried to make Aura hurt her friends back in the cave at the Demon Pool. Her mother was right. It *was* a bad thing.

Rhode sighed. "So. Your human Council and the Egyptian king will shortly be on their way to Lindos to ask the oracle if they should raise the Colossus of Helios? It's the perfect opportunity for us to avoid another war. We can use the Gift to communicate with them in the grotto, just like Kamira and Lindia used to do, and frighten the Council into leaving the Colossus where it fell. But we have to heal the Gift first, or it mightn't be powerful enough to let us communicate across the Barrier. I couldn't use it to contact Aura's father just now." She stood, her weight causing pebbles to roll. "Bring the chest ashore, and let's see how much of Poseidon's Gift we have."

Dusk was falling at last in the telchine world, and the first stars glimmered over the sea. King Ptolemy's ship rocked gently, its sail furled and its oars neatly stacked on deck. While they waited for the telchines to fetch the chest, Aura edged closer to her father and loosened the knots around his wrists. He smiled at her and whispered thanks. Out in the gloom, there was a splash. The telchines reappeared, swimming back towards the beach with the chest she'd seen so often in her visions floating between them. Her stomach fluttered as a blue halo glimmered over the water.

Rhode watched it come with narrow eyes. "These are the pieces Rhodes exported around the Mediterranean, and Leonidus has told us about his underwater store at Alimia. That leaves other pieces… where?"

"The Temple of Athene on Khalki island," Electra supplied, cheering up a bit now the telchines seemed to have decided not to fight.

"Easy. I'll send a message through the Gift instructing the chief priestess to bring it to Lindos. Any more?"

"Aura lost a piece in Khalki harbour," Milo said.

"Whoever goes with Leonidus to collect his store from Alimia can pick up that one on the way."

"The other statues in Rhodes City?" Chariclea whispered.

"Yes… someone will have to go to the City and steal them. That shouldn't be too hard, once the Council leaves for Lindos."

"Temple of Athene Lindia."

"Also easy, since that's where we're going. We'll take the king's ship to Lindos as soon as the Gift is healed."

Leonidus frowned at the Old One. "I thought you said you needed to get the missing pieces from Alimia and Rhodes City first?"

Rhode watched the telchines drag the chest from the ship up the beach, and smiled as the Gift glowed in response. "Not us. You. And you can take a few of these resourceful young Moths with you, in case you need help. You can use our sponge boats. They'll be less noticeable than the Egyptian ship. We'll keep the Half-and-Half and the rest of the human children here in our world to make sure you come back. You can meet us in the grotto at Lindos when you've collected the rest of the pieces, and then you'll have to persuade the Council to bring the Egyptian king down to the grotto to hear what the oracle says. Once we've successfully persuaded them not to rebuild the Colossus of Helios, we'll let the Half-and-Half and the human children go home." She turned to the telchines. "Sort the young ones out! Separate those who seem the best friends. Take the ones who need more time to recover to the village, and watch them. The human will co-operate while we have his daughter. Untie his hands."

There were protests and scuffles as the telchines waded into the huddle of captives and plucked moaning Moths from the arms of their friends. Milo fought to keep hold of Cimon, but was cuffed to the ground. Androcles had no choice but to surrender Chariclea when a telchine used eye-power to burn a hole in the shingle at his feet. Timosthenes exchanged a glance with the Moth leader, then limped to the village with the rest of the wounded and sick. Aura felt sure the boy was pretending to be weaker than he was, and wondered why.

When a telchine put a hand on her arm to lead her after the other hostages, she resisted. "You can't send my father away so soon! I want to talk to him!"

"He'll be back, Half-and-Half Aura," Rhode said. "Be sensible, please. You're my granddaughter. We won't hurt you."

"But—"

Electra gripped her hand. "I'll be staying with you, Aura," she whispered.

Aura cast a desperate look at her father, who was rubbing his wrists as the Moths picked for the expedition gathered around him. Androcles whispered something to him. Milo's eyes were dark and angry, his mouth set in a grim line. They'd fight at the slightest excuse, she knew. She eyed the glowing Gift, which the telchines were bringing out of their hut again. But she couldn't break her promise. At least the telchines had said they would help her mother. She bowed her head as

Leonidus and the others dragged the telchines' two sponge boats to the water's edge. The Moths clambered in, and oars were handed up to them. Leonidus stood waist-deep in the waves, staring back up the beach at her.

"Let me say goodbye to him," Aura begged. "Please, Old One."

Rhode gave her a hard look. "No tricks, Half-and-Half."

"No tricks, I promise." She met the Old One's gaze, and Rhode gave a curt nod.

Aura splashed into the sea, her mind a whirl. Maybe the Gift would refuse to send her father and the others back through the Barrier? Maybe she could jump in at the last moment and go with them... Leonidus put his arms around her and hugged her. She pressed her face into his damp tunic and burst into tears.

When she raised her head, she saw the telchines had gathered around the chest. Through a blur of tears, she watched Kamira throw out the layer of gold that had been used to smuggle the pieces of the Gift back to Rhodes. Presumably, the rest of the Egyptian king's treasure was still aboard his ship. She wondered if the telchines intended to give it back. They certainly didn't seem very interested in riches. The coins glittered briefly in the firelight, before being lost among the pebbles in the dark. Poseidon's Gift, freed of its wires, glowed brighter than the sun. Blue and green light rippled out of the chest, bathing the telchines' faces.

They stepped back and held hands in a circle around Rhode and the Gift, surrounded by that rippling light, singing softly.

"I meant to tell you everything when you were old enough to understand, Aura," Leonidus said. "But I was away too long, and you grew up so fast… I want you to know that I love you. I'm sorry I wasn't there when you needed me."

"I'll be all right," Aura said, putting on a brave face. "But you've got to be careful, Father! The chief priest still wants to kill you."

"Don't worry, I've no intention of revealing myself to Xenophon. But can we trust the Council, do you think? They never were much in favour of the Temple of Helios' more extreme policies. If they're going to ask the oracle about rebuilding the Colossus, that must mean they're not supporting the chief priest in this."

Aura frowned. She'd almost forgotten her strange interview with Councillor Iamus in the woods. "I don't know…"

Her words were drowned out by a crackle from the beach as Rhode lowered Poseidon's Gift into the chest. Pebbles and blue sparks sprayed into the air. The sky rumbled with thunder, and the ground shook. The Moths grabbed at the sides of the boats as a wave broke over Leonidus' and Aura's heads, knocking them to their knees. An intense blue light lit up the beach and turned the sea bright as day. She spluttered, not knowing whether to water-breathe or air-breathe. Her father's arms tightened around her, and she heard him cough as well as he regained his feet.

Aura wiped wet hair out of her eyes, afraid of what she might see. But the boats were still afloat, and everyone – telchine and human – seemed to have survived the reunion. Poseidon's Gift pulsed on the pebbles, its blues and greens fading to purple as the light died. It looked much bigger than before. King Ptolemy's treasure chest was on fire.

Rhode raised her arms triumphantly to the sky. "Poseidon!" she cried. "Send these humans back through the Barrier between worlds so they can rescue the missing parts of your Gift!"

Androcles and Milo picked up the oars. Leonidus planted a kiss on Aura's forehead. "I have to go now, Aura," he whispered. "Be brave. I'll see you in Lindos before you know it, and when we're back together I won't leave you again. I promise."

As her father climbed into the boat, Milo leant over the side and whispered, "We'll look after him for you. Keep an eye on Cim for me. We'll be back as soon as we can."

Androcles winked at her. "Don't you worry, telchine-girl," he called. "This bit of thievin' won't take us long!"

Aura stood in the edge of the waves and watched the two boats row out to sea. Blue light surrounded them briefly, and the hairs on the back of her neck prickled. An oar stroke... a glimmer of rainbows... and they were gone.

Chapter 13

LINDOS

THE TELCHINES LOST no time preparing for their journey to Lindos. They took Poseidon's Gift to the ship along with the Moths' slings and knives, lit torches that flared across the starlit sea, and readied the vessel for battle. Meanwhile, their hostages were confined to an overcrowded hut in the village.

Aura hugged her knees and stared at the two huge telchines guarding the door. She knew she should be doing something to help her friends, but she couldn't think straight. She needed time to come to terms with everything Leonidus had told them, but she didn't have any. Her mother might already be in danger at Lindos, and her father would be in just as much danger when he went to Rhodes City to steal the remaining pendants. Yet here she was, trapped in the telchine world without even a pendant to draw on the Gift's powers.

I should be grateful, she thought. At least the Gift can't burn out my eyes like it did to Mother's. But right now, she wished she *could* digest a slice of the creature and hold the power inside her like a telchine. Then no one would be able to take her family away from her.

The Moths discussed their situation in whispers.

"Why do they need to keep our weapons if they've got eye-power?" grumbled the boy who had suffered a broken leg back in the cave by the Demon Pool. Electra's splint still held, but the treatment the boy had received at the hands of the telchines had not helped much. "Are we supposed to catch and gut fish with our fingers? Don't see no handy villages in this world we can raid for food."

"And why the great rush?" said Chariclea. "If Aura's father's got to go to Alimia, and Androcles and the others have gone to steal pendants from the statues, that'll take a day or two at least – there's hundreds of them statues in Rhodes City! I always said we should smash 'em up, yet the moment there's some real fun to be had, I get left behind." The girl seemed almost more upset about missing a chance to smash statues than she was about being a hostage.

"Time's different here, remember," Electra reminded them. "They've probably been gone several days in human terms already. The chief priest might have recovered enough to travel by now, so the telchines have got to hurry or they'll miss the Council and the Egyptian king at Lindos and won't be able to give the oracle telling them not to rebuild the Colossus. Look on the bright side – the waiting won't seem so long for us."

The Moths muttered at this reminder of the time difference. Chariclea scowled and voiced Aura's private fear. "What if they don't come back for us? What if they decide to go through the Barrier and fight after all, an' the chief priest gets the Gift and wires it back up in his Colossus?"

"Yeah!" a boy said. "Even if they do come back, what's to stop 'em burnin' us all with their evil eyes once they've got their hands on the missing pieces of their Gift? We should've stayed with Councillor Iamus. At least we were in the right world then!"

Timosthenes made a face. "I didn't hear you complaining when I let you out of that hole the soldiers had locked you in! This is just the same – all we've got to do is work out how to open the door between worlds."

"How?" several people wanted to know.

"Yes, and how did you escape from Rhodes city?" Electra asked, but Timosthenes shushed her.

He eyed their guards and said in a low tone, "It's simple. We have to get our hands on the Gift before that ship goes through the Barrier. Those pendants the boss and Aura's father have gone to collect are attracted to the Gift, so we get it to take us home the same way it brought us here – only in reverse."

"Easier said than done," Chariclea said with another scowl. "That ship's swarming with telchines! And how are we goin' to make that Gift-thing do what we want, even if we do get it back? It never healed any of us unless it was feeling like it, did it? And it's free of its wires now. I bet it won't be so eager to take us back home, specially with that fat old telchine tellin' it all sorts of lies about us. It's more likely to bring Androcles and the others back here with its missing pieces, and then we'll *all* be stuck."

"Aura can make it work," Cimon said in a small voice. "She can ask it to take us home and trap the nasty telchines here in their world like Lindia did."

A hush fell as everyone looked at Aura.

She hugged her knees tighter. "I can't do that."

"Can't, or won't?" Timosthenes said. "Come on, telchine-girl! You owe us. If it hadn't been for your father collecting pieces of the Gift in the first place, we wouldn't be in this mess."

"That's not fair!" Electra said, putting an arm around Aura's shoulders. "Leonidus was only trying to help her poor mother. Anyway, you were the ones who decided to steal the Egyptian king's gold. If you hadn't done that, you wouldn't have been sailing down this coast when the god brought you through the Barrier."

Chariclea pulled a face. "*Gold*, yes... how were we to know one of those chests was full of talking sponges? We only sailed back this way because that Khalki boy Milo insisted we had to look for you two, and Leonidus wanted to go to the Invisible Village in case you were waiting there for him – gods, we were stupid! The rest of the Egyptian gold's still on the ship, and now the stupid

telchines are going to take it back to the Council! What a waste of effort. We sailed right into the trap. I wouldn't be surprised if the telchines didn't put you in this hut with us as a spy."

Aura stared at her webbed toes, too miserable to protest.

Electra glared at the Moths. "Don't be so horrible! Aura saved your lives. If she hadn't spoken up for you when you came through the Barrier, those telchines would have drowned the lot of you, no questions asked. Don't you understand? She promised to help them. That's why she can't make the god do what you want. She can't take it away from them again, like her mother did. It belongs to them. Besides, the telchines didn't say anything about giving the gold back, did they? I bet they don't care what happens to it – you saw the way they threw out those coins on the beach."

There was a short silence as the Moths digested this. Cimon began to sniff. "I don't want to stay in the Invisible Village until my brother and parents get old and die. I want to go home."

"We all do, Cim." Electra put an arm around the boy. "They can't keep us here for ever, don't worry. Besides, we only have to persuade the god to send us back home. We don't need it in the human world, so we don't have to take it with us. We'll leave it here with the telchines where it belongs. Aura will help us do that – won't you, Aura?"

Aura straightened her shoulders and gave her friend a grateful look. She had no idea if the Barrier would work like that, and was beginning to suspect the Gift didn't want to stay with the telchines, who ate slices of it every time they needed to recharge their eye-power. But she took a deep breath. "I'll try. I want to get back to the human world as much as you do."

Timosthenes clapped her on the shoulder. "Good enough. Cheer up, Moths! Since when did we let anyone push us around? Telchines might be able to kill people with their eyes, but Aura's got just as much magic as they have when she's touching the Gift. The Boss won't expect us to sit here and wait to be rescued, so this is what we'll do..."

The hostages curled up on their mats and faked heavy breathing and snores. When Rhode swam ashore to check on them at around midnight, it seemed they were sleeping off their exertions like normal children might be expected to do after such a strenuous, terrifying day.

The Old One smiled and rested a webbed hand on Aura's cheek. It was cold and damp from the sea. "I'm sorry it has to be this way, Half-and-Half," she whispered. "But after that trick you pulled with the ship, I can't trust you to come with us. If something goes wrong at Lindos, we can't have you interfering. You've a lot more skill with the Gift than we realized."

With an effort, Aura kept her breathing steady and her eyes shut. She wondered if Rhode would have said that, had she known she was awake.

The Old One instructed their guards to keep them in the hut until morning. The two telchines settled down outside, and they heard a faint splash as Rhode swam back to the ship. After a suitable pause, Chariclea crept to the door and peered out.

"The ship's leaving," she whispered.

Silently, Electra unbound the splint from the injured boy's leg. Timosthenes and Chariclea took one stick each and hid in the shadows either side of the door. The others clutched their blankets, ready to move. Then Timosthenes nodded, and the injured Moth started screaming. "My leg! My leg! Them sea-demons broke my leg!"

The telchines barged into the hut and bent over him, alarmed by his screams. As they'd hoped, their guards didn't seem to realize the boy had already been injured when he'd come through the Barrier, and assumed one of their number had broken his leg during the struggle in the water. While they were trying to help him, the other Moths threw blankets over their heads and Timosthenes and Chariclea knocked them out from behind. The telchines fell with two soft thumps. The Moths gathered round, panting, and stared at their guards with concern.

"Don't just stand there!" Timosthenes said. "They'll be all right. They're strong creatures. Better tie them up before they come round so they don't follow us. Anyone who doesn't think they can run to Lindos, stay here to look after the injured. The rest of you, let's go!"

Cimon and the others who were too weak to walk very far went to look for something to bind the unconscious telchines. The rest of them set out south along the starlit beach at a jog, following the ship.

For the rest of that night, they stumbled along moonlit beaches and splashed waist-deep around rocky headlands, afraid to talk above a whisper in case the Old One realized they had escaped the hut. The sun rose as they reached the last headland. Since it was too far to clamber round the rocks this time, and Timosthenes was worried they would be spotted by their quarry in the daylight, they left the beach and found a way up the cliffs. Breathless, they paused on top to stare out over the bay.

Below them, looking tiny, the Egyptian ship glittered in the rising sun. It was the only vessel in the natural harbour. The telchines had lowered sail, and were using the oars to get closer to the cliff. The white rocks soared over it, bare of houses or any sign of human hand. No proud acropolis crowned the skyline, nothing except birds' nests and screaming gulls.

"Are you sure this is Lindos?" Electra said.

The Moths muttered, uneasy. But Timosthenes straightened his shoulders. "Of course it's Lindos! The telchines know where they're going, and I recognize the landmarks. In the human world the Temple of Athene is up there on the highest point, and that hillside is covered in houses. The main street winds up that slope. Down there are the shipyards, and look – you can see the entrance to the grotto! That must be where the telchines are heading. We'd better hurry. We don't want to lose them now."

The final approach to the grotto turned out to be more of a scramble than a path. They had to be careful not to make much noise, because the ship swayed at anchor a short way off the rocks below. Aura made the mistake of looking down. Past the heads of the others, the sea waited, deep and blue. It made her dizzy, and she had an overwhelming urge to dive in. She resisted and continued down carefully, sitting back on her heels so she could use her hands to stop herself slipping.

Timosthenes waited until they were all safely at the bottom. "How many telchines do you see?" he whispered.

They crouched behind the rocks and peered at the anchored vessel. It seemed deserted, which no doubt explained why the telchines hadn't spotted them coming down the cliff.

"Maybe they've gone into the grotto already?" one of the Moth boys said. "We can swim to the ship an' steal the Gift while they're away."

"Maybe it's a trap," Chariclea said with a scowl.

"They've probably taken the Gift in with them," another girl said with a nervous glance at the cave mouth. "And if there are telchines in the water, I don't want to be in it as well."

"Me, neither!" several people agreed, obviously remembering how they'd nearly been drowned back at the Invisible Village.

Timosthenes looked at Aura. "Do you think you can sneak aboard and steal the Gift? If you can't bring it back here, use it to get through the Barrier and find your father. We'll wait in the grotto for you to bring us through."

Aura eyed the ship uneasily. But she nodded.

"You'd trust her to go alone?" Chariclea said, still scowling.

"Aura's the best swimmer, and the telchines are her family. They won't hurt her if they catch her, and she won't leave her friend stranded here. I trust her."

Electra gripped Aura's hand. "Don't forget you've got to persuade Councillor Iamus to bring the Egyptian king down to the grotto for the ancient oracle, Aura! Otherwise he'll just take King Ptolemy to the Temple of Athene Lindia instead, where the chief priest might interfere."

Aura nodded again.

Electra chewed her lip. "Be careful of the god. It might try to trick you again."

"Don't worry. This time, I'll be ready for it."

She wished she felt as confident as she sounded. She dived off the rocks with barely a ripple and changed to water-breathing. The tension trickled out of her as the underwater world welcomed her, colourful and magical. Down here, she didn't have to think about webbed toes, or scars, or being the Half-and-Half. It was a third world, where she could be herself. It was tempting to keep swimming out to sea, leaving the humans and telchines to fight over the Gift. But she couldn't abandon her family and friends. And the Gift needed her, too.

The ship loomed ahead, its anchor stone scraping mud from the seabed as it rocked on waves. Underwater, she had a better view of the grotto – a narrow crack in the cliff that seemed to go down forever. The entrance was nearly flooded, which was why the telchines couldn't take their ship inside, but glittering light beyond suggested the grotto opened out under the cliff.

She stared at the grotto, shivering. That was where, fifty-six years ago in human time, her mother and father had destroyed the balance of two worlds to save the life of a single man. Was she about to do the same?

She shook the thought away and swam quickly to the ship. She surfaced close to the anchor rope and used it to pull herself out of the water. The side of the ship reared overhead like a wooden cliff. The oars had been drawn up on board, so she had to brace her feet against the side and climb. Her arm muscles screamed. Once, she'd never have managed it. But she was leaner and stronger now. She bit her lip and struggled upwards, hand over hand.

"*Look out, Aura!*" Electra's cry came faintly from the cliff.

Aura froze as a line of heads peered over the side above her, their skin shining blue and their yellow eyes fixed on her.

"I might have known you'd try something like this, Half-and-Half," said Old One Rhode, shaking her head. "Looks like your father isn't here with the missing pieces, so we're going to have to take the ship through to the human world. You're not coming with us. Let go of the rope." She leant over the side and prodded Aura's shoulder with an oar.

It hurt, but Aura clung on. The sea glittered. The crack in the cliffs wavered in her vision.

"Let me try to contact him, Old One!" she said, desperately trying to think what might have gone wrong. "Please! Maybe he's just not had enough time? The earthquake damaged his store at Alimia, and the Moths say there are hundreds of statues with pendants in Rhodes City..."

"I'm sorry, Half-and-Half. The way time works in the human world, he's had more than enough to get back here with the missing pieces. Even if those young thieves are having trouble in the city, Leonidus would bring the pieces from Alimia here as fast as he could to rescue you and find Lindia. Something must have happened to stop him coming, so we're going through the Barrier to find out what."

"But if you go through the Barrier it could mean war!" Aura said.

"So be it," Rhode replied. "Now be sensible and let go, or we'll be forced to hurt you." Rhode gave her another prod with the oar.

Aura slid back out of reach and wrapped her arms and legs around the anchor rope. If the ship went through the Barrier, they'd have to take her, too.

Rhode sighed and muttered something to the male telchine beside her. He leant over and sawed at the rope with one of the knives they'd taken from the Moths.

Aura dropped back into the water and swam round to the stern to get a hold on the rudder instead.

The Old One used eye-power, sizzling into the sea, to warn her away. Aura dived again, thinking to come up underneath the ship. But the telchines had raised sail. Without the anchor rope attached, the bottom scraped over her head and drew away.

She gave chase, cursing herself for being so stupid. If they went through the Barrier now, she'd be left behind. She ought to have waited until she was sure the telchines weren't on board.

Just as she was about to give up hope, something splashed into the water ahead of her, pulsing blue. She felt the power coming off it and shivered... the Gift! At first, Aura couldn't understand why the telchines had thrown it overboard. Wouldn't it work on the ship? Had they sent it to burn out her eyes, as it had burnt out her mother's? A telchine dived in after it and tugged it towards her, and she surfaced in panic.

Phaethon's head surfaced beside her. "Quick!" whispered the boy, thrusting the Gift at her. "Take it to the grotto! I've been thinking about what you said, and you're right – it's wrong to restart the war. Can you use Poseidon's Gift to get through the Barrier and find your father? I'll do my best to delay the others until you've gone."

There was no time to think. More telchines dived off the ship and arrowed towards them, their yellow eyes gleaming in fury at Phaethon's betrayal. Underwater, they were frighteningly powerful, their long hair billowing in silver clouds around a blur of rippling muscle. Aura grabbed the Gift and swam for her life. It was heavier now it had absorbed the pieces her father had brought to the Invisible Village, but underwater it floated along easily enough. It glowed brighter as they approached the crack in the cliffs. Rainbows flickered at the edges of her vision.

Inside the grotto stalactites as big as temple columns hung from the roof and plunged, sparkling, into the water around her. Phaethon stayed behind at the entrance to block the telchines' way. The Gift was almost too hot to hold. It filled the entire grotto with light, and ragged holes appeared in the water around it, like the holes in the sky at the Invisible Village. Through them, Aura glimpsed entrances to underwater tunnels, but there was no time to look for her mother because overhead, through one of the holes in the Barrier, she saw the bottom of a boat.

Father! she cried silently, kicking for the surface. *Father, can you hear me?*

The telchines had got past Phaethon. A webbed hand grabbed Aura's ankle. She kicked free and swam towards the boat, dragging the Gift after her, willing it to take her through to the human world. But the Old One reached for the Gift, too, and they struggled for possession of the slippery creature.

The blue light brightened. Everything went quiet. For a horrible moment, Aura didn't know which way was up

and which way down, or if she was water-breathing or air-breathing. She lost her hold on the Gift. There were bubbles everywhere—

Then she surfaced.

Shouts and screams sounded faintly out in the bay. The air, that had been so clean in the telchine world, was heavy with incense, rotting fish, and sewage. Human noise, human smells.

Aura trod water in relief, trying to see where the Gift had gone, and if any of the telchines had got through the Barrier with her. The grotto was gloomy on this side. "Father?" she whispered, not sure that anyone was in the boat, after all. She peered into the depths beneath her feet, but couldn't see anything in the shadows.

Even as she hesitated, something whistled out of the boat and a net fell over her head. Before she could get free, the weighted ends whipped around her legs and tightened. She was forced under, got a lungful of water mixed with air, changed to water-breathing, then air-breathing again. She choked and struggled with increasing panic as she was dragged towards the boat like a trapped fish.

She came up spluttering, tangled in cords, and saw three cloaked figures bending over her. Human hands hauled her out of the water and dropped her in the bottom of the boat, still tangled in the net. Aura struggled desperately as one of the men rolled her face down and sat on her. Cords bit into her wrists and ankles and a cloth went over her eyes, snagging in her hair as he knotted it behind her head. This was followed by a hood, tied around her neck so she could hardly breathe. She heard the splash of oars, and felt the boat move.

Her senses returned. The noise outside… it sounded like a fight. She screamed as loudly as she could, knowing it would be muffled by the hood, and writhed against her bonds.

"Stop that!" A stick whacked the backs of her legs, and she froze as a voice from her nightmares said, "I know all your tricks, Aura of Alimia. You're mine now, and I have your father the traitor as well. Helios has delivered you both into my hands for punishment. You won't escape again."

Chapter 14

PUNISHMENT

THE CHIEF PRIEST had captured her father, too. The knowledge stole Aura's remaining strength, and she trembled in the bottom of the boat as it carried her out of the grotto. The hood and the blindfold meant she couldn't see what was happening, but if the chief priest had known about their rendezvous then it must be bad.

They rowed through a confusion of shouts and splashes. Aura screamed again, but Chief Priest Xenophon chuckled and gave her another prod with his stick. "Don't get your hopes up, Aura of Alimia! No one's going to rescue you this time. The Egyptian king wasn't very impressed when your Moth friends stole his ship and all his gold. He insisted that Councillor Iamus round them up for punishment. They made a mistake coming here."

The shouts faded behind them. Coolness fell across her as they entered the shadow of the cliff. Aura felt the boat bump against rock. The men rolled her out of the net and searched her carefully. "She doesn't have it, Your Holiness," one reported. He sounded a bit relieved.

The chief priest grunted. "I didn't think she'd be so stupid as to bring it with her, but I bet she knows where it is. All right, bring her up to the Temple of Athene."

The boat tipped to one side as the men climbed out. It was very quiet. They must have rowed around the headland. Aura considered struggling as they lifted her ashore. But tied like this she wouldn't be able to swim, and she couldn't see if there was anyone near enough to help her. Xenophon's men dumped her face down across something warm and hairy that shifted under her weight, and ropes were tied around her arms and legs, securing her to what smelled and felt like a donkey. The animal lurched into motion and began to climb.

Aura gritted her teeth against a sudden wave of nausea. The hood clung to her face, making breathing difficult. She tried to ease herself on the animal's spine, but the ropes were too secure. At least I won't fall off, she thought with a crazed little giggle, then immediately felt herself slipping. A vision of being trampled under the donkey's hooves flashed behind her eyes.

By the time the path levelled out, she had terrible cramp. The donkey stopped. She heard Xenophon's heavy breathing as he limped closer.

"Comfortable?" he said, prodding her bound feet with his stick. "I notice your ankle's healed. That was Helios' Gift, I suppose. I can see I'm going to need something a bit more drastic to slow you down this time." The stick forced its way between her webbed toes. "Your feet don't match your hands, do they? You can't be half-and-half all your life, Aura of Alimia. There comes a time when you have to choose which side you're on. So, which is it to be? Human or telchine, eh?"

Aura's skin crawled. Up to now, she'd simply been relieved the climb seemed to be over. She wondered if her father was being kept prisoner in the temple as well, and if she'd be taken to the same place. At least they'd be together. But something in the old priest's tone chilled her. It was the same tone he'd used before, when he'd hit her injured ankle in the Temple of Helios. She braced herself for a blow, hoping he wouldn't miss and hit the donkey instead. If it bolted back down the cliff path with her still tied on its back, she'd be killed.

"Since we can't very well stick your finger webs back on," the chief priest said in the same chilling tone, "the toe webs will have to come off. Do it quickly, and let's get her inside before Iamus finishes rounding up those Moths."

Horror rippled through Aura as Xenophon shuffled back. Someone turned the donkey, and a hand pressed on her ankles. Her stomach heaved as she felt the first cold touch of the blade, slicing the tender web between her big and second toe.

The pain made her vomit into her hood. She screamed, in case someone was nearby and might come to stop it. But the blade did not stop. It cut the other three webs, then moved to repeat the operation on her other foot. Before it was over, Aura fainted.

She came to her senses lying on cold marble. The hood had gone. But the blindfold was still tight across her eyes, and her hands had been bound behind her so she couldn't take it off. There was such a fiery trickle, hot and wet between her toes, that it took her a moment to realize the ragged breathing she could hear was not her own.

"Father...?" she whispered into the blackness.

"My poor darling! You're awake at last." She heard a rattle of metal. "Aura, listen! The pieces of the Gift I brought from Alimia are in here with us. They might help you. But I can't reach you, I'm sorry. I'm chained to the wall. You'll have to come across."

Aura gritted her teeth. Stiffly, she got to her knees. She tried putting her weight on one foot, but abandoned the idea when pain arrowed up her leg. "Where are you?" she said in a shaky voice, terrified by the thought of being blind like this forever, like her poor mother.

"Over here, darling. It's not far. Take your time."

But it was far. An ocean of cold, hard marble lay between them. She shuffled across it on her knees, trying to keep her injured toes off the floor. Because she couldn't see, she kept losing her balance and falling, which hurt her arms.

She bit her lip, determined not to cry. "How did he capture you?"

Leonidus made a frustrated sound. "His men were waiting for me at Alimia. Milo was with me. We dived to collect the pieces I'd stored underwater. It was quite a long job, because you were right about them being scattered by the earthquake. Xenophon's men threw a net over us when we came back up. I stayed to delay them so Milo could get away. Androcles took the second boat straight to the city. Did he manage to get the pendants from the statues back to the telchines?"

"I don't think so." Aura explained about the struggle in the bay. "The chief priest said the soldiers are rounding up the Moths for stealing the Egyptian king's ship and his gold."

Leonidus sighed, and his chain clanked again. "Don't give up hope. Young Androcles is more resourceful than Xenophon realizes. But how did the chief priest catch you, my darling? I thought you'd stayed behind with the hostages in the Invisible Village?"

"We followed the ship to Lindos, and Phaethon helped me. But the others are still trapped in the telchine world. I don't know if the Gift came through the Barrier with me. If it didn't, Old One Rhode will use it to bring the ship and the telchines through, and if the soldiers are still in the bay that'll start another war."

Leonidus went quiet. "Do you think you can use these pieces I collected to contact the telchines and warn them to stay on their side of the Barrier?"

"I don't know. I made contact through the Barrier when I was in the Invisible Village with the telchines, but I don't trust it. Sometimes it just refuses to work for me." Aura fell for the fifth time and lost her fight with the tears. "I'm sorry, Father! This is all my fault. Mother warned me the Gift would trick us, but I didn't listen. It did such a horrible thing to her, yet she only brought the Gift into the human world to help you. How can something done for love go so wrong?" She couldn't even cry properly through the blindfold.

Leonidus made a choked sound. "Aura, stay there. Don't try to move any more. I can see what he's done to your feet, now. It's worse than I thought. When I get free, I'm going to kill him." His voice was hard and tight.

Aura struggled to her knees again. "It's only the same as I did to my fingers," she said, alarmed by his hatred. "You remember, don't you? How I fainted afterwards, and you had to carry me back to Mother? They healed, and so will my toes. I'm fully human now!"

She shuffled a bit further across the marble. She could sense the pieces of the Gift now. Ahead, close. She bit her lip as her wounded toes banged against the floor again.

"Chief Priest Xenophon's got no right to treat us like this," Leonidus said. "When we get out of here, I'll lodge a formal complaint. The Council will strip Xenophon of his priesthood and banish him from Rhodes. Then I'll make him pay for what he's done to you. A bit further to the left, darling. That's my brave girl. You're almost there."

Aura's elbow scraped against something hard. She wriggled round and felt wood knobbly with barnacles. Her heart sank slightly. "They're in a chest!"

"Yes, darling. I had to store them in something. But you should be able to lift the lid. It's not that heavy, and it isn't locked."

This was easier said than done with her hands bound and her toes too sore to use for balance. Aura bruised her shoulder on a corner of the chest as her fingers slipped. She fought tears, heaved herself upright again, and after several painful attempts managed to lift the lid far enough to wedge her elbows inside. She groped blindly behind her, and at last touched one of the pendants her father had collected.

"Can anyone hear me?" she whispered, building a picture of the grotto in her head.

The piece she was touching warmed. Rainbows flickered in her head, and the pain of her toes dulled a little. Aura barely noticed. She was too busy trying to make sense of the vision that came in snatches.

Magical blue light, glittering off rock... an underwater tunnel, partly lit, the rest in darkness... a telchine, holding her hands out towards Aura with a look of terror and wonder on her eyeless face...

"Mother!" Aura cried, almost dropping the pendant she held. "Where are you? Which world are you in?"

But there was a blue flash, as if someone had hit her in the eye, and the vision changed.

Telchines and humans splashing in the grotto, haloed blue by the Gift... the rainbows so bright she cannot see faces, only silhouettes... a jumble of excited voices... then another blue flash, and Electra's unmistakeable cry, "Where's Aura? Did anyone see what happened to Aura...?"

"Electra!" Aura shouted. "Can you hear me? You must tell the Old One not to fight the humans! I think Councillor Iamus is on our side. We're prisoners of the chief priest in the Temple of Athene in Lindia. If you can hear me, please help— " The lid slipped off her elbows and came down on her wrists, making her drop the pendant she held with a cry of pain.

"Never mind, darling," Leonidus said. "It was worth a try."

Aura fought a wave of dizziness. Obviously, he didn't realize she'd made contact. "Father, listen! I saw Mother in one of the underwater tunnels. The Gift's still in the grotto where I dropped it, and I think it sent Electra through the Barrier into our world when I contacted it just now. But I couldn't see if Timosthenes and the other Moths got through as well, or what happened to the telchines. I have to get one of those pendants out of the chest and try to contact them again. Maybe I can hide it in my hand so I can use my eye-power when the chief priest takes this blindfold off— "

"I think not, Aura of Alimia," said the chief priest's creepy voice from across the room. "That's more than enough to tell me what I wanted to know. Now be a good girl and get away from that chest before I have to make you, eh?"

Aura froze with her fingers trapped under the lid, her skin prickling.

Leonidus' chains clanked. "You son of a mule!" he shouted. "If you so much as *touch* my daughter, I'll—" There was a whistle and a thud. Leonidus gave a sharp cry and fell in a rattle of metal.

"May I remind you," Xenophon said, "that you're the traitor here? Stealing the gods' holy pendants and substituting them with common sponges! Did you really think I wouldn't notice the difference? I'm quite within my rights. You'll find the Council has no power over temple affairs when someone has betrayed the gods."

Aura lurched to her feet and took two stumbling steps towards the chief priest's voice. "Leave him alone!" she cried. "He's not a traitor. *You* are! *You* were the one who stole Poseidon's Gift from the telchines and used it to pretend to be a god! It's *your* fault the Gift tried to make Lindia use her eye-power on my father. If you hadn't sacrificed my grandfather to your stupid Colossus, my mother might still be able to see!"

The chief priest tapped across the marble floor towards her and touched her mutilated toes with his stick, making her stiffen.

"On your feet already?" he said. "You're tougher than I thought. Or did the Gift heal them when you contacted it just now? Thanks for the information, by the way. I'd hoped you'd find out more, but no matter. If any of those telchines come through the Barrier, the soldiers will deal with them. Your thieving Moth friends seem to have disappeared again, no doubt off hiding the Egyptian gold they stole, but we'll soon hunt them down and make them tell us where it is. Councillor Iamus is currently reassuring the Egyptian king as to the power of our gods. As soon as I've used the pendants to tell the stupid oracle-priestess breathing her smoke in the sanctuary of Athene what to say, I shall have the Council's permission to rebuild the Colossus of Helios – and when we find the Moths, I'll have the Egyptian gold to finance it. All I need now is Helios' Gift so I can put it back where it belongs." The stick crawled across her big toe. "So, you think the Gift's in the grotto, do you? And you can obviously use those pieces your father so kindly retrieved from Alimia to trace it. Good! Then perhaps you can save his life by co-operating with me a little more fully than you did last time. Remember what I did to your grandfather Chares? Helios is hungry for another sacrifice, and your father's heart should do nicely."

Aura's knees weakened as she realized what he meant. The feel of the stick creeping around her throbbing toes made her feel sick. She crumpled in a heap at the chief priest's feet, and he chuckled.

"Maybe not so tough, after all. What's the matter? Did you think I was going to hit your poor toes?"

"Leave her alone!" shouted Leonidus, clanking his chains again. "You hurt her again, and I'll tear out *your* heart and put it inside your precious Colossus! I swear it."

The chief priest laughed. "Oh, I think the telchine brat's learnt her lesson. You're afraid of me, aren't you, Aura of Alimia?"

She tried to control her trembling. "No."

He grunted in annoyance. "You don't fool me. You're going to be a good girl and do exactly what I tell you. Later, when the oracle-priestess of Athene has passed on the word of her goddess to satisfy the Egyptian king, I'm going to take you down to the grotto and let you dive. You'll find Helios' Gift and bring it back for me, because if you don't find it your father will die. As a small precaution, I'm going to take out his heart before you dive. As you know, the Gift is the only thing that can save his life. That should make sure you don't dawdle. You've got a sponge diver's lungs, so you should manage to find the Gift all right before his body rots. Oh, yes, and I almost forgot... if you come across any of those telchines while you're down there, you might have to choose sides. But I think you'll make the right choice, all things considered, won't you?"

"You're mad," Leonidus whispered.

The chief priest chuckled again. "The physicians tell me having your skull cracked by a falling stone can do that to man," he said. "But in my case, it has merely made things clearer. Helios has spoken to me. I am his chosen one. If you don't want to suffer the same fate as your father Chares did, I'd suggest you do everything you can to persuade your daughter to help me get Helios' Gift back."

Aura swallowed. "I'll need a pendant from the chest. I can't find the Gift without one."

"That will be arranged when the time comes. I have to prepare the pendants for the oracle-priestess' question. Tiresome, I know, but a necessary deception with the Egyptian king here. Meanwhile, another precaution..." The chief priest's stick tapped away across the floor and back again, dragging something that rattled across the marble. Aura heard her father protest, and her heart sank as she felt a manacle click shut around her ankle.

"Can't have you meddling with the god's property, can we?" The chief priest said, giving her leg a pat. "Save yourself some pain, and don't bother trying. The chain's too short. I checked."

When the door thudded shut, neither of them spoke for a long time. Was the chief priest still watching them through some hidden spy-hole? Listening, as he had done before? The thought chilled Aura almost as much as what he had threatened to do to her father.

Finally, Leonidus sighed. "I think he's gone, Aura. We told him everything he wanted to know, anyway. I guessed he must have put you in here with me for a reason. I thought he meant to weaken me, by letting me see what he'd done to you... I had no idea how crazy he was. I'm sorry, my darling. I was stupid to get myself caught."

"I won't let him take out your heart!" she said fiercely. "He'll have to take off my blindfold when I dive. And he'll have to give me a piece of the Gift, so I'll be able to use my eye-power on him."

"We're going to get out of here before then," Leonidus said, with an attempt at cheerfulness. "You might have to run a bit on those feet, my brave darling. But we'll get these chains off, I promise. Then we'll escape."

Aura bit her lip. She'd been trying to rub the blindfold off against her shoulder, but it was too tight. She didn't see how they were going to remove metal manacles without help. She kept thinking of all the things she wanted to tell her father, all the silly little confessions and questions she'd been storing up over the years he'd been gone. But the thought of the chief priest possibly still out there, listening, imprisoned her tongue.

She rested her head against the wall. "He's wrong about the Moths having the Egyptian gold, though – the telchines still have the king's treasure chests on the ship. Why is it so quiet? Do you think the Council could have taken the Egyptian king down to the grotto to hear the ancient oracle already? Electra might have persuaded Councillor Iamus to go down there. But if we've got your Alimian pieces up here, and Androcles hasn't brought the pieces from the statues in Rhodes City yet, the Gift mightn't be powerful enough to communicate through the Barrier, anyway, so it'll all be for nothing... oh, I wish I knew what the telchines were up to!"

Leonidus grunted. "Let's hope they wait. I expect the priestess and the Council are in another part of the temple. I think we're in some sort of underground storeroom. It's empty, though. I could do with something to drink."

"So could I," Aura said, dry-mouthed after the time she'd spent unconscious.

"Maybe the chief priest's men will decide to feed us, and we can escape when they bring the food?"

"I don't think they'll fall for that trick twice." Aura recounted with a heavy heart how she and her mother had escaped the Temple of Helios. "If they do feed us, they'll be careful."

"Your poor mother… I wish I'd had a chance to say goodbye. I left you alone so much while I was off searching for pieces of the Gift. She didn't deserve it, and neither did you."

"We'll find her," Aura said. "As soon as we get out of here, I'll dive into the underwater tunnels and look for her. I think she's still in the human world. She's too scared of the Gift to use it to get through the Barrier."

It was Leonidus' turn to sigh. "She might go if the telchines help her, my darling. I don't think she'd have left you while you were small. But if Old One Rhode's forgiven her, I expect she'll go home."

Aura wanted to protest this wasn't true. But she remembered how her mother had said she was up-grown now. She tugged in frustration at the chain. Her toes did feel a little better… maybe. That wouldn't help them now.

"If I were a proper telchine, I'd get us out of here in no time," she said. "I wouldn't have to touch the pieces of the Gift. I could have simply digested a slice of it and kept the power inside me. Then I could have contacted someone and asked them to help us… except there aren't any pendants left in the temples, and all the priests and priestesses think the messages come from the gods..." She blinked away another tear and eased her bruised wrists. "Oh, it's hopeless, isn't it?"

There was a pause.

"Maybe not," Leonidus whispered.

Aura's skin prickled. "Why?" she said, her heart thudding.

"Because the chest's glowing. There's blue light coming from under the lid."

Hope surged as she remembered the Old One bending over her when she thought she was asleep, saying: *You've more skill with the Gift than we realized.* "Electra must have heard me, after all!" Then she had a more chilling thought. "Or the telchines have come through to the human world to fight with the Gift…"

"Or Xenophon might have caught Androcles, and be bringing him down here with the pendants he stole from Rhodes City."

They held their breath as a single set of footsteps passed the door. No tapping stick. No limp like the chief priest's.

"Help!" Leonidus shouted. "We're in here! Help us!"

The footsteps paused, as if someone were listening.

"Help!" Aura screamed. "Please!"

The footsteps faltered to a stop, hesitated, and came back. The door bar scraped, and fresh air flooded their prison. There was an intake of breath.

"Aura of Alimia!" exclaimed a woman's voice. "What are you doing in here, dearie?"

Aura's entire body sagged in relief. It was Priestess Themis from Khalki.

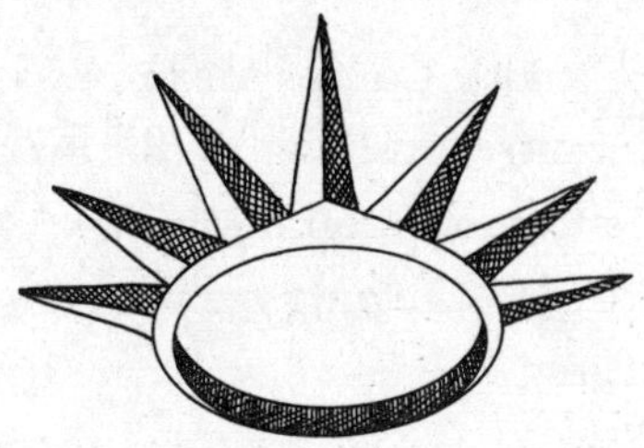

Chapter 15

JUSTICE

AT FIRST, AURA couldn't think what Priestess Themis was doing in the Acropolis. Then she remembered the message the telchines had sent through the Gift, instructing her to bring the pendant of Athene Khalkia to Lindos.

"Who trussed you up like that, dearie?" the priestess exclaimed. "And what have you done to your poor toes? Let's get that blindfold off, shall we…?"

Aura drew breath to tell the priestess everything. But before she could order her thoughts, there was a shout from the corridor, and the sound she'd been dreading tapped through the door. The chief priest snapped, "Leave it, Themis!" and Aura's heart sank in fresh despair as the fingers that had started to loosen the knot behind her head retreated.

"But what's this girl doing in here, chained up like a slave?" Priestess Themis sounded confused. "I sent her across to Rhodes with Councillor Iamus so she could be properly looked after! And who's this man?"

"The man is a dangerous criminal," said the chief priest. "And the girl is helping me with important temple business. It's regrettable you have to see her like this, but the bonds and the blindfold are there for her own good. She kept trying to mutilate herself, as you can see. Look at her feet! She's not right in the head."

"That's a lie!" Aura said desperately. "He told his men to cut off my toe webs! Are they there? Ask them!"

Xenophon sighed. "Priestess Themis is quite aware of how you cut off your own finger webs when you were younger, Aura. And now you've cut your feet, as well. There's no point denying it. I'll take you down to the sea soon, like I promised, and you can bathe your poor toes. Salt's good for wounds."

"Don't listen to him!" Aura cried.

"Those cuts look quite serious to me," Themis said. "The girl needs a physician. She oughtn't to be kept in here with a criminal."

"This is only temporary," the chief priest said impatiently. "They're both restrained for good reason. I assume you came to Lindos to witness the oracle? If so, you're in the wrong place. Guards! Escort the priestess upstairs."

Leonidus said in an even tone, "Priestess, I am Aura's father, Leonidus, son of Chares of Lindos. Please go and tell Councillor Iamus where we are. Tell him Chief Priest Xenophon is going to try to deceive the Council by using the gods' pendants to send his own message and pretend to be the oracle."

Themis hesitated. "Does this man speak the truth, Your Holiness?"

The chief priest laughed. "Would you believe the word of a criminal over that of Helios' chosen one?"

"I believe the word of my goddess," Themis said, and Aura stiffened as rainbows flickered behind her eyes.

Leonidus whispered, "She's got a pendant, Aura! It's glowing like those in the chest."

The chief priest hissed through his teeth. "Who gave you permission to remove that from the statue of Athene Khalkia?"

"The goddess herself did," Priestess Themis said. "I thought it a strange request, but now I see why she told me to bring it to Lindos. It guided me to this place. Obviously Athene has sent me here to help this poor girl and her father."

There was a silence.

"Ah yes, of course..." The chief priest gave a little cough. "The goddess sent you here, Themis, but not to rescue the prisoners. She means you to help me."

"Help you, Your Holiness?" Priestess Themis sounded confused again. "Help you with what?"

The chief priest chuckled. "At this very moment, the Council of Rhodes and King Ptolemy of Egypt are consulting the oracle. I'd hoped to manage this alone, but since the Sun God fell I've had some difficulty speaking with the gods. This stupid girl stole the pendant of Helios

Rhodos, and her father has tampered with the pendants in this chest and removed their wires, so they're no longer working as they should." Aura heard the lid of the chest being thrown back, and the rainbows brightened in her head.

"The pieces of the Gift are still glowing, Aura," Leonidus whispered.

"But they seem to have woken up since you arrived," continued Xenophon. "Come over here and bring your pendant. Shortly, we will hear the oracle-priestess of Athene Lindia asking if the Council should rebuild the Colossus of Helios. When she asks her question, I want you to answer *YES*."

Priestess Themis sucked in her breath. "You want me to help you interfere with the oracle?"

"Just do what I tell you, Themis! We're running out of time. I'll explain everything in more detail later. Goddess Athene told you to come here, remember? Helios must have told her to send you to me."

"She didn't say anything about interfering with the oracle." The priestess was firm. "I think I'd better check with her first."

The chief priest's stick whacked the wall. "She won't answer you, you stupid woman! She's busy. The oracle-priestess is already speaking to her to get the oracle for the Council!"

"Then I'll wait until she's finished."

Chief Priest Xenophon made a frustrated sound, and Leonidus laughed.

"What's the matter, Xenophon? Your gods not getting the messages you want them to these days? Couldn't have something to do with the telchines removing those wires you so carefully threaded through their Gift, could it? What do you think they're going to do to you when they catch you? If they're here in the human world, I'd say you're in a lot of trouble."

"Silence, traitor!" Xenophon's stick whistled again, this time striking flesh. Leonidus gave a grunt of pain, and Aura's heart clenched in sympathy.

"Your Holiness!" exclaimed Priestess Themis, a waver of fear in her voice. "I will not stand by and watch this treatment of your prisoners! Even if this man is a criminal, he deserves a fair trial before being punished. And I demand you let me organize proper care for the girl."

"*After* you've helped me with the oracle!" Xenophon snapped. There was a scuffle, as if the priestess had made a run for the door. Xenophon drew breath and continued in a more reasonable tone, "Come on, Themis. You know we're going to have to rebuild the Colossus of Helios eventually. Everyone on Rhodes wants their Sun God to stand tall again. It's our symbol of pride and independence. We can't just let it lie on the ground and rot."

"If we should rebuild it, then the oracle will tell us so," said the priestess in a righteous tone.

"And why do you think Goddess Athene sent you here with her pendant, if not to make sure the oracle speaks correctly?"

"I… she said to bring the pendant to Lindos and take it to the place where the oracle speaks…" Themis wavered.

"Exactly! She meant here."

"But she might have meant the grotto, where the ancient oracle used to speak. I was on my way down there when I got her second message, telling me to come and help these prisoners."

The chief priest sighed. "She sent you here so you could help me, Themis. As Chief Priest of Helios, I only want what's best for Rhodes. Telchines are dangerous sea-demons who do not recognize Helios or Athene. You know that, don't you?"

"I suppose…" Themis hesitated, and Aura heard her move away from the door.

"Priestess Themis!" she called, afraid she had given in. "The goddess didn't speak to you in the temple on Khalki! It was Chief Priest Xenophon, *pretending* to be her! He's been using the gods' pendants to send messages to all the temples – they're pieces of a sea creature that Poseidon gave to the telchines ages ago so they could defend themselves from the humans who were hunting them. But because I'm half telchine, I can use it as well to send messages and activate my evil eye. That's why he's blindfolded me. If you don't believe me, ask your novice, Electra! She's here in Lindos somewhere. She and I used the pendants in the sanctuaries to talk to each other, the night I was a prisoner in the Temple of Helios. That's why she stole your temple funds and ran away to Rhodes. I told her to do it, only she thought I was Goddess Athene at the time, so it wasn't her fault and—"

"Don't children invent such amazing stories?" Chief Priest Xenophon said with a little laugh. "Ignore the girl, Themis, and let's get on. We've wasted enough time."

But Priestess Themis didn't laugh. "Electra," she said. "I wondered why she left like that in the middle of the night. It was so out of character for her. And I *thought* that last message didn't sound much like the goddess speaking." She paused. "So… that's why there's one of these pendants in the sanctuary of Athene Lindia, is it? So you can pretend to be the voice of the goddess, and control the oracle?"

"Yes!" Aura and Leonidus said together.

Themis said tightly, "And all this time I've been hearing the goddess' statue on Khalki speak to me, it was you, Your Holiness?"

Aura thought the chief priest was going to deny it again. But he heaved a sigh and snapped, "What did you think, Themis? That you'd suddenly been given the ability to speak to the gods? There's no such thing as a real oracle, you know that, only priests tricking everyone into thinking there is! It's the same thing everywhere. At Delphi we had to sit and listen to the old priestess talk nonsense, sitting in the smoke and chanting like she was in a trance. It's always been the chief priest's job to make sense of it all – to work out what needs to be said for the good of all. This isn't so different, not really. All I'm asking you to say is a simple 'yes'. The Temple of Helios will reward you, don't worry about that. And if that doesn't work, you can help me make this girl reply for us. She's stubborn, but I think I've found a way to persuade her to co-operate. All we need to do is take out her father's heart, and—"

"*Now* I understand why I was brought here!" Priestess Themis said.

She moved fast for an old woman. A surprised grunt came from the chief priest, and his stick clattered to the floor. Aura's blindfold was tugged down. Firelight flared to join the rainbows in her head, making her eyes water. She saw her father, covered in bruises and chained by the wrists to the wall opposite her. An overturned lamp had spilt burning oil across the floor. The chief priest sprawled across the open chest and the glowing pieces of the Gift, his jewel-encrusted robes stained with salt from the grotto, and drool coming from his lips. His stick had rolled against the wall, and without it he could not get up.

Priestess Themis untied Aura's hands and pressed Athene Khalkia's pendant into her numb fingers. It warmed them at once, bringing back her circulation. "Use it, dearie," she said. "I see now how crazy Xenophon is. I'm sorry I didn't listen to you, back on Khalki."

The pendant glowed brighter, matched by those in the chest, haloing the chief priest's body in blue light. Aura closed her eyes as the rainbows filled her head in a fierce, wild rush. There was no fighting the Gift, even had she wanted to.

As the pieces in the chest under him grew hotter, she heard Xenophon shriek, "No, don't let her—!" Then her eyelids flew open, and the power roared from her in a blaze of blue lightning.

Vengeance, whispered a voice in her head, *is mine.*

The lightning struck the chief priest, lifted him up, and flung him against the wall, where his robes burst into flame and his withered old body jerked inside them. He shrieked like an animal. The pain she was causing him made Aura feel ill, and the smell of his burning flesh made her want to throw up. If she could have stopped it then, she might have done. But she was as helpless to deny the Gift the use of her eyes to channel its power, as the chief priest was to escape its revenge.

And at last, she understood. The Gift's final trick had not been played on her. Xenophon had cut pieces off the poor creature, and wired it up in his Colossus to serve him like a slave for fifty-six years.

The creature desired justice.

It was over very quickly. The blue light faded to violet, and the pendants became dull once more. The chief priest's body thudded to the floor, blackened and shrivelled. His once fine robes were smoking rags, his mouth stretched wide with his final scream. The door hung off its hinges, burning. The guards raced in and stared in confusion at the frazzled corpse.

Priestess Themis had flattened herself against the wall and shielded her eyes from the blue light. But when Aura collapsed, she pulled herself together and closed the lid of the chest.

"A horrible accident," she explained. "He knocked over the lamp, and his robes caught fire. There was nothing I could do. It was Helios' will. Please take the body somewhere it can be prepared for its return to the city, and release these prisoners. They are from Alimia, which is under the protection of the Temple of Athene Khalkia. I'll be responsible for them from now on. Tell me, has the Lindian oracle answered the Council's question yet?"

The guards eyed the body of their chief priest, clearly unsure whether it had been the accident she claimed. But with no evidence otherwise, they decided to respect Priestess Themis' white robe and authoritative tone. "No, Priestess," one said. "But they've been in there a while. It shouldn't be long now."

Aura tightened her hand around the pendant Priestess Themis had given her and listened carefully with the inside of her head. But she couldn't hear the oracle-priestess' voice. What if the priestess had asked her question while Aura had been using the eye-power?

She was not sure the chief priest's men would go so far as to free them, and hoped she wouldn't have to use the eye-power again. But one of the guards patted her cheek as he unlocked her manacle. "Don't worry, love, we'll soon have you out of here. I, for one, am not sorry old Xenophon's dead. He was crazy enough before, but he's got ten times worse since he had that bang on the head. None of us liked it when he ordered us to cut your toes like that. Hold your breath and close your eyes, now, while we go through the flames at the door." He held her firmly, but to support her rather than restrain her. "Priestess, where do you want us to put the Alimians until you're ready to take them home?"

Priestess Themis eyed Aura's blood-crusted toes and grimaced. "Take us to the oracle-priestess' private quarters. And bring that chest, too, before it burns. We've some important things to talk about, and we don't want to be disturbed."

One of the guards carried Aura up some steps, and they emerged into a glorious sunset that stained the marble around them delicate pink. As they climbed through the avenues of columns to the temple on the highest part of the acropolis, the bay shimmered below them, quiet and peaceful. If the telchines were in the human world, they were staying out of sight. Below, the tiled roofs of Lindos tumbled down the hillside through terraced gardens and marble streets. There were statues and flowers everywhere. Aura's eyes watered with the unexpected beauty of it all.

"There, there," said the guard, mistaking her tears for fear. "No need for that. You'll be all right with the Priestess of Khalki. Old Xenophon's gone now. He can't hurt you any more."

Aura couldn't help wondering if the man carrying her had been one of those who had cut her toe webs and beaten her father. She sighed. It didn't matter now. They had more important things to think about.

Novices and slaves stared curiously at them, but no one questioned Priestess Themis' white robe. They hurried down a colonnade and entered a small, but comfortable, room.

Two slaves, tending the lamps inside, jumped and bowed their heads. "Pr– Priestess?" they stammered, glancing at Leonidus and Aura. "We weren't expecting you! Priestess Melito is breathing the smoke for the Egyptian king!"

"I know." Priestess Themis indicated the men should put the chest near the door. "We'll wait. Go and help these men look for my novice from Khalki. Her name's Electra. If you find her, tell her I want to see her at once. And bring us bandages, warm water, herbs and something to eat."

"Yes, Priestess." The slaves bowed again, and left with the guards.

The food and medicines arrived. Priestess Themis bandaged Aura's feet, tutting over the state of them. But she seemed pleased by the way Aura's ankle had healed. It was easier to let the priestess think this was due to her care back on Khalki, rather than explain about the Gift's healing powers. Aura nestled under Leonidus' arm in the cushions, afraid to lean too hard against him in case she hurt his bruises. He, in turn, held her gently as he told Priestess Themis the whole story of how Chief Priest Xenophon had been deceiving priests and priestesses by controlling oracles across the entire Mediterranean.

Aura let his voice wash over her. Safe in her father's arms and with her belly full, a warm glow filled her. The pendant she held remained dull after the chief priest's death, and the rainbows had gone from her head. The room was cosy with its rugs and cushions. Lamplight glittered off the gold threads in the hangings that covered the walls. The scenes showed Goddess Athene springing fully-grown and armed from the skull of Zeus, Goddess Athene victorious in battle, Goddess Athene the Champion of Justice... they wavered in her vision, until she dozed off into a beautiful dream where she swam with her mother through the underwater tunnels, harvesting sponges from the rocks, and her mother could see again.

A tentative knock at the door jerked her back.

Electra's voice said, "Priestess Themis?"

The priestess smoothed her robes. Her face assumed a serious expression as she told the novice to enter.

Electra slipped inside. Her hair was dishevelled and her novice's robe even dirtier than the last time Aura had seen her. The girl looked pale, but her eyes lit up with joy when she saw Aura.

"Aura! Thank Athene you're safe! We went into the grotto after the telchines, and I thought I heard you calling me as the god sent us through the Barrier. Timosthenes said you must have joined up with your father as planned. But when we emerged in the human world and couldn't find you, we thought the worst... what happened to your feet?"

"Never mind that now, Electra," Priestess Themis said in a stern tone. "You betrayed a sacred trust when you stole funds from the Temple of Athene. By rights, I should dismiss you from your duties, but Aura tells me you were tricked into thinking the goddess spoke to you."

Electra coloured. Her gaze darted to Aura, trying to guess how much she'd told the priestess.

"It wasn't her fault, Priestess!" Aura reminded her. "Please don't punish her for it."

Themis waved her quiet and said with a wry smile, "But it seems you weren't the only one tricked into thinking the statue spoke with the voice of the goddess, so I'm going to give you a chance to redeem yourself. Open that chest."

Electra obeyed, still nervous. She smiled when she saw the pieces of the Gift. "You got them!"

"Leonidus' collection from Alimia," Themis said. "And Aura's got Athene Khalkia's pendant. Since you two apparently used two of these... ah... pieces of the Gift to communicate with each other after the Colossus fell, I'm going to let you see if you can persuade them to send a message to the pendant in the sanctuary of Athene

Lindia where the Egyptian king is listening to the oracle, just as the chief priest planned to do – only not the message he would have sent. Well, take a piece then, and go sit by Aura. She can't get up. Her toes are bad."

Electra dropped into the cushions, slipped a cold hand into Aura's, and squeezed tightly. "The Moths are all right," she whispered. "Milo's with them. They're hiding down in the shipyards with the pendants they stole from Rhodes City. After we got through the Barrier, the telchines took the god back to the ship and brought it through after us – but we persuaded them not to fight, and they've gone to the shipyards to make the god whole again. They've still got the Egyptian gold that was on board—"

"Shh!" Priestess Themis hissed. "We don't want the Council to hear that!"

Electra held her piece of the Gift tightly, rigid with the desire to prove herself worthy of being a priestess. "What shall we say?" she whispered.

Aura shivered as the pendant she held began to glow again. She could think only of her mother in the underwater tunnels. She wanted to run down to the grotto, dive in, and look for her at once. But she supposed they ought to tell the Council not to rebuild the Colossus first, and thanks to the chief priest she could barely hobble, so she couldn't get down to the sea on her own.

"*Please help me find my mother*," she breathed to the Gift. "*If you do, I promise I'll help you escape.*"

Priestess Themis chewed a nail. "We need a genuine oracle to tell us what to do," she decided, as if she had received a message from her goddess. "I want you to instruct Priestess Melito to tell the Egyptian king and the Council to go down to the grotto to ask ancient Lindia's advice, like people did in the old days."

Chapter 16

PROPHECY

WITH LEONIDUS CARRYING the chest containing the pieces of the Gift, and Electra helping Aura hobble, they followed Priestess Themis as fast as they could along the temple corridors. They arrived at the sanctuary in time to see the door crash open and King Ptolemy of Egypt stride out.

The king's robes glittered with even more gold and silver threads than the late chief priest's. The collar about his neck contained so many jewels, he gleamed brighter than the lamps lighting the shrine behind him. His eyes had been blackened with kohl, and he wore the same strange crown with a snake's head curling from his forehead that Aura had seen in her vision of his ship. He looked furious.

As his bodyguard hurried to catch up, the king turned and snapped something in Egyptian that did not sound very polite. Councillor Iamus rushed out after him, apologizing for the confusion. In a soft, persuasive voice, he managed to calm the king and draw him out of the temple, promising that the oracle in the ancient grotto would give them a better answer and tell him where to find his missing treasure chests. The other Councillors followed, muttering and casting dark looks over their shoulders at the priestess.

"It worked!" Electra whispered. She giggled. "What we said wasn't very popular with the Egyptian king, though."

"Quiet!" hissed Priestess Themis. "We've got to get Athene Lindia's pendant from the sanctuary so no one can use it that way again. Where are the novices, the lazy good-for-nothings? Poor old Melito's going to fall off her tripod in a moment!"

Aura peered into the sanctuary. A statue of Athene stood in the centre, wreathed in smoke. The pendant between her marble breasts was still glowing faintly. The oracle-priestess perched on a tall, three-legged stool at the goddess' feet, her head bent to her knees and her hair falling across her face. As Themis spoke, novices rushed into the shrine and eased the swooning woman off the tripod on to a stretcher.

Electra sobered as they carried her out. "We're as bad as the chief priest, tricking her like that."

"She knew enough to invent the words of the goddess when it suited her," said Priestess Themis, less sympathetic than before. "Quickly, now. Get that pendant from the statue, and let's get down to the grotto. I want to hear the ancient oracle speak."

The pendant came free easily with the aid of Athene's spear, and Electra added it to the chest. Moonlight, reflecting off the marble, lit their way as they hurried from the temple. Priestess Themis found a donkey to transport the chest. The very sight of the animal made Aura's toes throb, and she was glad when her father insisted upon carrying her down the steps himself. Athene Khalkia's pendant, safe inside her tunic where she'd slipped it out of sight after sending the message to the sanctuary, grew warmer as they descended. She closed her hand about it and tried to contact the telchines, but received only a jumbled vision of tunnels and moonlit sea.

"We have to tell Councillor Iamus the truth about the telchines and the ancient oracle," she whispered. "If he asks his question before the Gift is reunited with the rest of its pieces, he won't get an answer."

Leonidus tightened his arms around her. "I'm more worried they might be in the grotto already, and try to assassinate the Egyptian king. That *will* start a war – a human one. Rhodes will be caught in the middle and destroyed."

Aura's stomach tightened. "They wouldn't do that." But she wasn't so sure. The Gift had a lot more power than any of them had realized. What if the telchines decided to use it as a weapon? The wounded Moths would remain trapped in the Invisible Village, and her poor mother would stay lost in the underwater tunnels for ever.

She wished she had wings so she could fly down to the sea. But every ten steps or so Leonidus had to stop and rest, and the donkey was spooking at shadows, nervous of its glowing cargo. Priestess Themis kept looking round, as impatient to reach the grotto as they were.

"Put me down," Aura whispered. "I'm holding you up. Let me walk so you can carry the chest."

"You can't walk with those toes, don't be silly."

"Then take me to the cliff edge. I can dive off and find the telchines, tell them you're bringing the remaining pieces of the Gift and the councillor's on his way to the grotto to consult the ancient oracle, so they don't have to fight."

Leonidus looked at the dark sea below them. He shook his head. "That's too risky a dive at night with those rocks down there, and I'm not leaving you to face danger alone again. We'll go to the shipyards where Electra said she left the Moths, and see if the telchines are still there."

Aura told herself this was a sensible plan. She settled for gripping the pendant and sending a whispered message to Old One Rhode, though she had no idea if the telchine heard.

"*This is Aura, the Half-and-Half! We're on our way. We have the remaining pieces of the Gift. The Council and the Egyptian king are on their way to the grotto as planned. You don't have to fight. Please wait!*"

By the time they reached the bottom of the cliff, quite a crowd had gathered. Torches flared, lighting up the rocks as bright as day. A boat carrying Councillor Iamus, King Ptolemy and his bodyguards, could be seen rowing round the rocks to the mouth of the grotto. The rest of the councillors stood on the shore, their robes fluttering in the night breeze, shaking their heads after it as if they disapproved of the whole matter. Priestess Themis tried to push through them, but a line of Rhodian soldiers blocked their way.

"No one is to pass while the Egyptian king is out on the water," an officer told them. "His safety is our prime concern."

"You fools!" Leonidus said. "Don't you know there are telchines in the bay? You won't be much use out here if they attack. You should be in the grotto with him."

The officer frowned. "And who might you be?"

"Leonidus, son of Chares of Lindos! And this is my daughter, Aura. Let us through. We need to get to the shipyards."

"And I have to see Councillor Iamus at once," Priestess Themis added. "I have some important information for him concerning the chief priest and the oracles."

The officer shook his head. "I'm sorry, Priestess. But no one is to pass while the Egyptian king is in the grotto. Orders from the Council."

The crowd was growing larger and noisier as more people heard about the visit to the ancient oracle and streamed down the hillside to see if it would reply. Someone waved a torch in the donkey's face, and it shied at the flames, ripping the lead rein out of Electra's hand. Priestess Themis made a frustrated sound. "This is no good. We need to find a boat—"

"Will a ship do?" said a boy's voice behind them, and Aura's heart gave a peculiar little jump.

"Milo!" she breathed, twisting round in her father's arms.

The Khalki boy smiled at her with his dark eyes. "Aura," he said quietly. "I knew you would come back, but Old One Rhode thinks you've sold out to the humans. She took the telchines back to the grotto to lie in wait for the Council – the Moths are waiting with the ship just around the headland. They took it over when the telchines abandoned it."

He led them over the rocks out of sight of the crowd, where Leonidus at last put Aura down and hurried off to signal the ship. Electra and Priestess Themis dragged the donkey after him. Milo guided Aura to the edge of the water so she could sit.

In the darkness, he slid an arm around her shoulders and said, "I've so much to tell you! After your father got captured, I dived for the piece of the Gift you'd dropped in Khalki harbour and took it ashore to see if it'd heal Father before I brought it back to Rhodes... but he was already healed! The priestesses of Athene said the goddess' pendant lit up the whole temple with blue light a few days ago, and all the injured got better.

They said it was a miracle, but it must have been the day the telchines took the wires out of the Gift. I had to make up a story to explain why Cim wasn't with me so Mother wouldn't worry, then I brought our boat back here and joined up with the Moths." He stared after Leonidus' bruises. "Did the chief priest do that to him?"

"Yes," Aura said tightly. "But Xenophon won't hurt anyone again." She told him how she'd used the telchine eye-power in the storeroom.

He whistled, impressed. "Good for you!"

She shook her head. "It wasn't me. It was the Gift. I couldn't stop it. It wanted revenge for what the chief priest did to it, wiring it up in his Colossus and cutting pieces off it to put in the other statues. It used me, that's all."

Milo eyed her bandaged feet and said in a fierce tone, "He hurt you, as well!"

"Never mind that now." Although part of her wanted to sit with Milo on this rock under the stars forever, she knew they were running out of time. She wriggled out from under his arm and tugged at the linen. "Help me get these bandages off, Milo! I can't swim properly with them on. I have to find the telchines before they start another war. I can't wait for the ship. The last pieces of the Gift are in that chest of my father's. Get them on the ship and bring them to the mouth of the grotto. I'll meet you there with the telchines... I hope."

Milo's eyes darkened when he saw her blood-crusted toes. Then he pulled off his tunic.

Aura frowned at him, distracted. "What are you doing?"

"I'm coming with you, of course. Your father will know to bring the chest."

"No, Milo—"

"Just you try to stop me. Sponge divers' code, remember?"

Aura pulled out the pendant, which brightened at once, casting blue ripples over the water. It knew the Gift was close. She tightened her scarred fingers around its glow. Somehow, she had to make Milo stay.

"Forget the stupid code!" she said. "You want to know why I didn't drown in the Demon Pool? I'm a telchine, Milo! I can breathe underwater. That's how I stay down so long – it's got nothing to do with having a sponge diver's lungs or holding my breath. It'll never work between us. We're too different. When Helios loved Rhode, they created a war between telchines and humans. And the Gift punished my mother for loving a human by burning out her eyes. You can't come where I'm going. You'll drown."

He stared at her, hurt.

There was no time to regret what she'd said. Before Milo could stop her, Aura slid off the rocks into the dark sea. She changed to water-breathing and dived straight down, fast and deep. She put the Khalki boy out of her mind and concentrated on the pendant. It lit up the bay

with eerie violet light, illuminating the sponges that clung to the surrounding rocks, and glinting off shoals of tiny fish.

The cuts on her toes were bleeding again. Biting her lip against the pain, she swam through the crack into the grotto, staying as deep as possible so that the councillor and the Egyptian king wouldn't spot her.

She didn't see the telchines at first. But as she swam further into the grotto, there was a flare of blue light from one of the underwater tunnels and they arrowed up past her with the Gift, knocking her aside with their solid bodies. Aura twisted round, her heart thumping. But they were not heading for the councillor's boat, as she had feared. They streamed towards the entrance, where the oars of the King Ptolemy's ship, stolen by the Moths and now containing the rest of the Gift, dipped beneath the surface. She saw them grasp the wood and pull themselves out of the water in a mass of bubbles. The Gift had obviously sensed its remaining pieces on the ship, and the telchines were going to retrieve them at any cost.

In fresh fear for her father and friends, Aura gripped the pendant and kicked for the surface. The Egyptian ship blocked the entrance, its mast scraping the rock. Between the stalactites, she saw a confusion of kicking legs and struggling bodies. The soldiers on the shore, seeing the stolen ship, were throwing spears at the Moths, and the Moths were slinging stones back at the soldiers. The telchines, thinking the stones that fell short were aimed at them, had joined in the fight. Spears, stones and bolts of eye-power sizzled into the sea around Aura's head. She dived again in alarm. It was all going wrong.

Then her father yelled something and threw his chest of pendants overboard. There was a crackle and a wild flare of light, and the telchines were thrown backwards as the Gift reformed itself. Huge, pulsing, powerful, it sank towards Aura, sensing the pendant in her hand.

Aura hesitated, her heart racing. Several telchines were chasing the Gift. She forced the wires of Athene Khalkia's pendant apart, ripping off a fingernail in her panic. The final piece of the Gift melted into the halo surrounding the creature, making it complete. Soft as a sigh, it settled into her arms, and the ragged holes in the Barrier closed up with small sounds like kisses. Warmth flowed through Aura as the rainbows enveloped her, and she realized her finger had stopped bleeding and her toes didn't hurt any more. She glanced down, a little afraid of what she'd see. But her toe webs were still missing, their cuts scarred over with pink skin.

She looked at the telchines, reaching their webbed hands to take back their Gift, and knew what she had to do if she wanted the Gift to help her find her mother. Tightening her arms around the creature, she kicked for the surface.

As she changed to air-breathing, there was a terrible crackle like a summer storm, and a sheet of light divided the grotto in two, drowning her in rainbows. Her breath came faster as both worlds became visible at once – the telchines thrown back into their world on one side and the human delegation on the other, staring at the rainbows around them in wonder and terror.

Aura shivered. This must be what the grotto had looked like, before her mother had taken the Gift into the human world.

When they realized the Gift had restored the Barrier between them and their enemies, the furious telchines swam towards the boat and pushed at the light-wall with their webbed hands, trying to reach the humans. King Ptolemy's bodyguards leant over the side to jab at the telchines with spears that blurred in the rainbows and sprang back. On a ledge near the mouth of the grotto, Milo struggled with a soldier who was trying to raise his bow to shoot Aura.

Ragged figures lined up along the rail of the Egyptian ship, their faces bathed by the rainbows. One of King Ptolemy's bodyguards panicked and threw a spear at Aura, but it bounced off the Gift and splashed harmlessly into the water. The Moths yelled and slung stones at the boat.

In the middle of all this, Aura climbed on to the ledge, heaved the dripping Gift above her head and yelled, "STOP!"

A hush fell as everyone stared at her. Waves slapped and echoed against the stalactites and the rock walls. The top of the ship's mast broke off as Leonidus abandoned the tiller and rushed to the side calling, "Aura, be careful!"

Councillor Iamus' eyes widened as he recognized her, and Milo shouted, "No, Aura! Get out of here! Something bad is about to happen!"

Aura smiled. The rainbows were pouring off her skin like oil. She felt shivery, yet unafraid. The power was building behind her eyes, as it had in the storeroom. But this time she was in control. Old One Rhode climbed out of the water on the telchine side of the Barrier and tried to grab her arm, but could not touch her through the rainbows. The soldier pushed Milo aside and tried to seize her as well, but had the same trouble.

"Give us Poseidon's Gift, Half-and-Half!" Rhode said. "It's ours."

Aura shook her head. "No one owns it. It's alive, and it wants to be free."

"Is that Helios' Gift?" said Councillor Iamus, signalling the boat closer to the ledge. "I thought you'd been killed when you fell off that cliff! Does it have the power to bring people back from the dead? Give it to me, there's a good girl."

Aura shook her head a second time, gritted her teeth against the rainbows that were roaring in her head, and said, "I'm going to let it go back to the deep where it belongs. When that happens, humans and telchines won't be able to speak through the Barrier again. So you have to make peace, right now. *All* of you." She included the Moths in her glare. "Otherwise, I'll use my evil eye to cause an earthquake and destroy this grotto

and everyone in it. You know I can do it. The Gift will give me the power."

Councillor Iamus looked askance at the Gift and Aura's shining skin. He eyed the telchines. "They came into our world and attacked us."

"They won't be able to do that any more, once the Gift is gone. They'll stay in their own world, and they won't bother you again. All they want is to be left in peace. Humans hunted them first."

The councillor stroked his beard. "I'll need a promise from them."

"Old One?" Aura said, turning to Rhode. "Will you agree to let the Gift go free, and not try to cross the Barrier again?"

The old telchine frowned. "But that means the humans will have Rhodes! It belongs to us."

"You'll have Rhodes, too, won't you? The Rhodes of the telchine world. And you'll be safe there, because the humans won't have the Gift, either."

The Old One rested a hand on Phaethon's head. "How do we know the humans won't try to find the Gift and use it to hunt us again?"

"You have my word," the councillor said. "The humans who used to hunt you before the Barrier was created are long dead."

"You must both promise on the Gift," Aura said, holding it out.

Warily, the councillor touched the glowing creature. The Old One did the same. The Gift brightened, and the promise passed through Aura, every word, so she knew it was made.

"Xenophon's not going to like this," the councillor muttered as he withdrew his hand. "I still think it'd be better if I kept Helios' Gift somewhere safe..."

"The chief priest is dead," Aura said quickly. "Things have changed."

The Egyptian king, hearing only half this conversation, grew impatient. He leant out of the boat and squinted at Aura. "Is that the priestess who gives the oracle down here, Iamus?" he called. "Because if she is, tell her to get on with it! We've messed around in this quaint little town quite long enough, and now you've found my ship and the gold I brought for your earthquake fund, I have to get back to Alexandria. Did I hear her say that crazy old priest of yours died?"

Councillor Iamus gave him a distracted look. His eyes narrowed as he realized what Aura had said. "Xenophon's dead? How?"

"Helios struck him down!" called Priestess Themis from the deck of the ship. "I saw it happen. You're going to need to appoint a new Chief Priest for your Sun God."

Councillor Iamus gazed around the rainbow-filled grotto. "Xenophon's dead..." He gave a sly little smile and announced with perfect assurance, as if he'd arranged the entire thing, "Yes, your majesty! This is the oracle-priestess of the ancient grotto. She might be young, but as you can see, she is blessed. She will give us the oracle."

He whispered to Aura, "For Helios' sake, say no! We can't afford to rebuild that monstrosity of Xenophon's, especially not now we have his funeral to organize as well as all our cities to rebuild."

The councillor and the Egyptian king, Old One Rhode, Phaethon and the telchines, Milo and the confused soldiers, Priestess Themis and Electra, Leonidus and the Moths… everyone held their breath to hear what Aura would say. She closed her eyes and took a deep breath. But before she could speak, the rainbows surged in her head and a huge, booming voice filled the grotto.

IF THE COLOSSUS OF HELIOS IS RAISED AGAIN, THE ISLAND OF RHODES WILL BE DESTROYED AND DOOM WILL COME TO ALL WHO DWELL UPON HER SHORES.

The Gift burnt her fingers, and Aura dropped it into the water. Stunned, she opened her eyes and watched it sink into the depths, growing smaller and smaller, a purple star, sucking the rainbows after it and darkening the light-wall as it fell until the telchines disappeared behind the restored Barrier. Only then did she realize it had tricked her one last time.

It had left her in the human world, and her mother was still lost in the underwater tunnels.

"No, wait!" she cried. "You're supposed to help me find my mother! Wait for me!"

She dived off the ledge and plunged after it.

The Gift was already out of sight. She swam desperately downwards, chasing the final flickers of light.

The tunnels were black holes ahead of her. Hundreds of them. Aura stared at them in dismay. Which one had she seen her mother in, when she'd had her vision in the temple storeroom?

She had gone past the point where her lungs ran out of air and she had to change to water-breathing, before she realized Milo, the idiot, had dived in after her. He grabbed her ankle, and she looked round at his pleading face. His cheeks bulged with holding his breath. He was already too deep to reach the surface on what remained of his air, yet he clearly had no intention of going back without her. Bubbles trickled from his lips and then stopped coming. His dark eyes gazed steadily at her and then rolled up in his head as water entered his lungs and he began to drown.

Aura's heart twisted. Her mother would be safe in the tunnels, whether she found her or not. If she had gone back to the telchine world, the Old One would look after her. But if she left Milo down here, he would die. There was only one choice she could make.

She put her arms around the boy and headed back for the surface. Far below them, a BOOM shook the seabed and sent shoals of fish whirling away in panic as the Gift vanished from the world. Aura and Milo were thrown upwards, clinging to each other and spinning uncontrollably in silver bubbles.

Up, up, and up towards the light of a new day.

Chapter 17

CHOICES

THE ORACLE'S ANSWER echoed around Lindos Bay and whispered up through the rock to the Temple of Athene, where Priestess Melito stirred in her drugged sleep and sighed. After so many people had heard, there was really only one decision the Council could make. The councillors thanked King Ptolemy for his generous financial aid, told him they would not be rebuilding the Colossus because it was obviously too tall to withstand earthquakes, and sent him back to Egypt with his recovered ship. They assured him that the Moths would be suitably punished for the theft. The Egyptian king was not upset. He had seen strange lights in the grotto and heard a genuine oracle speak. That was worth the journey on its own.

After Aura had surfaced under Councillor Iamus' nose with a half-drowned Milo, and the Moths had been escorted ashore by the soldiers, there was little point in running any more. Priestess Themis dragged Electra off to check on Priestess Melito, while the rest of them were taken to the acropolis to await the Council's decision concerning the theft of Helios' gold and the Egyptian king's property. Timosthenes was separated from them without explanation in the marble courtyard, and the soldiers would let none of them leave the room, so the atmosphere was tense.

Androcles paced the floor, scowling at the door each time he passed it. Chariclea tried to persuade him to eat some of the cheese and olives the Council had provided, while the others huddled in little groups making whispered plans to escape if things turned bad. Milo, revived somewhat after his lung-bursting dive, rested on a pile of cushions. Aura sat beside him, too tired to think about what had happened in the grotto. She knew only that, for the first time since the earthquake, her head was quiet and the rainbows had gone. Leonidus put an arm around her shoulders and held her in sympathetic silence.

Finally, the door opened and Timosthenes slipped into the room. He wore a tunic with red and green sleeves, and his hair had been curled around a circlet of silver. He smelled of rose petals and looked very grown-up.

Everyone stared at him in surprise. Milo stirred and blinked at the blond boy. "What's going on? Is that really Timosthenes...?"

"Shh," said Aura, beginning to suspect what Timosthenes had been hiding from the Moths all along.

Androcles' scowl deepened. He planted his hands on his hips. "Where'd you get them fancy clothes?" he demanded. "Sold us out, have you? I'm warnin' you now… if you've told the Council where the gold we took from the Colossus is hidden, I'll kill you. I trusted you like a brother!"

Timosthenes moistened his lips. "Of course I haven't told them where your hiding places are. Listen. Fath— Councillor Iamus has offered us a deal. I think it sounds good. But you're the boss, so it's up to you."

He explained the details. Any Moths who wanted to could go home to their families without reprisals. The others could return to Ialysos and live there with their own rules as before, but on condition they helped the Council from time to time with various undercover jobs that might involve sneaking in somewhere quietly, listening to people's conversations, and getting out again without being caught. This way the Council could obtain the sort of information previously controlled by the priests through Helios' Gift, and use it for the good of Rhodes. In return for these services, the Moths would be paid in food and a small amount of coin, so they could live comfortably without having to steal from the Rhodians. Anything they'd stolen to date that had not been retrieved during the raid on the ruins, they could keep. But any Moth who broke the agreement and was caught stealing in future would be treated as a criminal, and the others would suffer a corresponding cut in pay until the debt was repaid.

Androcles considered this with narrow eyes. Chariclea started to say it didn't sound so bad, but the Moth leader cut her off. "And?" he said.

"And what?"

Androcles tugged the sleeve of Timosthenes' tunic. "This! Do we all have to ponce about in fancy clothes and wash in rose water every day?"

Timosthenes smiled. "Not unless the job requires it. The Council will probably use people suited to each task. If we have to mingle with civilized people, I could do it. Whereas if it's in a rougher place, you or Chariclea would blend in nicely."

"Good," Chariclea said. "Because you pong!"

Androcles gave her a warning glance. "So how come you get all the special treatment? It's like what happened back in Rhodes City, when we were prisoners – you go off alone with the soldiers and come back, free as a bird, to rescue us. We're not stupid, you know. You were goin' to say something else just now. You were goin' to say 'Father', weren't you?"

"Oh, I *get* it!" Milo whispered. "Timosthenes is Councillor Iamus' son!"

Timosthenes went scarlet. "I was going to tell you, Boss, when the time was right."

"You sneaky *spy*!" one of the boys said, leaping to his feet. "I always thought you spoke like one of them stuck-up boys who go to the oratory school. And I thought you weren't too keen to attack the councillor, when he trapped us at the Demon Pool. Now we know why! You told your dear father we were taking the Gift to the Invisible Village, didn't you? No wonder the soldiers were lying in wait for us there! How long have you been rattin' on us to the Council, you sneak? Let me teach him a lesson, Boss—"

Androcles held up his hand. "Wait. We haven't finished, and I'm the one who'll do any teaching that's needed here." He shook his head at the blushing Timosthenes. "Right, let's get this straight. We can go free as long as we promise not to steal? It'll be difficult to stop some people. We haven't all had the advantage of a rich upbringin', you know."

"I know it won't be easy. But it's as good a deal as I could get. You won't really need to steal, if the Council gives you food. And you'll get to keep the gold from Helios' crown – since they're not rebuilding the Colossus, they won't need it back."

Androcles narrowed his eyes. For a moment, Aura thought he would refuse. Then he grinned. "Done! It'll be hard work makin' the Moths change their ways, but these jobs of the Council's sound like they might be fun. We'll give it a try, any rate."

Timosthenes looked relieved, but Chariclea scowled. "Don't think we're going to trust you with anything again. You'll be kept well away from any plans we make in future!"

"I don't blame you," the blond boy said. "If it's any consolation, I feel bad about betraying you. I really thought that Gift thing was going to get us all killed. It was only when Aura and Electra fell off the cliff at the

Invisible Village that I realized Father was just as afraid of the Gift as we were. But you needn't worry, because I won't be going back to Ialysos with you."

Chariclea frowned. "Aren't you goin' to stay a Moth, then?"

Timosthenes glanced at the door. "Well, it's part of the deal I go home..." As Chariclea's face fell, he smiled and said, "But that doesn't mean I can't visit you from time to time. The whole lot of you need lessons in speaking properly. Father's charged me with starting a school up in Ialysos— "

"A *school*?" Androcles scowled. "What's wrong with the way we speak, you stuck up councillor's brat? And you know the penalty for rattin' on your fellow Moths." Before Timosthenes realized what was coming, he'd knocked him to the floor.

Aura pulled her feet out of the way as the two boys rolled in the cushions, punching and kicking, while the rest of the Moths formed a circle and cheered them on. Chariclea folded her arms and grinned as Timosthenes' fine clothes got torn and bloodied.

The guards at the door rushed in to see what all the noise was about, but Leonidus motioned them back.

"Don't worry, they're just celebrating," he said with a smile. "I think you can tell Councillor Iamus the Moths have accepted his offer."

In the morning, they said goodbye to Electra, who was going to accompany Priestess Themis back to Khalki. The Moths were allowed to take an old fishing boat north along the coast to find the friends they'd left behind in the Invisible Village and tell them the good news. Aura, Leonidus and Milo went with them – Milo to pick up his little brother and Aura to show her father the Demon Pool where Lindia had dived into the underwater tunnels.

They made a real group of invalids. Androcles had cuts on his face and a sprained wrist from his fight with Timosthenes the night before. With Leonidus' bruises turning green, Aura's newly scarred toes, and Milo still weak from his dive, it was left to Chariclea to sail the boat – which she did with unexpected skill, making good speed up the coast.

Aura had been a little afraid what they might find, not trusting the Gift not to have played one last trick on them all. But the beach was alive with ragged figures, dancing and singing around bonfires they had lit to guide their friends back to the cove. There seemed far too many of them to be the Moths they had left behind the night they followed the telchines to Lindos, and as they sailed closer they saw grown men and women holding hands around the fires, their clothes in rags.

"Those must be the villagers who vanished when Lindia brought the Gift through the Barrier to heal my father's heart," Leonidus whispered. "Fifty-six years, and they've hardly aged!"

Cimon swam to meet their boat, shouting about how the earth had shaken and the sky had torn in two with lightning and rainbows. Apparently, the villagers had been living rough in the wood, hiding from the telchines, but had come to investigate when they saw the rainbows. Their two telchine prisoners had been left behind in their own world when the Barrier reformed – no doubt already back with the rest of their people, trying to explain to the Old One how their hostages had escaped. While they were waiting, the invalid Moths had collected up the coins Kamira threw out on the beach, so they were rather pleased with themselves, particularly when they heard that the Council had written off the missing treasure so they could keep them. When Androcles had calmed the Moths down and told them about the Council's offer, the party began all over again. They all wanted to clap Aura on the back for returning everyone to the right world and restoring the Barrier. Aura felt hollow inside, thinking of her mother. As soon as possible, she and her father slipped away to the Demon Pool, taking Milo and Cimon with them.

It was nearly sunset when they arrived. Bronze light slanted through the trees and skimmed the surface of the pool, making it seem magical and mysterious. Aura stopped at the edge of the clearing, her breath tight with memories, and Milo – who had barely left her side since they had surfaced together in the Lindian grotto – squeezed her hand.

"I know it was a hard decision to make, Aura," he whispered. "But you wouldn't really have been happy living with the telchines… would you?"

Aura bit her lip as she watched her father approach the pool. He stared into the depths, knelt and bowed his head. They watched him cup his hand, bring it to his lips, and kiss it. He whispered something and let the water slip back through his fingers.

"I'm glad I chose to stay," she said. "Really, I am. It's just—"

Cimon, who had been peering curiously into the depths, leapt back and pointed in excitement at the pool. Aura's skin prickled. Her father was staring into the water with a look of wonder. She gulped and ran to the edge, dragging Milo with her.

There, just beneath the surface and surrounded by a halo of rainbows like a vision from the Gift, floated her mother's face. Aura gazed down at the telchine, afraid to move or speak.

Two perfect yellow eyes stared back at her through a cloud of swirling silver hair. Lindia gazed first at Leonidus, then at Aura, as if fixing their features in her memory. Then she smiled, raised a webbed hand in farewell, and sank from view. Her beautiful, newly-healed eyes were the last to disappear.

Aura's heart twisted with loss for herself mixed with joy for her mother, who could see again. Leonidus sighed, and a single tear dripped from his cheek into the water. Milo held on to Aura tightly as the last of the light left the pool. He seemed afraid she might try to dive in after her mother, like she'd done the last time they were here.

Seeing the question in his eyes, she smiled. "It's all right, Milo, I'm not going anywhere. It was a vision from the Gift in return for me helping it escape. Mother's gone home now. She was never really happy in our world. I'll miss her, but she's right. I'm up-grown now. I don't need her like I did when I was younger, and I've got Father back. I'm glad he had a chance to say goodbye, and I'm glad she got a chance to see me. The Gift must have grown her new eyes, like it grew Chares a new heart. It's forgiven her." She rested her head against his shoulder with a sigh. Milo's arms sent ripples of warmth through her. Her feet felt strange without her webs, but nice in a peculiar way. She'd never felt grass between her toes before.

"Do they still hurt?" Milo asked, touching one of the scars.

"No. The Gift healed them, like it healed Mother's eyes. And it gave the oracle in the grotto. Maybe Electra was right all along. Maybe it was a god."

"Poseidon or Helios?" Milo asked with a teasing smile.

"Does it matter? It's gone now, and it won't be back. Let's forget about it, Milo, please."

He regarded her thoughtfully. "So you're fully human now?"

"Looks like it." Aura smiled and wriggled her fingers and toes. "See, no webs!"

"That's not what I meant."

She looked into his enigmatic eyes and sobered. "I know what you meant. I didn't mean what I said before, you know, when I dived into the grotto. And I've been thinking. Things might work out for us, after all. Helios and Rhode were god and telchine. They had to meet on land, where neither was happy. Lindia and Father are telchine and human. They had to choose which side of the Barrier to live, and whichever side they chose one of them would have been unhappy if they stayed together. We're different. I'm half human, and we were both born in the same world. So maybe…"

Milo hugged her tighter. "Never mind all that! Of course it'll work. We've more in common than our human blood. We're both divers, aren't we? We're bound by the—"

He didn't have a chance to say it.

As Leonidus looked up from the water and smiled at them, Cimon clapped his hands and jumped up and down.

"Sponge divers' code!" he shouted. "Milo and Aura will be together for ever, because they promised on the sponge divers' code!"

GUIDE TO AURA'S WORLD

AURA AND HER friends lived on Rhodes and its neighbouring islands during the devastating earthquake of 227BC, which toppled the Colossus of Helios (also known as the Colossus of Rhodes), one of the Seven Wonders of the Ancient World. The Colossus had stood for only 56 years, but an oracle warned the islanders not to rebuild it, prophesying doom and destruction if they did. It is interesting to note that another big earthquake struck the island just three years later.

The prayer to Helios in Part 1 was probably part of a dedication inscribed on the Colossus of Helios. The prayer to Poseidon in Part 2 is my own invention, as is the world of the telchines.

acropolis	A fortified hill inside a Greek city.
Alimia	A small, uninhabited island off the coast of Rhodes.
Athene	Greek warrior goddess, born full-grown from the head of Zeus. She had many temples on Rhodes and her surrounding islands. To avoid confusion, each statue of the goddess was named according to where her temple stood, e.g. "Athene Khalkia" for the one on Khalki, and "Athene Lindia" for the one at Lindos.
Barrier	Created by Helios to stop the war between the telchines and the humans. The Barrier separates two worlds existing in the same space but invisible to each other – one where telchines live, the other where humans live.
colossus	A large statue. There were over a hundred colossi on Rhodes.
Colossus of Helios	A huge bronze statue of the Sun God Helios, largest of all the colossi. It stood in Rhodes City until it fell down during the earthquake of 227BC. One of the Seven Wonders of the Ancient World.

Demon Pool	A very deep pool with underwater tunnels linking it to the grotto at Lindos. Today known as "Seven Springs", and supposedly favoured by nymphs.
eye-power	A telchine power that comes from the Gift, enabling them to kill with lightning from their eyes. Known to humans as the "evil eye".
Helios	Sun god (also known to the Greeks as Apollo).
Ialysos	The hideout of the Night Moths gang: a ruined city on top of a mountain in the north of Rhodes, abandoned by its population when Rhodes City was built below it.
Invisible Village	A village on the eastern coast of Rhodes, where the Barrier between worlds is thin. Based on the modern village of Afandou, which means "hidden".
Kamiros	A city on the west coast of Rhodes.
Khalki	A small island off the coast of Rhodes, famous for its sponges.
King Ptolemy	King Ptolemy III of Egypt, who offered gold to rebuild the Colossus after it fell down in the earthquake.

Lindos	A city on the east coast of Rhodes, with a grotto beneath it where the oracle of the ancient goddess Lindia used to speak.
oracle	A place where gods or heroes speak to humans and give prophetic messages (the messages themselves were also called oracles). A priestess usually delivered the oracle in a drug-induced trance, and her message was interpreted by "prophetai-priests" for the questioner.
Poseidon	Zeus' brother, god of the sea.
Poseidon's Gift/ Helios' Gift	A blue sponge-like creature with magical powers.
sponge	A sea creature found in the Mediterranean – technically an animal, although it looks more like a plant. In ancient Greece, sponges were harvested for padding helmets and for washing. Most sponges today are synthetic, but real sponges are still sold on Rhodes.
telchine	Legendary race of sea-demons, who lived on Rhodes before humans came to the island.

water-breathing	A skill that enables telchines to swim underwater for long periods, obtaining oxygen from the water like a fish.

THE SEVEN FABULOUS WONDERS

THE GREAT PYRAMID ROBBERY

Magic, murder and mayhem spread through the Two Lands, when Senu, the son of a scribe, is forced to help build one of the largest and most magnificent pyramids ever recorded. He and his friend, Reonet, are sucked into a plot to rob the great pyramid of Khufu and an ancient curse is woken. Soon they are caught in a desperate struggle against forces from another world, and even Senu's mischievous ka, Red, finds his magical powers are dangerously tested.

000 711278 5